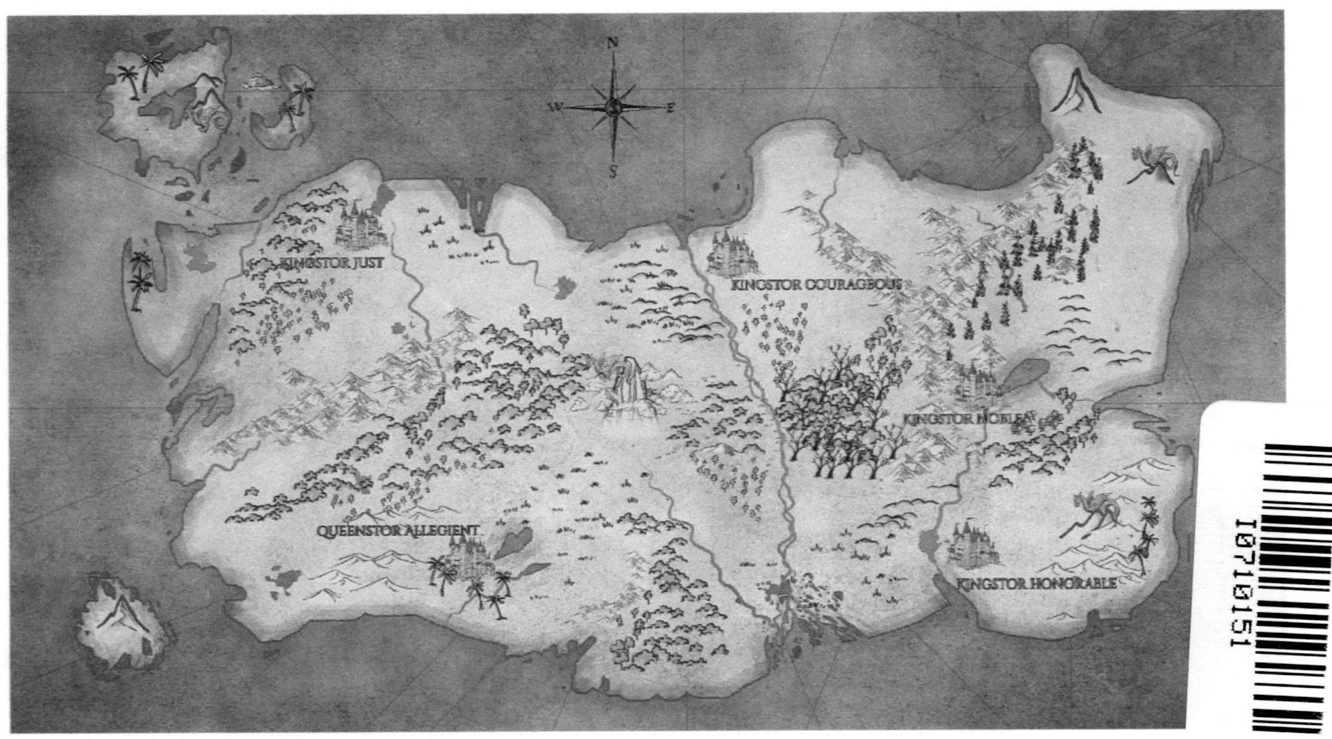

N
W E
S
KINGSTOR JUST
KINGSTOR COURAGEOUS
KINGSTOR NOBLE
QUEENSTOR ALLEGIENT
KINGSTOR HONORABLE
I0710151

THE GATEKEEPER
OF DEATH

<u>Dragons of Avonoa Series</u>
The Gatekeeper of Death (Book One)
The Champion of Justice (Book Two)

Also by author HRB Collotzi:

<u>Avonoa Series</u>
The Secret of Avonoa (Book One)
The Shadow of Avonoa (Book Two)
The Heart of Avonoa (Book Three)
The Traitor of Avonoa (Book Four)
The Krusible of Avonoa (Book Five)

<u>The People of the Storm Series</u>
People of the Storm
People of the Storm 2

THE GATEKEEPER OF DEATH

HRB COLLOTZI

DRAGONS OF AVONOA SERIES BOOK ONE

ISBN 13: 978-1-962628-03-7
Library of Congress Control Number: 2024907114
Ingram Spark
Published by HRB Collotzi
Rosemount, Minnesota

www.avonoa.com
www.hrbcollotzi.com

For Jason,

who has always made my dreams come true!

For my kids,

Josh, Ashley and Ryan,

For helping me with brainstorming, beta-reading,

and supporting me every step of the way!

CONTENTS

1

SUMMONS

"He's there again."

"I know, he's there."

"We *all* know he's there."

"He's always there."

"When has he ever left?"

Jassan silently cursed the little twig he had stepped on before peeking out from behind the tree again. He could hear every word being said and everyone in the group ahead of him in the clearing knew it. The creatures in the clearing took turns to glance or blatantly glare into the trees at him. He had worn a brown cloak in hopes of being somewhat camouflaged and to possibly protect himself from the rain, but neither idea worked. Rain seeped into the holes for his faerie wings and the cowl of his hood and trickled down his back, slicking his black hair in place like paint. His pale blue skin shone like a beacon in the muted light.

"Why don't you just come out from there?" Emma called into the trees after stacking her last stone on a large mound.

Emma. She was the reason Jassan persisted in following the young group of friends. The most beautiful part-human, part-dragon in all of Avonoa. Even dripping in the heavy mists of fall, her curly yellow hair seemed so light compared to his own lank, black hair. Her smooth, golden-brown skin glistened wherever it peeked out from under her silvery waterproof cloak. Every time he saw her, he disliked his freckled blue skin more. To his disappointment, he wore the skin of a faerie, the most reviled creature in all of Avonoa. He knew the group of disparate beings didn't like him and he shouldn't spend his time following them, but Emma's glowing blue eyes, like the sparkling twilight sky as the sun escapes the horizon, beckoned him toward freedom and he responded.

"Don't say that," Lokna growled through his long fangs at her. The brown dragon used his length to tie a damp flag in the trees above them with a sense of superiority, as if Emma couldn't do the same thing in her dragon form, but Princess Emma wasn't in her dragon form at the moment.

Emma and her younger brother, Burk, kept to their human forms most of the time, but Jassan had seen her true dragon form. To start with, she was less bulky than Lokna and thus had a prettier shape, but Jassan most admired her dark blue scales which matched the dragon wrappings under her cloak. While in human form she always wore them tightly wrapped around her body, from below her knees to up over her shoulders.

Dragon wrappings, the majikal material part-dragons wound around themselves when in human form, was the easiest way to spot a part-dragon. The specially made material changed with the human and melted into their dragon form scales. As long as they were the same color as the dragon, they disappeared. The only other way to tell if someone was part dragon was by the wing markings on their backs. But in the current rainy season, not many humans wandered around without their cloaks.

"Why not?" she shot back, spinning on the brown dragon.

"Because he might actually show himself," he snapped back, tying the last flag and landing with a thump in the soft mud. "And we might actually have to talk to him."

"I'm with Lokna," one of the centaur twins spoke up. She always argued against staying within eyesight of Jassan. She dumped an armful of wood into a pile in the center of the clearing. "Go away!" she said into the trees, waving her hand in Jassan's direction.

Emma looked away from the trees to purse her lips at the centaur.

"Don't be mean, Tyla," the other twin chided her sister, dumping a second armful of wood on the immense pile.

"We don't want him to know what we're doing, do we?" Jassan didn't look around, but he was almost certain it was the goblin who had spoken. Her curly purple hair could hardly be seen behind a stack of rocks as she carefully piled hytocomp moss on top of the pyre.

"He's been stalking us for months, Dasha," Lokna growled, baring his fangs toward the woods as if all their comments were Jassan's fault. "He probably knows exactly what we're doing."

Feeling emboldened that they were including him in the conversation, Jassan moved farther out around the tree toward them. "It's not going to work," he said, then mentally berating himself as he slid back behind the tree. *Stupid. Stupid. Stupid.* His awkward action would give them even more reason to disdain him.

"Oh, please," Tyla said, rolling her large eyes at him. "You don't really know what we're doing, you just like snooping on us."

"And why would we listen to you anyway?" Lokna said, shaking his head to rid himself of a few raindrops that had accumulated on his horns, letting the water drip down the short barbels on his jaw. Jassan suspected that Lokna had made the display in his direction to show off the fact that he was a dragon while Jassan was a mere faerie. Lokna stepped into the trees closer to him. Jassan assumed he was going for intimidating…because it worked. He pulled himself tighter into the tree. "You're a faerie and faeries can't be trusted."

Jassan frowned. He knew that was what all the other races of Avonoa thought. But it wasn't his fault that seventeen years ago most of the faeries had used the powers of majik at their disposal to betray their longtime allies, the dragons, and had tried to kill them off. If it hadn't been for Emma's father, Hirowyn, and her mother,

Priyanna, the faeries might have succeeded. Her parents found the traitor to the dragons and stopped the war. They were legends.

Everyone in Avonoa knew about the first two beings who had become both dragon and human, able to change between species. Emma's mother, Priyanna, had been born the first part-dragon, part-human as a shocking result of a tragic love between a dragon and a human. When Emma's father, Hirowyn, fell in love with Priyanna, he too changed from a full dragon into a part-dragon, part-human. Together, they discovered the fatal betrayal of the faeries and eventually brokered peace between all of the Avonoan species, who had been dragged into the war.

After their loss and rebuke, the faeries had retreated and gone into seclusion. Their withdrawal from the world back then is why Jassan felt obligated to keep his distance now. Even though he and the others here were close in age, and both dragons and part-dragons aged at the same rate as faeries did, none of them had been alive during the faerie betrayal and the dragon war that changed the course of Avonoa. Gizi, the orange dragon and only full dragon female in this group, was the oldest and she had only been in the egg at the time. Jassan didn't feel any of them had the right to judge him based on the culture of suspicion toward faeries for reasons they had never actually experienced.

But it wasn't just they who he felt judged by. He really didn't like being around other faeries either. He would take reproaches from dragons any day over what he usually got from his own race.

"Faeries are better at majik than any other species," Jassan bit back defensively, loud enough for the group to hear him. "My aunt told me how to do it properly. She studies it."

When no answer came from the clearing, he dared to peek around the tree. Everyone was glancing at each other, wondering about what they'd just heard. Jassan could see the uncertainty in the seven faces. Lokna and Tyla shook their heads at Emma and Gizi.

"Do you know what we're doing?" Emma's little brother finally spoke up, addressing Jassan. He had been hiding behind his sister, as he usually did. Jassan felt a connection to Burk's innocence, sensing that the little part-human, part-dragon was even more shy than he was, as well as being younger. Burk was the youngest and smallest in the group but he never let on to the others when he caught Jassan following them, and instead let them discover him on their own.

Because it was the most timid person in the group who had spoken to him, lowering his fear, Jassan fully stepped out from behind the tree. He pointed to the fire they were preparing and the ingredients nearby in confirmation. "Torgana root, mint, hytocomp to build the smoke. The totems you've built," he indicated the piles of rocks and twigs surrounding the group in the clearing, "as well as the banners," he pointed to the green flags hung in the trees and dripping with rain, "you're trying to summon from the World of Souls. You want to talk to the dead."

Jassan watched Lokna narrow his eyes at him. "We must be doing it right," Lokna said, "since you can see all the signs of it. So we don't need you, you can leave us alone now." The dragon turned his back on Jassan and swung his tail as if waving goodbye. Although he was more than twice the faerie's height, Jassan noticed that the dragon moved with surprising grace, able to avoid each of the carefully built pyres while circling the more substantial one in the middle.

"But he said it won't work," Emma said.

Lokna sighed and glanced at the others in the circle, who each shrugged or looked away.

"It's up to you," the centaur said reluctantly. "It's your uncle we're summoning."

Emma stepped forward. "She's right," she said, "it's your choice. But this might be our only chance to get it right. If the parents find out, they'll never allow us to see each other again. You know that."

Lokna sighed again, but turned to Jassan.

"Alright, Mister Thinks-He-Knows-Everything," he grumbled, "what are we missing?"

Jassan walked into the clearing with his chin a little higher. He inspected the dishes of ingredients and totems like his aunt would when she checked over his writing for incantations. As he sidled past Lokna he could feel the dragon's eyes glaring down at him and the contempt pouring from him in waves of heat.

"You have all the ingredients, although they should be in sequence of the spell around the circle going east," he said.

"We knew that," Tyla huffed, picking up one of the dragon-scale dishes.

"We were just about to order them," her twin finished, moving another dish.

"Then you know the incantation?" Jassan asked.

"Of course we do," Lokna snapped. "I memorized it and taught everyone else. We have everything we need."

"Except the one biggest thing," Jassan said, genuine worry creasing his brow. "You're trying to create a tear in the boundary of the World of Souls, and you don't have the one most important and necessary item. The one and only thing that is probably the reason your parents haven't allowed you to even *know* about the spell. The one most dangerous and vile thing. The one—"

"I know!" Lokna snipped to cut him off.

"What is he talking about?" Burk murmured, pushing his dark cowl away from his face to look at the brown dragon.

Rather than respond to the confused looks running through the group, Lokna glared at Jassan.

"What were you going to do?" Jassan uttered to the dragon. "Sacrifice yourself?"

"I'm not so stupid," Lokna growled back. "I only wish *you* were a dragon."

"Lokna," Emma said, stepping toward him, "what is he talking about?"

Lokna ground his teeth together, but turned back to Emma. "In order for the spell to work, a dragon must die."

Muttering and cursing rumbled through the group.

"What?! What are we going to do now?"

"I knew we would never make this happen!"

"Why didn't you tell us?"

"What were you thinking?"

Lokna turned to face his friends. "It's ok," he said. "I spoke with Sha Orna before we met. She said that if we sacrificed something *from* a dragon, like scales or blood and stuff, they would have the same effect."

"You worm!" Tyla shouted. "You promised this would work!"

"We are going to get in so much trouble," the goblin, Dasha, muttered to no one in particular.

"We haven't done anything yet," Tyla's twin said to the goblin.

"And we don't have to," Emma said. "We can go home as if we've been having another grand adventure in the woods, like always."

"Yeah," Burk said, pleading. "Let's just go home."

"No!" Lokna yelled. "I told you, it will work! I promise! You all said you would help me. I want to see my uncle and this is the best and only chance I'll have!"

His voice broke at the last statement and Jassan inspected the dragon, surprised at his emotion. Jassan hung his head when he realized that Lokna had never known his uncle Milah. Lokna had probably heard stories about his heroic deeds from his sire, Milah's brother, Mitashio. Jassan's aunt had told him lots of stories about the dragon war. Lokna's uncles were among the most famous heroes, along with the other dragons' sires and Emma's parents.

Jassan knew enough about Lokna's family to understand how extremely close the brothers had been before Milah's death. He could understand how Lokna desired to meet his uncle's soul to know him for himself.

Jassan ground his teeth. "He may be right," he said before he could stop himself. "The spell might work if you all turn into your dragon forms and sacrifice something. Maybe if you all put in your own blood ..."

Lokna glanced down at Jassan. They only had to lock eyes for a second for Jassan to see that Lokna didn't appreciate his tentative input.

"Yeah, ok," Lokna said begrudgingly, lifting his head to his friends. "Can we at least try?"

"If you're going to risk using this altered spell," Jassan added, despite the centaur's eyeroll, "my aunt says the best time of the year to summon a soul is in fall."

"This time is better than any other?" Emma asked.

"Yes," Jassan said, "because the sky is falling, and it weakens the boundary."

They all looked into the sky as the rains of the fifth season of Avonoa began to fall in earnest, steady drops.

"That is believable," Emma said. "I've heard that the World of Souls is in the sky."

"It is," Jassan said, "and doing the spell now will make the majik stronger."

"But how will the spell work with only dragon blood?" Emma said. "And how can we sacrifice our dragon blood if it turns to ash when we bleed?"

"Yeah!" the other dragons grumbled.

One of the centaurs perked up. "We could cut ourselves when we're not in our dragon forms," she offered. "Then our blood won't turn to ash."

"What about Lokna and me?" the orange full dragon, Gizi, said. "Our blood will just turn to mush in this rain."

"No," the brown dragon said, "I've thought about that too." Lokna stepped to the pile of firewood they had gathered in the center of the clearing. He picked up a small knife from the ground and showed it to everyone in the circle. Even under a dark and cloudy sky, the glittering multi-colored hue shimmered across its edge in the faint light. A majikal blade. A blade specially designed to prevent the blood of an injured dragon from turning to ash. If a dragon was killed by this blade, the belief was that their body wouldn't turn to ash or embers and their soul wouldn't go to the World of Souls. They would be stuck between the world of the living and the world of the dead, or go somewhere else, unknown and lost forever. The knife was too small to do any real damage to any of the dragons here; however, in the silence of the group Jassan could hear the emotional implications of the risk.

But Lokna, with a determined gaze at everyone in the circle, lifted the knife. "It will work," he growled, and ripped the knife across his claw.

The fire before them blazed the angriest Jassan had ever seen one burn. It hissed and sizzled as acrid raindrops assaulted it. But every time a wet drop pelted a piece of wood, the fire in that spot shot higher than before. It was as if the fire itself was angry at the rain for trying to stop it from burning, and fought back with a vengeance. Because the fire had been ignited by all the dragons around it, it only wavered a moment before it burned hotter and higher.

"Dragons only," Jassan was told as the group gathered closer around the fire. Since he wasn't a dragon, he couldn't be in the circle, but the others consented to allow him to watch. He stood close by to assist Lokna if need be. However, he hadn't been entirely honest with them in his assessment of their spell. His aunt had allowed him to study things commonly considered "dark majik" but she hadn't exactly drilled him on the wording of this particular spell. It was entirely possible that if Lokna asked him to help with the chant, he might get it wrong. If he ever got the chance to do a summons, he knew exactly who he would contact. So he listened carefully and dreamed of seeing his parents again.

Jassan's parents had been killed five years ago when one of their experimental spells had gone horribly wrong. They never allowed Jassan to be present when they attempted new spells, so he had been safely tucked away at his aunt's home while they worked. The other faeries picked on and scolded him for his family's continued practice of majik and the rebukes only increased after his parents' death. As he watched the proceedings of the summons in front of him, he rehearsed in his mind the many ways he could ask his parents why they had continued such a dangerous practice.

Most everyone in the circle had shifted to their dragon forms. The five females stood in a loose circle surrounding Lokna. He began the incantation while the others used their fires to burn the ingredients in the smaller dragon-scale dishes next to them. Burk had opted to stay in his human form and stood outside the circle behind his sister, Emma. He wrapped his dark cloak around his shoulders tightly covering his dragon wrappings and hiding his dark, messy hair with the hood.

Jassan jealously compared the hues of the dragons around him. Emma was a beautiful dark blue with flecks of blue-green on her tail and spine. She looked like a glittering star streaking across a clear night sky. Small spikes jutted from her head like stunted hair but long, dangerous spikes on the end of her tail compensated in appearance. Back when her parents were young, most females had no spikes or horns, but over time and with hybrid dragons mixing into the genetic pool, many things about them were changing rapidly and Jassan thought the threatening spikes only added to Emma's allure. She was easily the smallest dragon in the group gathered around the fires, but Jassan assumed Burk would be even smaller in dragon form due to his age difference.

Gizi was bright orange overall, but Jassan could just make out a darker orange-red on the tips of her scales, tail and claws. Her eyes were widely separated on a large head, making her look much more distinctive than the others, and her jaw curved up, giving her a natural smile.

Sitting next to Gizi, Dasha lashed her tail. Her greyish, stone-colored goblin skin was reflected in her soft greyish-blue dragon scales, but her belly and wings were a greenish-blue. Her curly purple goblin hair disappeared in dragon form, but similar numerous spikes surrounded her dragon head and swept down her neck, implying the look of a lion. Jassan wondered if she might prefer being in her dragon form because then she was as large as the dragon twins, while as a goblin, she was smaller than the others and only came up to Emma's human shoulder.

Next were the twins. Both dragons were the red of a brilliant sunset after a dangerous storm, but Tyla's body had spots of darker red. Jassan caught her casting narrowed eyes at him as if daring him to comment on her deep red marks. He had freckles too, but he couldn't begin to compare them to Tyla's spots. Hers gave the appearance of a ferocious leopard, and her personality matched. And even though Eleka, on the other hand, was different in appearance from her sister only in the stripes of darker red that looked like blood or acid dripping down her sides, she didn't give off the fierce vibe that Tyla did. The longest horns on the twins' heads curled back and down, like their centaur hair being whipped in the wind.

Jassan wished his cloak was majikally waterproofed, like Burk's and his sister's, which would allow the water to trickle away from the cloth without touching it. But only a highborn part-dragon would wear a waterproof cloak on a daily basis. The twins wore only short cloaks over their shoulders in their centaur forms. In their dragon forms, the cloaks would be stuffed under their dragon wrappings, which grew to match their size. He knew the goblin didn't usually bother with a cloak, but because of the fall rains, he figured someone had forced one on her. While in her dragon form, she simply tossed it aside.

The dragon-scale dishes of ingredients in the circle contained the same foul-smelling potion of snorgack root and whistleberry, among other things. As Lokna smeared the potion on his front claws, the flames waved in unison with his claws. He chanted the spell and the others in the circle echoed a repeated phrase, "Fire of blood, soul of flame." The repetitive drone of it should have lulled Jassan, but the knowledge of what it meant sent a chill of dread down his spine.

He watched as the knife with the majikal edge was passed to each dragon in the circle. When it was received, each sliced the pad of their claw and squeezed it over a dish to express the blood within. While the knife was passed around, Lokna started the melodic part of the incantation. The others harmonized with his words.

> World of Souls,
> dragons be,
>
> Fire of blood,
> soul of flame.
>
> Hear the cry,
> come to me.
>
> Fire of blood,
> soul of flame.
>
> Milah ido Maran, he.
>
> Fire of blood,

soul of flame.

Here the blood,
offered thee.

At these words of offering, each of the surrounding dragons dumped a clawful of blood into the fire. It hissed and crackled and Jassan sensed in the sound the goddess of the dead laughing at them.

Fire of blood,
soul of flame.

We all here,
call to see.

Fire of blood,
soul of flame.

Milah ido Maran, he.

Fire of blood,
soul of flame.

Rend the gate,
Soul be free.

Fire of blood,
soul of flame.

Come to us,

I order thee.

Fire of blood,
soul of flame.

Milah ido Maran!

FIRE OF BLOOD,
SOUL OF FLAME!

FIRE OF BLOOD,
SOUL OF FLAME!

FIRE OF BLOOD,
SOUL OF FLAME!

FIRE OF BLOOD,
SOUL OF FLAME!

The final repeated chants grew louder with every word. Jassan and Burk, who had edged closer to Jassan without realizing it, looked up into the rain, now pouring over all of them. Despite the deluge, the fire in the middle of the circle grew taller and hotter. The smaller fires in the dragon-scale dishes grew accordingly.

The entire circle cast their eyes into the sky with the last words. Burk reached out without thinking, grabbing Jassan's arm, but Jassan only noticed in the back of his mind. He and all the others watched as a dark image appeared in the clouds over them. Jassan couldn't discern its color in the dark sky, but it grew and grew in size before them until it fell into the circle they formed.

The shape appeared as a fully grown, brown dragon, very similar to Lokna. It had landed in the fire, scattering embers into the faces surrounding it. The dragons all cast their faces away or threw a claw over their eyes to avoid the burning debris even though they were all immune to it except Jassan and Burk, still in human form. When they turned back, they could see the form of a dark dragon. His eyes glinted with warmth and sparkle as he searched the dragons around him. A hint of a smile curled his scaly dragon lips.

Suddenly the rain falling on him seemed to drain him of color. The grin melted from his face. Black smoke rippled down his scales and billowed around him. All the fires in the circle sputtered out. The dark dragon's scales and flesh seemed to shrink into his body and wrap around the emerging skeletal figure inside, exposing ridges against his hide. His claws elongated and his horns and fangs stretched to sickeningly sharp points. His eyes that had at first flickered with kindness and warmth deadened and turned fully black. No pupil gazed out, no iris glinted, and the ridges around the sockets sank into his face, giving a hollow, empty appearance. When the smoke began to clear, the dark and unnatural form of a shadowy monster stood in the remains.

2

THE FAERIE

"Milah?" Lokna uttered. He blinked several times to clear water from his eyes before he squinted into the pouring rain. "Uncle?"

The dark apparition growled a low rumble, but said no words. He stood silently in the remains of the fire. Thick, pure black smoke fell over him as if the rain turned black when it touched him and fell from him as dark shadow. He swung his head. More shadow dripped from him, but not in synchronization with the rain. The rain met his shape and simply disappeared into gloom. His eyes, empty and dark, swept the clearing and dragged themselves over the young dragons. But no light, life or recognition shone from the echoing recesses. What once may have been bright and lively seeing orbs now echoed the emptiness reflected everywhere else from inside his darkened form.

"I thought your uncle was a brown dragon?" Emma breathed.

"He was. Or is," Lokna whispered back.

"Perhaps all souls turn black from the World of Souls?" Emma wondered aloud.

Jassan felt Burk trembling at his side, his small hands now both clasped tightly to the faerie's arm.

"He's not right," Burk murmured quietly.

"Something's wrong," Jassan agreed, saying so louder for everyone to hear.

"Uncle," Lokna tried again, "Uncle Milah, do you know me? I'm your nephew, Lokna."

The dark apparition of Milah stepped closer to Lokna, out of the wet pulp that used to be the fire.

"Lokna," Emma warned, "be careful." Jassan heard the caution echo around the circle.

"I'm Lokna," he repeated. "Your brother, Mitashio, is my dromdan, my father."

Suddenly several things happened almost at once. Milah's shadow pulled back his blackened lips into a fierce snarl. Baring his long fangs, he raised his claw to strike at Lokna.

Lokna threw himself to the side to avoid the razor claws as everyone else reached out to him, as if to help from a distance. Even Jassan. But as Jassan reached his hand out, something hard slammed into his arm knocking it to the side. It felt as if a searing rock had pelted from the sky to stab and cling to his forearm. Any pain it might have caused disappeared instantly. Jassan turned his arm over to see a hole burned through his sleeve and a sparkling silver gemstone majikally stuck to his arm. He shook his arm quickly to see if it would come off, but the gem stayed fastened tighter than even his aunt's glue potion could work on a faerie's skin.

His gaze was torn away when Jassan noticed through the rainy haze that someone else had appeared next to the dark apparition in the circle. The muscular form of a man wearing a hood stepped next to the black creature. He placed one hand on its back leg and Jassan saw a soft glow coming from the man's other hand before he and the shadow dragon disappeared together in a swirl of what seemed like a miniature tornado.

"Where'd they go?" Lokna yelled over the suddenly torrential rain.

In reply, they heard a roar behind Jassan. The group turned to see the shadow creature strike at the strange man after they appeared in the woods together. The stranger held up a hand to protect himself from the roaring threat, but only for a moment before the wings on his back spread and lifted him from the ground just out of reach of the creature's claws. The faerieman flew swiftly back to the group with the dark dragon following him. He stopped briefly, his eyes falling first on Jassan and then on the gem embedded in Jassan's arm that had first burned a hole in his sleeve.

"Run!" he bellowed before he flew to Jassan's side.

He grabbed Jassan by the arm in a tight grip and pulled him toward the forest to escape the stampeding monster. The entire group fled with them.

"We should fly!" Lokna called as the group splashed through the bracken of the forest toward the safety of the portal they used so often.

But the stranger quickly corrected him. "No!" he said. "That will make it easier for him to follow! Stay to foot!"

The group crashed through the trees and brush with the menacing presence right behind them. Burk continued to cling to Jassan's arm as they ran, with the stranger clasped to Jassan's other arm.

"Let go of him!" the stranger cried to Jassan indicating Burk.

Jassan glanced at the faerieman, confused about his intentions. The stranger nodded hastily, again indicating for Jassan to shake off the younger boy. Jassan looked at the human boy, shaking beside him. He was much smaller and with his shorter legs would be much slower than Jassan on foot. Burk held his brown cloak high out to the side as he jumped over a log. Under the cloak Jassan could see a dark teal-colored wrapping similar to the dragon wrappings he'd seen on the others when not in dragon form. As confused and scared as the young boy looked beside him, Jassan didn't think he could be so heartless as to leave him in order to save himself.

"Let go of him!" the faerieman shouted.

Hearing the anger in his voice, Jassan pursed his lips and used the hand of the arm Burk gripped tightly to reach over and shake the faerieman's hand from his other arm. If the faerieman wanted Jassan to abandon a younger helpless human, Jassan didn't want the stranger's help. Unfortunately, Burk's grip let go in the chaos and the faerie's grip was stronger. In an instant Jassan landed at a run, stumbling on the uneven ground. He fell to the mud and looked around.

He had landed in a spacious depression in the forest. Roots wrapped around the edges of it, creating a hollow. The canopy of branches overhead made a shelter, keeping the soil beneath him somewhat dry.

"Stay here," the faerieman said. "Keep quiet."

"But—" Jassan started urging the man to also save the others, but the faerie interrupted by holding up his hands.

"I'm going back for the others," he said. "Keep everyone quiet when they get here."

Before Jassan could ask anything else, the faerieman disappeared.

Jassan tried to calm his breathing. Before he'd taken two breaths, the stranger reappeared with Dasha, in her goblin form.

Dasha was on the ground, on her side, mid-scream. Her small, grey goblin hands awkwardly covered her pointed ears and purple curls with her cloak tangled around her.

"Keep her quiet!" the faerie said over her noise and disappeared again.

"Dasha!" Jassan said as her cries abated into whimpers.

"What's going on?" she asked, sitting up. "How did we get here?"

"I don't know," Jassan admitted, "but he said to stay quiet."

"Who is he?" she asked, tugging her cloak from her leg.

Jassan could only shrug.

The stranger reappeared with Lokna.

"What about the boy?" Jassan said. "You can't leave him."

"These," the faerieman paused for a short breath, "were closest to the monster. Would you rather I have left them to it in order to rescue the boy?"

Jassan didn't respond and the faerie disappeared in a cloud of vapor again.

He materialized next with Burk, then Emma. Burk handed Emma her cloak as she shrank back into her human form. The two huddled together whispering, but neither met Jassan's eye.

As each person appeared in turn with the stranger, the questions flowed faster and louder from everyone present.

"Stay quiet," Jassan insisted.

"Who put you in charge?" Lokna shot back much louder than Jassan knew the faerie had advised him to allow.

"He did," Jassan pointed at the stranger as the faerieman reappeared wordlessly, dropped off Eleka and disappeared again.

Lokna scoffed. "He has no idea—"

"Quiet," Emma said. Her voice was firm but low. She stood and stared into the dripping sky. As Eleka began to speak, Emma held a finger to her lips.

"But—" Lokna began before Emma shushed him too.

"I hear something," she said under her breath.

The group silenced, everyone searching the dark, wet forest surrounding them. Jassan turned his head and tilted it in the direction Emma looked. His pointed faerie ears were better at finding sound than the humans' ears were, but not the dragons'. Since he was surrounded by dragons and part-dragons, he held no advantage. They all heard it at the same time; Tyla's scream.

The noises grew louder. They heard the monster roar, they heard branches breaking with a boom like a cannon. Out of nowhere Tyla and the stranger suddenly stood together in front of them. The faerieman hovered over her as the centaur crumpled to the ground.

Tyla opened her mouth to cry again, but the faerieman clamped a hand over it. He held a finger to his lips as Emma had just done, and everyone held their breath.

The woodland sounds increased as the monster got closer, accompanied by its low rumble of frustration. The trees and branches snapped with loud popping noises, making Burk jump. The stranger searched the forest around the depression that sheltered them, then waved for the group to gather under the roots to one side. Jassan sat down with them and was immediately squashed between Emma and Dasha, with Lokna taking up the rest of the space in front of him. The warmth of dragon scales against his cheek and Emma on his other side made Jassan flush.

They listened from their refuge, no one breathing as they heard reverberating footfalls behind and over them. Low growls bounced between the trees. Jassan closed his eyes for a moment and could notice the singular musk scent of damp earth and even the sharp tang of pine surrounding them. He could feel the mud in the wall they huddled against compress from the weight of the shadowy creature, then ooze over Jassan's shoulders and onto

Dasha's purple hair. Seemingly holding back the urge, Dasha didn't make a move to clear the mud. She simply shrank back further into the soft wall.

Finally, the growling above them calmed. The footfalls ambled away. The faerieman held up his hand, signaling the group to wait before they came out of hiding. He peered out first, looking over the edge of the depression. He held the rest of them back against the wall as the noises of the creature retreating in the trees slowed. The occasional thump of footfalls drifted back from farther away. Branches cracked in the distance. The monster's distant roar and grumble faded to quiet. Dasha finally wiped the mud from her forehead once the noise stopped altogether. But the group tucked together in the depression remained quiet, listening to the sound of rain trickling through the branches.

The rain eased momentarily, but still no one moved. Then the rain began to pour harder. Despite the cover of the trees overhead, rain dripped through their hair and scales, but they remained motionless.

"Slowly, and quietly," the faerieman said as he eventually lifted his weight from the group first.

The rain returned to a gentle mist, the best alleviation the fall season could give, allowing Jassan his first good look at the stranger. He saw a purple faerie under the dark hood. Jassan found the purple and green faeries more attractive than the blue faeries like him. As he rubbed life into his legs, he took in the stranger's plain black cloak with sleeves. The cloaks he had worn were sleeveless and fell all the way to the ground, one long piece of cloth that covered everything from the top of a faerie's head down to his feet. The stranger's cloak had a hood, but the hem reached only to his knees. Jassan had never seen one like it. Black pants visible under the cloak stopped above thick cloth bindings on his feet. None of the faerieman's clothing showed a drop of mud or water so Jassan assumed it was all majikally enchanted. Jassan thought he might be a highborn faerie, but he didn't recognize the faerieman.

"We have to get somewhere safer," the faerieman said softly, almost to himself. Then he pointed to Jassan. "I can only take one of you at a time. You come first."

Feeling the eyes of the others on him, Jassan started moving toward the man, but stopped when he heard Lokna.

"Wait," Lokna said, as he quietly shifted his weight away from the others. "What about Tyla? She's hurt."

Only then did Jassan allow his eyes to search out the young centaur in the dwindling light. A broad slash had been torn across her meaty horse rump.

"It's just a scratch," Tyla whispered. "I'll be fine. Let the faeries go first. Odds are that monster is probably after them."

"My uncle did despise faeries," Lokna agreed.

"No," Jassan said before the faerieman could take hold of him. "Take Tyla and Eleka first. Get them out of danger."

The faerie seemed to clench his jaw ever so slightly, but walked over to the injured centaur and placed his hand gently on her muddy shoulder.

"The rest of you stay quiet until I return," he hissed. His eyes swept the area beyond them briefly, seemingly to make sure the monster hadn't returned.

No one spoke. Jassan listened to the rain dripping in the leaves. He tried to keep his arm curled against his body so the others couldn't see the glistening gem that had attached itself. Hugging his meager cloak against his soaked skin helped his cover. But the tips of his ears felt stiff with cold, so he tried to pull the hood closer to his head and face. The wet cowl stuck to his cheeks and more water dribbled down the front of his tunic.

"What's that?" Lokna growled. Jassan turned to look at him and saw the dragon pointing one massive claw at Jassan's arm and the shining gem.

"I don't know," Jassan said quickly, re-covering his arm the best he could and tucking it back inside his wet cloak.

"Is that what the monster wants?" Lokna growled. "Did you use that against my uncle?"

He took a step closer to Jassan but stopped when the faerieman abruptly reappeared beside them.

"It looks safe enough for now," the faerieman said, then noticed the atmosphere between Jassan and Lokna. His faerie eyes locked on Lokna's. "Perhaps I'll take you next," he said. Placing one hand on Lokna's shoulder, the two of them disappeared in a cloud.

Jassan could feel the eyes of everyone on him again. He thought it might be best to go last so the others didn't think he was running away, so he curled into the muddy bank and kept his head lowered. His breath against his chest did nothing to warm him. He wished he could go back to curling up against one of the dragons.

The faerieman returned and disappeared with everyone in the group in turn. Emma and Burk went last before Jassan, with Emma only barely able to let go of Burk's hand when they had to separate.

Once everyone was gone, Jassan listened in silence to the gentle rainfall in the forest around him. He thought he could hear the monster crashing through the woodlands miles away. A jolt of fear shot through him as he wondered whether the faerieman might leave him behind. Maybe he had done something bad to Lokna's uncle without realizing it. The spell may have gone horribly wrong and Jassan was to blame. If he ever got back home and saw his aunt, he would have quite a bit to tell her about the entire process and he knew he would have her full and rapt attention.

Then he wondered if he should just leave this place under his own power and not wait for the other faerie to transport him away. He had gone a long way from home following the dragons to their meeting place. He had often wandered far to follow the dragons. From here he thought he could probably get above the trees and find his way home on his own. He looked into the canopy of branches overhead and shook a little from fear at the idea that the monster was still nearby. He knew it would find him with no trouble at all.

Jassan also knew that if he left on his own there was a chance the strange faerieman would hunt him down too. The faerie might be able to find him through some majikal means with this thing attached to his arm. But he knew the others didn't want him around, they never had. He had not gained their friendship and had achieved little else by following them; in fact, look where he found himself now. Wouldn't it be merciful not to force his presence on them any longer? He might even give them the satisfaction of thinking the monster had gotten him.

He tried to picture the forest around him in his head. He didn't know where he was. He had scurried through the woods with the others in a direction he wasn't familiar with. He thought he was on the far reaches of the area closest to Marrack Forest, where he lived, but he hadn't recognized anything around him. He sat up and tried to peer into the darkness. If he left now, would he be able to avoid the dragon monster? And would he be less safe going home to his aunt? If he left now, any route from here would be a long distance, but traveling by himself might be easier than the stop-start of following the others, or safer than trusting the faerie to take him. His plans were interrupted when he thought he saw movement in the dark distance, so Jassan pulled himself back into the mud wall. No, he wouldn't be going it alone.

Jassan was both relieved and a little disappointed when the faerie suddenly reappeared before him. Jassan stood slowly, hugging himself for warmth, and sad that he had missed his opportunity to slip away.

He walked over to the faerie, but the man didn't reach out to him as he'd expected. "Are we leaving too?" Jassan asked, wondering if the faerie's reticence confirmed Jassan's thought that he might not want Jassan to be with the others he had already transported away.

"I thought we might talk first," the faerie said. "I can explain that thing on your arm."

Jassan tucked his arm tighter to his chest. "No," he said, surprising himself.

"Don't you want to know what it is?" the man said. "What power it holds?"

With these last words, Jassan's chin lifted to meet the faerie's gaze. But he swallowed his curiosity. "It doesn't matter," he said, surprised his voice held so steady. "The others, they wouldn't believe anything coming from me if I had to explain it to them later. You should explain it to all of us together."

"They don't matter," the faerie said, waving his hand. "I can get them home and you'll never have to see them again."

Jassan's gaze dropped again. The faerie could take him home too, but then he might never see Emma again. Could he bear never seeing her again? Besides, he had the sinking feeling that one or two of the dragons in the group would hunt him down for answers anyway. He shook his head. "They deserve an explanation too, especially Lokna," he said. "And I would hate for you to have to explain it twice."

The faerie sighed. He put out his hand and Jassan reached for it, but the man grabbed Jassan's wrist and pushed back his sleeve to expose the silvery gem embedded in his arm, almost as if making sure it was still there. The faerieman pursed his lips, thought for a moment, then nodded.

In the blink of an eye and a swirl of clouds, Jassan and the stranger stood side by side in a dark cave.

"Alright," the faerieman said. "It's time for explanations."

3

TRIVNOR

The cave walls were a burnt-gold color striated with reds and oranges, the likes of which Jassan had never seen. The cave opening yawned down a short tunnel off to the side. Jassan could see swirling mists of fog outside and instinctively knew the rains and mists of the forest they had left were somehow far away from here.

"Where are we?"

"Who are you?"

"Why did you bring us here?"

"What was that thing?"

"When can we go home?"

"How did we get here?"

The questions started as soon as the faerieman appeared in the cave with Jassan, but they seemed to have been stirring for a while among themselves. Gizi and Tyla's twin, Eleka, hovered over the injured centaur. Dasha,

Emma and Burk huddled together against the wall nearby and Lokna sat stoically glowering at the proceedings.

As Jassan attempted to hide next to the wall of the cave, the faerie ignored the questions coming at him. Instead, he sat down on a stone next to Tyla, pulled a small satchel out from under his cloak and produced a rag and an elixir that he began applying to Tyla's wounds.

"Ow!" she flinched as he splashed the pungent-smelling liquid on her hind quarter. Everyone else, obviously concerned, quieted down around them. "What is that stuff?" she asked him in the silence.

"Flarote," he said. Tyla recoiled as if he had threatened her with further pain. The entire group of youth gasped. Even Jassan, though he wasn't a dragon or part-dragon, knew the stories. Eating too much flarote would kill a dragon, and flarote had been used to make a dragon poison back in the days of the dragon war. The name of the herb was now synonymous with killing dragons of all types and in all ways, although Jassan also knew many of those stories weren't true, according to his aunt. Through misinformation, secrecy and stories, it had been forgotten that flarote was also a healing herb. His aunt had taught him from a young age the intricacies of the little fire-shaped mushroom, including that it was illegal for a faerie to use or possess it.

"Are you crazy?" Tyla said, her large eyes growing larger. "Get that away from me!"

"Does it look like it's hurting you?" he asked, indicating the slice on her back end that was slowly closing. "The flarote is diluted with mint and other healing herbs. It won't hurt you."

"What happened to you, Tyla?" the goblin Dasha asked.

Tyla shrugged, "I tried fighting the thing, unlike the rest of you who just ran away."

"Did you hurt it?" Burk asked, his eyes lighting up for the first time since the spell and summons had worked.

"No," Gizi said with a giggle, fitting for her name in better times. "She blew fire in its face! When that didn't stop it, she threw her cloak over its eyes, but it knocked her down anyway. The scratch is from a branch scraping her as she fell."

"It was a good tactical decision!" Tyla insisted as everyone else chuckled. "Better than yours, Dasha. You just shrank into your goblin shape, hoping for, what? That its claw would land later rather than sooner? You didn't even try your fire!"

"Fire won't hurt a dragon, monster or otherwise, it would only light the forest on fire. If I hadn't shrunk down underneath it," the goblin shot back, "it would have clawed me to pieces."

"And once you were smaller, it wasn't touching you," the faerieman said, quelling the spat, "I was able to pull you out." His job with Tyla's wound done, the faerieman returned the supplies to his bag and moved from the stone to sit down next to Jassan. Dasha gave Tyla a smug grin, but Tyla rolled her oversized centaur eyes away from her.

"I'm sorry," Jassan finally spoke up when it seemed no one else was going to ask what everyone still wanted to know about the man sitting next to him, "but, who are you?" A hush fell over the entire group. They all wanted to hear this.

The faerieman sighed and tipped his head to Jassan. "That's more like it," he said. "One question at a time."

"But—" Lokna started before the faerieman cut him off with a look.

"—AND," the faerieman said louder, "you must let me speak."

Lokna huffed and curled his cumbrous body against the wall. He glared at Jassan without blinking but Jassan did his best to ignore him.

"My name," he turned back to Jassan, "is Trivnor. I'm not sure how many answers I can give you to your questions, but I'll do my best."

"Where are we?" Jassan asked first, staring out at the rolling fog. The cave felt much warmer than anything he had yet experienced in the forest. The persistent clouds of fall gave most of the kingdom darkness for three months of the fifteen-month year. But this place was bright, and as the fog shifted outside, Jassan thought he could see golden sand on the outside.

"We're on the far reaches of the east side of the Allegiant Queendom. I'm sorry, they call it Sandarin now, don't they?" Trivnor said. "This was the farthest and most secluded location I could think to go in the moment."

"Sandarin?" Jassan breathed. He had always wished to visit other kingdoms, but never dreamed he might. "How did we get here so quickly?" Jassan asked. He had never been farther from his aunt's home than the clearing where he had found this group of friends, let alone out of Marrack Forest.

"With this," Trivnor said. He held up his hand to show the group a gemstone the same size and cut as the one embedded in Jassan's arm, except instead of the solid silver of Jassan's, the colors in the man's were a swirl of grey, white and silver, and the gem was attached to the palm of his hand. The gem looked like half of a dragon's heart, tear-drop shaped, with crisp facets along its face and edges. "This gives me the power to move myself and one other person instantly to anywhere I've been before or I can see ahead of me."

"Where did you get it?" Jassan asked, enthralled. He remembered the faerie asking him, only moments ago, if he wanted to know what kind of power the gem in his arm held. He tried not to rub his arm or the silver gem, only wondering and hoping it might give him the same kind of powers he'd only heard about.

Several months before this Jassan happened to see the group of dragons flying overhead when he was out gathering herbs. He had followed them and shadowed their adventures in the forest. He followed the group again and again after that first time, reaching them with less and less trouble, but since their dragon wings could take them to their meeting place farther and faster than his smaller faerie wings could take him, he had to get up earlier and search longer each time. He had never been to where they lived and could only imagine going to the Noble Kingdom to see Emma. Or being able to easily find the friends wherever they gathered.

"You're not asking the right questions," Emma said, interrupting Jassan's reverie. "What was that thing that attacked us? And when can we go home?"

The others murmured their agreement. Burk whimpered, "I want to go home."

Trivnor sighed. "I'm not sure that's safe right now," he said gently to Burk. "But we will try when it is. First, I must know who you all are and where home is for each of you."

His gaze swept the group, but no one seemed willing to respond first. The twin centaurs looked at each other, avoiding eye contact with Trivnor. Jassan assumed none of them would trust the stranger right away because he was a faerie, so he decided to speak up. Perhaps the faerieman would feel sympathy for him.

"My name is Jassan," he said. "I live with my aunt in Marrack Forest."

Trivnor touched his forehead in a casual salute and glanced around the group again. When no one else seemed forthcoming, he turned back to Jassan. "And who is your aunt?" he asked, waving him on to continue.

"She's no one, really," Jassan mumbled, prompting an exaggerated eyeroll from Lokna.

"I doubt that," Trivnor said. "Perhaps I know her?"

"Probably not," Jassan said. "She's Shaman Bitra."

"Not many faeries practice majik anymore," Trivnor said, without the accusing tone Jassan usually heard when others talked about faeries and majik. It sounded as if the faerieman was truly interested when he heard his aunt was a shaman.

"And well they shouldn't," Lokna grumbled. "Dragons have long memories."

"That happens when you can literally pass memories to each other," Gizi added.

"Which is why I share the memories of my sires. We remember the times when faeries practiced whatever sorcery they wanted without considering the consequences," Lokna said. "They should have been banned from majik entirely."

"My aunt is a good faerie," Jassan said, his voice rising at the accusation he felt now. "She tries to help other beings and races and she doesn't do anything dangerous. The things she's taught me helped you, didn't they? With your summons?"

At this, Lokna raised his top lip to reveal his fangs, but Jassan knew he was right about this. He had helped Lokna summon his uncle. He just didn't want to let on that he had no idea what had gone wrong.

"What type of majik does she practice, Jassan? What is her specialty?" Trivnor insisted.

Jassan's eyes bounced and couldn't quite fix on Trivnor as he admitted, "She studies the World of Souls and summoning majik. But she does lots of other things too."

Lokna growled. "It was either her ineptitude or your meddling in things you don't understand that summoned Milah the way he is." Jassan jumped to his feet to face Lokna, but had no immediate idea what to do or say, so he settled with standing tall and trying to look bold. He folded his arms across his chest to avoid plucking at the bunching of his breeches.

"If I hadn't helped you the summons wouldn't have worked at all," he told the large dragon.

"If you hadn't stalked us and shoved your way into our group, Milah wouldn't have been...ruined!"

"That wasn't Jassan's doing," Trivnor said gently. "I believe he was just trying to help. Someone else is the real enemy here."

Lokna and Jassan turned away from each other. Jassan seethed, but in the back of his mind he knew there was a real possibility that Lokna was right, no matter what the faerie said. He might have done something wrong with the spell. He wouldn't know if Lokna had gotten the wording right. He couldn't be certain of the ingredients and he most certainly had made up the idea that the ingredients had to be set out in a certain order. He might have caused whatever darkness had come over Milah because he didn't fully understand his aunt's practice and teachings. When it came down to it, he had really just listened to her stories and gathered the herbs she needed.

With their silence, Trivnor sighed and looked over the rest of the group. "Anyone else?" he asked. "Or would you rather find your own way home from here?"

"I'm Emma," she said quietly, "and this is my brother Burk. We'd like you to take us back to the Noble Kingdom. Please."

"That one might be tricky," Trivnor said, "but like I said, I will try."

"Well, I don't need anything from a faerie," Lokna spoke up. "Gizi and I can make it home ourselves, right, Gizi? The Rock Clouds aren't so far from here."

"Lokna," Gizi grunted, "you just told him my name."

"And you just told him mine!" Lokna growled.

"And you told him where we live," Gizi growled back.

They both jumped into an attacking crouch. Before the dragons could pounce on each other, Trivnor stood and held out a hand to each of them. "Either way," he said firmly, "Lokna, Gizi, the Rock Clouds are probably the most dangerous place to go right now. Of all of you, I will have to try to get you home last."

"What?" Gizi blinked in surprise.

"Why?" Lokna barked.

Trivnor shook his head. "We'll have to discuss it later," he said. "For now, I'd like to hear more about the rest of you." He sat back down, folding his legs under him. "Centaurs, where are you from?"

Tyla vehemently shook her head at her sister but was waved off. "I'm Eleka," the centaur said. "This is my twin Tyla. We live on the plains at the north end of Centaur River."

The twins were nearly mirror images in their centaur forms. Both had earthy horse bodies and dark skin with dark wings imprinted on their backs. Other than their personalities, the only way Jassan could tell them apart was from the way Tyla wore her dragon wrappings, the cloth that melted into her dragon scales when she changed species, stretched across her chest in an 'X' from shoulder to hip. Eleka, the friendlier centaur, simply looped them around her midsection. The X that Tyla wore seemed to warn everyone not to mess with her.

Jassan didn't need the diffused light from the fog enhancing the brightness in Tyla's red irises or the large size of her eyes to notice them roll at her sister. He thought Eleka wanted to say more, but Tyla threw her hand out and touched her sister's arm.

"And we ask that you return us to the plains immediately," Tyla finished for her, then threw her twin narrowed eyes.

"And I will try to do such as soon as I can," Trivnor said. He bowed his head and touched first his forehead, then the bridge of his nose and his chest as if in salute to the centaurs. Jassan saw the twins glance at each other with confusion.

"That's a very old centaur salute," Eleka acknowledged out loud.

"Antiquated," Tyla added.

"No one uses it anymore," Eleka continued.

"Where are you from?" Tyla finished suspiciously.

"Far away," Trivnor said. "And I still use it because I'm older than I probably seem." Then he turned to Dasha to end their questioning. "And you, goblin, where can I return you?"

"Kirlik," she snapped back at him. "And my name's Dasha and I don't appreciate being kidnapped nor will my father, seeing as he's one of the generals for the goblin army."

"Would your father have preferred I allow you to die at the hands of the monster?"

Dasha allowed her chin to lower slightly before she cast her eyes away from the faerie.

"Now, as I have said," Trivnor continued, "I will try to get you all home as soon as possible, but the travel will not be exactly safe."

"Why won't it be safe?" Gizi said, the ready giggle in her voice all but gone. "Is it that thing? That monster?"

"Hey!" Lokna snapped. "That's my uncle."

"No," Trivnor said, "that was not your uncle. Not the way you would know him, anyway. You might have recognized his soul, but the being you saw here was a shadow of it, corrupted… and controlled by…an evil man."

"Who?" Jassan blurted out before he could stop himself.

"He's no one you need concern yourself with," Trivnor said, looking at Jassan. "For now, I need for you to give that to me." He pointed to Jassan's arm.

Jassan pulled his sleeve back to look down at the silvery gem. Now that he looked at it closer, he noticed that it wasn't purely silver. It was shiny and smooth and…reflective. It was a mirror. Swirls of fog or mist appeared to drift through it, but mostly it reflected either his appearance or the world around him.

Jassan gently ran his hand over the gem attached to his arm. His aunt concocted a mixture of sap, honey and drained hytocomp to make saen, the most powerful adhesive known in Marrack Forest, and the most highly sought after, even from the faeries that couldn't be seen with her. Jassan had once accidentally dripped the saeny glue onto a dish, adhering it so strongly to the table where it sat that his aunt needed dragon fire to release it. And they had to get a new table. But this gem seemed painlessly attached more strongly to his arm than even his aunt's adhesive would ensure. He feared the pain he would feel trying to remove the gem. But before he could reply to Trivnor's prompt, he heard himself say, "How do we know we can trust you?"

Everyone else turned to look at Trivnor. Jassan lifted his chin slightly when he realized that none of them had thought to ask that yet.

"Yes," Emma said, "you haven't told us anything about yourself except your name."

"How do we know *you're* not the evil man that created that monster?" Dasha said.

"And poisoned me?!" Tyla added.

"He didn't poison you," Eleka said quietly.

"We don't know that!" Tyla retorted.

"Isn't it illegal for a faerie to possess flarote?" Gizi asked, looking to Dasha.

"That's kind of a grey area when it's mixed with other things," Dasha answered Gizi before she turned to Trivnor. "Where did it come from? Why do you have it?"

"And how do you plan to use it on us?" Lokna growled.

"Alright," Trivnor conceded. He squeezed his eyes shut briefly and Jassan saw the edge of his lip twitch into a frown. "I'll tell you what I can, on two conditions. One, the questions must at least slow down, allowing me to answer. Two, and this one is not negotiable, you must all swear an oath upon your wyrd never to tell another living soul anything that I tell you here." He paused to let what he'd said sink in. "Will all of you give me your wyrd?"

The group settled down immediately. Eyes darted. Mouths fell open. To give one's wyrd was to give the one who asked for it one's most serious trust with an everlasting bond. If a dragon broke the wyrd they gave to another, they had to be ready to give up their life. They could be killed for breaking their wyrd or forgiven, but that's why giving one's wyrd was a stronger commitment than giving an oath or a promise. A dragon's wyrd equated to their life. Jassan knew immediately, as he was sure everyone else did too, that protecting whatever the faerieman was about to tell them was more dire than protecting any of their lives.

"I'll give you my wyrd," Jassan said, barely hesitating. "Who am I going to tell, anyway?" he asked rhetorically, with a half-hearted grin. Deep down, he hoped that being brought into whatever confidences this faerie was offering might help him keep the gem on his arm. It might give him power like Trivnor's and the secrets that go with it.

"If any of the rest of you don't want to give your wyrd," Trivnor said, "then I can certainly take you home and you'll never hear from me again."

"I want answers first," Lokna growled.

"Answers only come with your wyrd," Trivnor countered.

Lokna ground his jaw hard, but kept his silence for the moment.

"I'll give you my wyrd," Burk said suddenly.

"Burk!" Emma hushed him.

"It's ok," Burk said. "If it turns out that he's taken our wyrd on false pretenses, then the bond is void, right? That's what Aunt Tierni says."

Trivnor nodded to him.

Emma sighed. "Alright, I'll give you my wyrd too."

Slowly everyone agreed and gave Trivnor their wyrd with either a nod or an undertone consent. Agreeing last, Lokna slithered his enormous head in front of the faerie. "I'll give you my wyrd, faerie," he hissed, "with the understanding that, if you betray us, not only will the bond be void, but if you lie or deceive us in any way, shape or form, I will personally tear you limb from limb."

Trivnor didn't even blink. "Understood."

After a pause, Trivnor pointed a purple finger at his and Jassan's gems. "These are powerful, majikal keys," he said, "and more of them are out there. Now that you know of them and you've given your wyrd not to tell anyone what you learn here, the first thing I will tell you is that your help is required to retrieve the rest of them."

Murmurs filled the cavern. The wind outside whistled past the entrance as a maelstrom of fog and sand picked up. After a few moments, the questions poured out again.

"How did *he* get one?" Lokna said, jabbing a claw at Jassan.

"Where did they come from?" Eleka asked.

"Danger keys!" Gizi exclaimed.

"Do they all do what yours did?" Dasha asked.

"No, power keys!" Gizi corrected herself without prompting from anyone.

The questions (or ridiculous comments in Gizi's case) continued to rattle until Trivnor held up his hands for quiet.

"Again, you must let me answer one at a time," he said with a stronger hint of irritation. "No, they don't all do what mine did, each key has a different majik. The keys aren't dangerous, each one has valuable power. And they were blasted apart when Kelraz attacked me."

"Who's Kelraz?" Dasha asked.

"Alright," Trivnor said, pinching the bridge of his nose, hesitating before he knew what would have to come next. "I'll tell you everything. Let me start at the beginning."

4

KNOWING

"These are not just any gems nor are they random gems with power, like the ones the goblins mine," Trivnor said, looking into each pair of eyes in turn before landing on Jassan's. "They are the keys used to guard the gate to the World of Souls."

After a few gasps followed by another somber silence, he continued. "My home and village were destroyed by Kelraz. Only a short time ago." His voice broke, but he swallowed hard and continued. "I come from a small village that has raised and trained each successive gatekeeper down through time. Kelraz was my friend in our youth but today he…he attacked us. He killed the gatekeeper and tried to take the keys. I was able to send the keys to relative safety with the power from this key." He indicated the gem in his palm. "I was also able to follow that one." He pointed to the gem on Jassan's arm.

"Now," he continued, "I need to find the other keys before Kelraz does. If he gets them all, he'll…well, he'll do what he set out to do from the beginning."

"What's that?" Emma asked.

"Kelraz," Trivnor said, "even while being raised alongside myself and other potential gatekeepers, has somehow come to believe that with the power in these keys, in addition to being in charge of the border between the living world and the World of Souls, the gatekeeper should also rule over the entire world. He believes that, since the keys confer the powers of the gods, the gatekeeper should be allowed to exact their will over all of Avonoa. If Kelraz gets all the keys, he'll destroy the world as we know it. Damaging your uncle's soul," he said as he pointed at Lokna, "was only his first step."

"If you're telling the truth," Emma said thoughtfully, "then we should take this to my parents. My uncle will send out an army and find the keys for you."

Trivnor began shaking his head before she finished. "I remind you, it is vital to your lives that you keep your wyrd and don't share this with anyone outside this group. Finding the gems will be enough trouble. Besides, what would happen if someone doesn't want to give it up? Start a war to take it? Multiple wars? One faerie, who was raised to revere and respect the power of these keys, was willing to murder his friends and family to gain them. What do you think someone else with more status than you have would do to get them? Kings? Queens?...Villains? The wars that could ensue are unthinkable. The more beings who know about them and their power, the more dangerous they are.

"I was forced to tell you this is because you have seen these two keys. The mystery of the gateway has been kept secret since the dawn of Avonoa through strong majik from the gods themselves. If someone leaves our village to travel, they are bound not only by their wyrd but by powerful spells, sacred oaths and enchantments. As for the keys themselves, layers of majik surround and sustain them. Again, given by the gods. I, as the last remaining loyal guard from my village, must find and attain these keys and take my place as gatekeeper."

"I'm sorry," Gizi said quietly, "but that all sounds like exactly what this Kelraz guy would say." Her bright orange hue in contrast to the cold, grey skies set off the red tips on her wings, tail and head. Surrounded by the warmth of the cave, Jassan thought she glowed like a giant fire.

To Jassan's surprise, Trivnor nodded. "You're right," he said. "And to prove that I'm not the villain in this, I'll do two things. One," he stood and offered his hand to Dasha to help her stand, "I'll take you all home. We can decide what to do from there. But you must remember your oaths not to tell anyone else. And two, I'll even allow this young faerie to keep the key he has for now. Until I can earn your trust."

After he helped Dasha to her feet he said, "I will have to trust all of you to keep the secret of the gateway, and I'll trust you," he looked at Jassan, "not to use or give away that key until you do trust me or you find someone else you can trust to use it properly. The fate of the world of the living and the dead relies upon this trust between us. Do we have an agreement?" He offered his hand to Jassan.

Jassan allowed Trivnor to help him from the cave floor. When he stood looking up at the purple-skinned faerie, he nodded.

"Very well," Trivnor said.

In the silence that followed, Burk sniffled. "Emma," he said, "I'm hungry."

Emma looked down at him. "Trivnor," she said. "It's time we go. We wish you and Jassan luck, but we need to return home to whatever punishments might be meted for our summoning. Because everyone is sure to find out about it."

"Or they will when Milah charges the gate," Gizi muttered. Lokna backhanded her leg.

A palpable foreboding settled on the group. "Yes," Trivnor said. When he turned from the entrance to the cave to face everyone, the heavy fog of fall and the sands of Sandarin swirled around behind him and over the dunes in the distance. "I have been to many places in the land of Avonoa," he continued, "but unfortunately, I haven't made it to the Noble Kingdom."

"What does that mean?" Emma asked. "You can't take us home?"

Trivnor shook his head. "It means I can only take you back to where I found you, or thereabouts. We can find the way to your homes from there."

"What if that monster is still there?" Gizi said. "Can you kill it? Fight it?"

"Hey!" Lokna shot at her. He would not let any of them forget who Milah was.

Gizi shrugged, "I mean, if it's evil and he's not *really* your uncle."

Lokna looked like he wanted to defend his uncle further, but Trivnor waved a hand to hold his tongue. "I don't really have a means to harm the creature. Or stop it." When he said that everyone froze. "The best we can do is try to avoid it."

"He came from the World of Souls," Lokna said. "Won't he just return there after a short time? That's what all the spellbooks say about summoning. The souls always return after a brief stay here."

"I'm sorry to say," Trivnor said, "that the gate is wide open right now. Normally, the visitation of souls to the living world is closely regulated by the gatekeeper using all the keys. That's what the gatekeeper is raised and trained to do with these keys. But there is no gatekeeper right now. No souls will be restrained from crossing the gate between worlds until all the keys are restored."

"So," Gizi spoke slowly, "you're saying that we have to go back to the place where we summoned the soul and try to sneak home from there, only hoping it won't follow us home from there?"

"I'll do what I can to transport you all and protect you," he responded. "That will hopefully prove that you can trust me. But, yes, we will have to start by backtracking the way we came to the place you summoned his uncle," he motioned to Lokna, "and from there do our best to get you home. Before your uncle's damaged soul or Kelraz can find us."

"Thanks for not leaving me," young Burk said, looking up at Jassan as he tip-toed alongside him. Trivnor had transported everyone back to the clearing with the muddied and scattered remains of their fire and spellcasting attempt. Once no one had heard or seen the corrupted soul of Milah skulking about, they had set off quietly through the woods.

"You know I didn't want to," Jassan said. He didn't want the boy to think the worst of him, the way he felt the others did. He still felt bad about what happened when they were on the run together while escaping the dark dragon after the summons. Jassan remembered trying to remove Trivnor's grip on his arm but instead accidentally pulling free of Burk's smaller hand holding tight to his other arm. Jassan had a soft spot for Burk and hoped the younger boy didn't fault him.

"I know," he replied. "My fingers slipped."

"Yeah," Emma stepped up to join the two as they walked along and Jassan's stomach did a little flip, "thanks for helping Burk."

"Are you coming back to Kingstor with us?" Burk asked.

"My parents can keep you safe," Emma offered.

Jassan shook his head. "Trivnor said he would take me to my home after he gets all of you back to the portal."

"Will you be safe there?" Burk asked. "I mean, you won't have tall walls and guards and battlements and stuff to hide behind like at the castle where we live."

"No, I won't," Jassan said, "but I'm pretty sure that your parents, of all humans, don't want anything to do with my kind ever again."

"That's not true," Emma said, her silver embroidered cloak swishing over leaves on the ground, further reminding Jassan that she was royalty. "Faeries come to the castle all the time."

"No, they don't," Burk said.

"Yes, they do," Emma said. "You just don't know about it."

"Why not?" Jassan asked. "Why would he not know when faeries are in the castle?"

Emma shrugged. "It's just… our parents don't make a big fuss about it, that's all."

"You mean they hide it," Jassan said. "They're not exactly happy with faeries being there. Right?"

"Well…" Emma's voice trailed away. She pursed her lips and wouldn't lift her gaze from the ground.

Jassan's heart burned. He forced himself not to grind his teeth. Not only were these two part-dragons royalty, but their parents would be ashamed and possibly angry to know they had showed any deference to Jassan, a faerie.

Jassan began to lift his wings. He wanted to fly away. Leave, get away from them and the sadness of not feeling accepted, but before he could do anything they heard Trivnor from up ahead tell everyone to be quiet.

Everyone stopped. They had done this on their way a few times. Trivnor would halt them, and once he was sure the noise or sight was nothing of alarm, they would set off again. The trek on foot was longer than anyone liked. The group of friends usually came through a portal and then flew to their meeting place in the clearing. Trivnor reminded them that the monster could also fly and they would easily be seen in the air, so they lumbered through the forest instead.

"Alright," Trivnor called, "let's continue—"

Before he could finish, a colossal black shadow burst through the sparse canopy overhead, knocking into Dasha's greyish-blue dragon body before the two dragon forms crashed into a thicket of trees, sending branches and bark flying through the air. Dasha screamed, attempting to push the larger and heavier dragon off her body. This time she remembered her fire and blew flames into the monster's face. It didn't even blink. The monster dripped black shadow onto Dasha as she screamed and flung out her claws to ward off her attacker.

"No!" Trivnor yelled. In a flurry of clouds, he transported himself on top of Milah's form and grabbed him by the horns on his head. Wrenching the dragon's head back and forth, he was able to keep the dragon from snapping its jaws into Dasha's neck. Dasha got her legs between them and heaved her weight upward, throwing the shadowy dragon away from her and on top of Trivnor.

Trivnor scrambled free of the dragon and stood to face it.

The dark dragon rumbled in its throat. It took a swipe at Trivnor, but instead of attacking, it stopped and blinked. It glared at Trivnor and slowly began circling him. The dragon's growls gradually turned into the rough shape of words.

"Triv-nor," it gurgled.

The shock showed on Trivnor's face for only a moment before he narrowed his eyes. "Kelraz," he said slowly.

"Where – are – they?" The mangled words came haltingly at first.

"It knows you," Emma whispered from only a few dragon lengths away, but Trivnor and the monster both heard her.

"Yes," Trivnor answered.

"I—know—you—too," the beast rumbled. "Emmaleena—daughter of—Hirowyn—and—Priyanna—Noble Princess."

Emma gasped. Trivnor cast his eyes to Emma and pursed his lips as if he hadn't known of Emma's royal blood. Although Emma and Burk weren't first in line for the throne but only cousins to the heirs, they still lived at the castle and learned to rule the kingdom.

But the monster didn't stop there. "Prince—Burkyla," it growled low. His shadowed eyes turned to the others one by one. "Lokna—son of the—current Rakgar—Rock Clouds."

Lokna bared his fangs at the monster.

"Gizi," he continued. Jassan noticed that the words were coming easier, "daughter of—Rakgar's most trusted—advisor and close—friend of Hirowyn—feira Toggil."

Gizi crouched low as if she might attack and narrowed her eyes.

"Tyla—and Eleka—daughters of centaur—warrior leader—Ashel—and the dragon—Prakyndar."

Eleka's gaze swept the forest floor, obviously thinking furiously, but Tyla pulled a small knife from under her dragon wrappings.

"And   Dasha—daughter   of—General—Keeahrspi—of the—goblin army."

The greyish-blue dragon hissed.

"You—cannot—hide from—me." Milah's dark soul dripped shadow as he glared at the group through vacant eyes.

When another swirl of wind and clouds had cleared, Trivnor and the beast were gone. But the rest of them stayed rooted in their places by the fear that a dangerous, mad faerie now knew them all, and knew where they lived. He knew their full names. He knew of their parents and their families. The group of friends glanced at each other. No one looked at Jassan.

Then Trivnor reappeared in front of them alone and before they could react, he responded to Milah's challenge. "We can try," he said, and began pushing Jassan forward. "To the portal," he called to the group, getting everyone moving. They believed the faerieman was their best hope to get home safely, so they fell in line.

As he ran beside the older faerie, Jassan glanced over his shoulder, looking for the shadowy form he thought he could hear crashing through the trees after them. Then glancing up at Trivnor, he said through gasping breaths, "He knew you."

"Yes," Trivnor said, his voice unnervingly steady. "But he did *not* know you."

Finally, when Jassan thought the pain in his side from running would force him to collapse, the group burst from the trees to the little-used road leading to the portal. Jassan took a moment to gawk at the portal. A massive hole in a wall of rock, three dragons could easily fit through it side-by-side. It loomed as dark before them as the shadowy creature they feared was chasing them.

Jassan had never been through a portal before. His aunt would never allow it. She didn't trust them and she demanded that Jassan never go near one. He wondered briefly what his punishment might be for crossing her as he watched the others get swallowed in the dark when they entered before he did. When Gizi's red-tipped tail disappeared last into the blackness, Jassan turned to see the shadowy monster several dragon lengths away. It roared and tore at the bare branches, forcing its way through toward the portal.

Jassan's side hurt. His breathing came in ragged gasps. His thighs burned from running so far. Most faeries used their wings more than their legs to transport across distance and Jassan was no different. Since the way was clear, he sprang from the ground and allowed his wings to thrum, carrying him to the portal entrance a little faster. He closed his eyes right before he felt himself hit the barrier of darkness.

5

THE GODS

Jassan instantly found himself outside the portal exit on another cleared but lightly used road. He knew he was somewhere he had always dreamed of going, but had never had the opportunity until now. He had just crossed the portal into the Noble Kingdom. And this road would lead directly to the Noble castle, Emma's home. The home of King Philip, Emma's and Burk's uncle. Unfortunately, on his first visit here he was barreling through mud in a downpour behind beings that disdained him, and alongside a strange faerieman.

Nice first appearance in the Noble Kingdom, he thought to himself. *Dripping in rain, caked in mud, strange faerie at your side and a monster at your heels. They wouldn't welcome a highborn faerie to the castle, why would they allow you inside?*

Despite the miserable circumstances, he followed the others at a run, trying to ignore the ache in his side and the burning in his legs. He only slowed slightly to take in the sight of the kingdom before him.

The portal of Marrack he'd come through was named for the faerie forest it was near and passed its users into the lesser-used portal of the Noble Kingdom of the humans. It was a lesser-used portal because the humans rarely visited the faeries. This portal had been created by the goblin king to try to encourage relations between the faeries and humans. But the portal was rarely used by either species to start with, and even less so over time until it had been all but forgotten. Jassan believed that was why the group of friends ahead of him had chosen to use it for their secret adventures.

The portal was carved into the side of a mountain outside a village not far from the castle. Even the village had been specifically built there to allow humans and faeries mutual access for trade, but little trade had occurred and the village had shrunk over the years as many humans moved on.

The dark fall day had already turned to night and the few humans who still lived in the village outside the portal kept to their homes. There had been no sign yet that the black monster had followed them through the portal or found them otherwise, but in any case, the mixed group of friends splashed through the puddles on the road as fast as their trembling legs could carry them. Tyla stumbled once but pushed off Lokna's offer of assistance. Even Gizi slowed to a limping pace. Burk ran beside Jassan in his human form but kept slipping from Jassan's sight. When Lokna slowed, he glanced at Trivnor.

"Fly!" Trivnor finally shouted as they ran up the road toward the castle of Kingstor Noble.

Jassan took to his wings as he watched the others do the same. Emma, in dragon form, picked up Burk in human form and flew him toward the castle gates.

Jassan only had a moment to take in the towers and spiked merlons atop the battlements outside the keep. The flags announcing the royalty within hung damp on their posts. Although the rain had significantly eased here, the persistent drip from the sky covered all of Avonoa in some form or another. It trickled down from balconies and awnings. Jassan could barely make out the mountain beyond the king's forest, Teardrop Sea behind the castle and the great river flowing in front of the castle.

When they reached a turn in the road, Trivnor called for the group to hold up. No one complained about that. He pointed to a copse of brush around the bend that had been unseen from the portal. They all dove into the trees and tumbled over each other, falling to the ground in a heap.

"Wait here," Trivnor said. Jassan noticed that the faerieman was barely out of breath. Jassan and the others gulped for air and untangled themselves to huddle among the trees, exhausted. Although the castle gates were barely a few minutes' flight away, even the dragons took advantage of the rest.

The group waited as Trivnor stepped out to peer around the bend. Jassan could feel Lokna's massive chest expanding and contracting, although he doubted the dragon would ever admit to being overexerted. Those that could, shifted into their smaller forms to give each other space among the trees. Emma wrapped her arms around Burk, but continued to search the trees around them as if hoping for a glimpse of home.

"We can rest here a moment," Trivnor said. "Since we're so far from him, hopefully he can't sense where we've gone. But if I know Kelraz, he'll figure it out. You," he pointed to Jassan, "you might have to say goodbye to your friends here."

"We're *not* his friends," Lokna growled.

Jassan glanced at Emma, hoping for a different reaction. She and Burk hung their heads. Lokna, Tyla and even the goblin glared at him openly. Everyone else found something else to look at. Jassan hung his head. He knew these creatures had never liked him. He had hoped they would at least be interested to know what would happen to him after their shared trials, but instead he felt their rejection and knew they would never accept him. He could only wish for their approval and desire to keep him around. Jassan lowered his head and clasped his arms, wanting to melt into the forest floor. He stared at the root of a nearby tree, wishing he could crawl under it and disappear, when suddenly he felt a small pinch in his chest.

"Whoa!" the goblin yelped.

"What are you doing?" Lokna said.

"Oh, no," Trivnor muttered.

"What?" Jassan asked them, his eyes widening. His eyes shot directly to Trivnor, thinking the monster had reappeared, but knowing everyone else's eyes were on him. "What's wrong?" he asked again.

"You…" Emma began, but was unable to finish.

"You…changed!" Burk said. "But just a little."

"What do you mean?" Jassan asked. Relaxing his arms, he noticed a tiny glow coming from the gem attached to his arm. The fog and mist he'd seen in it before had cleared enough that he could see himself in it now despite the rain dripping over it. But rather than seeing his blue, freckled faerie skin, his face appeared to have the same cracked grey surface as the tree trunk he had been staring at, and a little twig protruded from his temple. "Whoa!" he squawked, his eyes darting between the image in the key and the tree.

"It's time to go," Trivnor said, grabbing Jassan by the upper arm and yanking him to his feet. "You've just given us away."

Trivnor called for everyone to fly ahead to the castle. He kept a grip on Jassan and the two lifted last into the air, following the others.

"Change back!" Trivnor shouted, giving Jassan's arm a shake. Behind them they finally heard the roar of the monster. It must have come through the portal.

"I don't know how!" Jassan said. He didn't even know how it had happened, but the sight of his skin so different, by *any* means, sent a thrill through him. He could change! He could be different!

"Remember your faerie face!" Trivnor said. "Cut the connection!"

"What are you talking about?" Jassan yelled back. "What connection?"

They heard another roar, louder and much more distinct. The monster had lifted into the air and pursued them over a clear path. Even through the dark and night and rain, they could see the creature rising above the trees behind them.

Everyone pumped their wings except Burk, who remained in human form and was being carried by his sister. Emma screamed ahead for someone behind the gates to help them.

As they neared the castle, five dragons lifted from the towers. Two massive grey dragons, appearing almost black in the cloudy night sky and much larger than the other three, flanked the guard. One of the other three was of fair purple and lavender colors and flew in the lead. Another was brilliant green and was sleek and smaller than any of the others. The last dragon was nearly invisible, being almost as black as the monster that was chasing them.

The smaller purple dragon roared and led the charge to intercept the arriving travelers. The five castle dragons met Jassan's group above the road that led to a bridge over the river. "Who goes there?" the purple dragon called to them as they met. The lead dragon focused her shining yellow eyes on Trivnor and Jassan.

"Leena?" the green dragon called to Emma. "What's going on? Where have you been?"

"Mother!" Emma called back. "The monster! It's coming!"

Both dragon groups angled toward the ground as they met, landing in the mud while Jassan and Trivnor caught up. The monster was only moments behind them.

As soon as their feet touched the ground, the black castle dragon jumped between the faeries and the other dragons. Growling low, he crouched to spring and allowed a small burst of fire to stop them. But Emma waved her claws, "No, father, not them!"

The black dragon hesitated before he spoke to Trivnor. "What are you doing here, faerie? And what is that?" he indicated Jassan, held tight in Trivnor's fist.

"That's Jassan," Gizi said. "Apparently, he's part tree."

"I'm trying to help," Trivnor said. "We're not the danger here. That is."

The castle dragons' eyes followed Trivnor's pointing finger and spotted the black shadow beast coming for them. It was above the trees next to the castle and would soon be over the road where they were gathered. Just as it reached them, Jassan heard growls coming from the other dragons, but the black castle dragon took in the sight of it and uttered, "Milah?"

Of course, Jassan knew this from the stories. The black castle dragon was Hiro, Emma's father, and he knew Lokna's uncle. Hiro had been present at Milah's death. The black castle dragon would be just as emotionally distracted at the first sight of the shadow dragon as Lokna had been.

That single hesitation cost him. Jassan had assumed the castle dragons would intercept the monster before it reached them, but the dark shadow beast aimed only for the faeries and the dragons from the castle hesitated.

Trivnor dove with Jassan out of its path before Milah's corrupted soul could reach them. He quickly flew with the younger faerie to the side of the sleek green dragon, but Priyanna flinched away from them as well.

Instead of scooping Trivnor and Jassan, the monster turned to slam into the black dragon at full speed. Hiro stood his ground, but the monster held nothing back. All four claws and an open jaw were bound to find purchase. The back leg claw sank deep into the black dragon's leg joint. Hiro bellowed in pain as the other dragons jumped in.

"What is it?!" Priyanna shouted to Trivnor just as she was ripped off the monster's back and thrown to land next to the group.

"An abomination," Trivnor insisted.

"Well, that's as clear as a faerie," the green dragon said with exasperation, rolling her eyes. "What can be done?"

"Nothing can be done," Trivnor said. "Fire won't hurt it."

"Of course not," she snapped. "It's a dragon."

"But it might at least distract it," he said. "You have numbers, you might scare it away, but you'll never hurt it or kill it."

"What does it want?" she asked.

Trivnor's eyes motioned to the young group behind them, then to Jassan at his side.

"Get them inside the castle," Priyanna said, jerking her head toward the Noble stronghold.

Trivnor shook his head. "It won't help. More of his kind will come until you're overpowered. As long as one of these creatures knows where these young ones are, more will follow."

Priyanna's eyes darted back to the monster, who was now fighting the swift lavender dragon. She was fast enough to avoid the monster's claws, but her own claws against him didn't leave a scratch. "What can be done?"

"I must hide them," Trivnor said. "They can't remain here or your kingdom will be overrun. And we will all be killed. Leaving them with you would only put everyone in more danger."

The green dragon's lips lifted to bare her fangs a moment, then she said, so low Jassan almost couldn't hear it, "Take them."

"Whatever you do," Trivnor told Priyanna, "don't let it kill anyone."

Trivnor spun toward the others, keeping Jassan in his steel grip. "We have to go," he told them. "Now."

"What?"

"Why?"

"Where will we go?"

"No! We can't leave!"

"Mother?" Emma said expectantly, turning to the green dragon.

"Go with him, we'll hold it back," Priyanna said firmly, then she turned back to Trivnor. "I'm trusting you, faerie. Keep them safe. All of them." She glanced down at Emma before she gazed briefly at Burk, then shook her head and launched back into the fight.

The beast fought ferociously. He swung his claws at the castle dragons with speed. When their claws succeeding in finding their marks, the shadow dragon would roar in pain, but it continued the assault without slowing. The only purpose any of the dragons' fire retained against the monster was as a veil to hide behind. Jassan watched the black castle dragon, Hiro, drag himself out of the fight using only his front claw, to be replaced by the much smaller green dragon, Emma's and Burk's mother.

Jassan was shaken from his transfixion on the fight by Trivnor, who spun him to face him. Trivnor bent down, nose to nose, to make sure that Jassan could only see his face. Jassan stared into the faerie's grey eyes, still thinking about the fight going on behind him.

"Look at me," Trivnor said. "Think about your own face. Your skin is blue. With dark freckles. Where are the freckles placed on your face? Tell me."

Not wanting to have to recall his own loathsome appearance, Jassan forced himself to think of the skin on his face. He had always found it so grotesque that he had spent countless hours staring in his aunt's mirror, singing majikal songs and willing it to change. "They're mostly on my cheeks," he said grudgingly. "In clumps at the top."

He glimpsed another gentle glow from the key on his arm and he felt the tiny pinch in his chest being released. Looking down, his all-too-familiar face was reflected back at him in the mirrored key.

They heard a vicious bellow from the monster behind them.

"Good," Trivnor said. He turned to the others. "Run!" he told them, pointing down the road away from the castle gates.

As the young dragons tried to get away without attracting the monster's attention, they stole glances behind themselves at the continuing attack at the castle.

"Can't you just transport us away from here?" Tyla asked Trivnor as she trotted down the road.

Trivnor shook his head. "That would call attention to us and where we're going," he said. "He can sense it."

Another terrifying roar brought their attention back to the attack just before they turned at the bend in the road. They could see the green and purple dragons darting in and out of the fight to swipe at the monster's legs and face. The grey guard dragons tore at the monster's sides, keeping his claws busy. But the frustrated beast had chosen an opponent. Kelraz, in Milah's form, grabbed one of the grey dragons by the shoulders and shoved him into the other's claws. The grey dragon, already weakened, roared as three sets of claws sank into his neck and shoulders. He roared again as his body crumbled to ash on the ground. In its place arose a shadow dragon, dripping darkness. The two menacing monsters turned to face the others together.

6

NEED

"NO!" several voices screamed. Jassan's breath caught in his throat. Luckily, the sound of the younger group's wails from down the road didn't attract attention because the older dragons still in the fight bellowed even louder at the loss.

"Go, go!" Trivnor hissed, finally releasing Jassan to reach out both arms and shove the others to continue their escape. "They won't be able to hold them off much longer," he said, urging them on.

"What happened?!" Eleka cried, allowing Trivnor to push her into a faster trot. Everyone matched her speed as they ran down the road.

"I'll explain later," he said, stealing glances behind them.

"He—they—will know which way we've gone," Tyla said. "They'll just follow us."

"I know," Trivnor said. "But this is all we can do for now."

"The river," Eleka said. "We should head for the river. Maybe they won't think to follow us there."

"And do what when we get there?" Lokna said. "Drown? Dragons can't swim!"

"You're the only dragon who can't swim," Gizi said, snickering.

"We can walk in the shallows just to get around the port," Eleka insisted.

Trivnor nodded. "It's our best bet, let's go."

"Wait," Emma said, getting her bearings, "the river is behind us. We can't go back now."

"We can go through town," Eleka replied quickly, pointing at the buildings they were running past, "to the bend farther down."

"I can't fit through those streets," Lokna said. "I'll knock down a building or something."

"You're not as big as you'd like to think you are, worm," Gizi said. "If I can fit through the streets, so can you."

Lokna sneered before retorting, but Trivnor cut him off. "You'll both fit," he said, shutting down the bickering.

The group slipped between two buildings, but a tall wooden fence blocked their way. Jassan flew over it quickly, staying low enough for the tall structures on either side to block most views of the fugitives from the sky.

It was a tight fit, but Gizi scrambled over the wooden fence. Then she lifted her front claws to catch the front half of Tyla's centaur form and set her on all fours on the other side as if she had easily leapt the fence on her own.

"Don't wait for us or anything," Tyla said snidely, reaching Jassan's side.

"You could have just changed into a dragon and flown over," he said, watching Gizi help Eleka over the same way.

"And get stuck or give our location away?" she scoffed. "We'll leave that to you."

"Quiet," Eleka chastised her sister, as Gizi helped the goblin over the fence next. "We can't raise the alarm."

After Emma and Burk had also been helped, Lokna climbed over the fence last, scraping the sides of both buildings. Once everyone else was safe, Trivnor flew over the fence and pointed to Eleka. "Lead the way," he directed. Eleka panted a couple times to think for a moment then nodded before taking off around a corner.

The group scampered through the port town, splashing through the unavoidable mud and puddles of the fall season. Jassan noticed that Eleka led them through smaller passageways, earning grumbles from Lokna each time. Eleka's dark hair dripped with rain where the hood from her short cloak didn't cover it. The rain began to fall at a steady drip that soaked through Jassan's cloak. As they charged through the streets, he noticed that everyone was wet except Emma and Burk, who huddled tighter in their majikal cloaks. Tyla had lost her cloak in her fight with the monster, but she didn't seem to miss it.

"Emma," Burk whispered from between Jassan and his sister, "I need to chinkle."

"Can you wait until we get to the river?" she responded.

The younger boy shrugged and nodded.

After a few more minutes of sneaking through the town, Burk whispered again.

"Emma," he said, "I'm hungry."

Emma didn't have an answer for this request, and it only served to force Jassan's thoughts to his own whining stomach.

Emma looked at Jassan. "We're going to have to find something to eat soon."

Jassan nodded. He turned to see Trivnor at the back of the group. "Tell Eleka to stop," Jassan said to Emma. Then he slipped past Gizi and Lokna behind them to join Trivnor.

"Burk is hungry," he told the older faerie, "and so am I. We need to stop soon. We can't go all night without food."

"Would you rather be turned into a soulless monster if we get caught?" Lokna said as the group slowed to a stop.

"Too late for that," Gizi sneered. "He's already a faerie."

"We have to have lost them by now," Emma said, coming back to join them. "Can't we stop?"

"There's an inn up ahead," Eleka said, "of sorts. If we can get out of the town and down the shoreline a little way, the town has been building a wayside rest for visiting dragons. I don't think it's anything fancy, but it's dry and hopefully safe."

"Is there food?" Dasha asked.

"I don't think so," Eleka said. "From what I've heard, it's literally just a structure with walls for protection from the elements."

"We can't stop before we reach it, we'll have to find something to eat along the way," Trivnor said. As if to make his point, they heard a roar coming from the direction of the castle. Everyone put their heads down and soldiered on.

Trivnor instructed Eleka to guide them to the port on the edge of Teardrop Sea instead of to the river. He claimed he wanted to stay as far from the castle and the road as possible. But the river led directly to the castle that loomed over the small city, and served as one of the castle's major defenses. They did their best to keep out of view of the castle and finally the port with several docked ships sprawled before them.

Trivnor told the group to go to the farthest end of the docks. They waited for him there while he slinked between the enormous sailing ships. When he finally reached them where the docks ended at the edge of the city and the seaside coast passed into open waters, he carried with him a hefty bag.

"Where did you get that?" Lokna asked. "Did you steal food from the ships?"

"We don't have much choice," Trivnor said. "Or would you like to go find the ships' owners and ask nicely if we can have some of their food?"

Emma answered for him. "Of course he doesn't, and we don't have time for niceties, anyway."

"Besides," Gizi added, jerking her head toward Burk, "if they knew who it was going to, they would probably tie it up with a bow for us."

"Eleka," Trivnor said, ignoring the conversation. "Where is this inn you were talking about?"

"Um," she pointed around the curve of the trees, "it's just around those trees. Farther down the shore."

"Have you been there?" Trivnor asked.

Eleka shook her head. "I just happened to hear about it and my father said he might take us there once it was finished. It will give us all a place to visit Emma together within the Noble Kingdom."

Another roar punctuated the night sky and the rain began pouring again.

"Alright," Trivnor said. "Let's just hope it's dry."

The group slogged through the embankment and around the bend. Several times they were forced to wade in order to go around trees and brush hanging over the water. Lokna could be heard complaining any time they had to take to the water. Jassan thought the fact that Trivnor and Jassan could fly when Lokna couldn't probably added to his displeasure, because they could stay low and out of view of the castle and port.

"Finally!" Lokna exclaimed, as they turned around another bend and an immense rock-walled building, open to the sky, stood before them at the water's edge.

The structure reached to the tops of the trees and looked as if it was either designed to be open or it was still unfinished at the top. As they got closer, they could see through the open rock walls on two sides that the structure had three levels, a ground level on the dirt and two higher levels with wooden floors. Each level could comfortably fit fifteen sleeping dragons. Two opposing walls extended up the full height of the structure, but the other two sides were open, allowing easy access to each level.

Just as the rain began to fall in earnest again, the group scrambled into the bottom level of the shelter and collapsed on the dirt floor. Even Trivnor sat down heavily with his back against a rock wall. Jassan wondered if he'd been putting up a strong front to encourage them to continue on.

"Do you think we're safe here?" Jassan asked the older faerie.

"For now, yes," he said with his eyes closed. "If Kelraz hasn't caught up to us by now, we should be able to get a few hours of sleep. Don't waste it."

"I don't plan to," Lokna grumbled before he curled into a ball and closed his eyes.

After a few more rumbles of agreement, everyone silenced. Jassan briefly marveled at the fact that he was lying in a dragon shelter with several dragons and part-dragons and a mysterious power source attached to his arm. With visions of himself as a dragon flying alongside friends, sleep swiftly overtook him.

7

THE DRAGON

Jassan woke to heavy rain and pounding thunder. Though the sky was still dark, Jassan could tell it was morning. Most creatures of Avonoa could instinctively tell the time of day or night in the fall. The sun's visible position in the sky made the time of day apparent during the other seasons of spring, summer, autumn and winter. But in fall, with the sky falling, creatures became instinctively aware of the sun beyond the clouds. Jassan scanned the shelter and when a bolt of lightning split the sky, he found Trivnor standing just short of the rain's reach inside, staring out into the maelstrom.

Jassan tip-toed to his side, hoping not to startle the older faerie. He reached for the bag of food that lay nearby but jumped when he heard his name.

"Jassan," Trivnor said quietly, "I'm glad you're awake. We need to discuss when you should pass that key to me."

"I wouldn't know how," he said, wondering what had happened to allowing him to keep it.

"It's a simple incantation," the faerieman answered.

"But you agreed to gain our trust by letting me keep the key." Jassan said. "I'd like to hear what the others have to say first." He wasn't ready to admit the hopes he had about the gem and what it might do for him.

Trivnor sighed. "I suppose it's wise to consult with your friends," he said.

"They're not my friends," Jassan reminded him.

"Why do you say that?"

"They've said it themselves, and besides, I know they don't like me."

"That's not true!" The two faeries turned toward Burk's interjection as he sat up. Their voices must have awakened him from his slumber, curled against his sister's warm dragon belly with both his and Emma's cloaks thrown over him. "I like you," he said. "I'll be your friend."

"There, you see," Trivnor said to Jassan before he turned to Burk. "Burk, isn't it? Prince Burk? Burkyla?"

"It's just Burk."

"And your sister is Princess Emmaleena?"

Burk nodded.

"Your mother called her Leena," Trivnor pointed out.

"Yeah, she does that," he said. "Our parents call her 'Emma' when she's a human and 'Leena' when she's a dragon. It's an old tradition. But she likes to just be called Emma and I like to be called Burk."

"Does that mean your parents call you 'Kyla' as a dragon?" Jassan asked.

Burk hesitated and looked back at Emma, slowly awakening. Sitting up, she rubbed the back of her claw across her scaly eyes.

"We just like the names Emma and Burk," she said. "Having two different names is something from the old days for our parents. The same goes for changing names as you reach milestones in life or achieve great accomplishments; they do it, we don't. It just gets confusing to have so many names. Our friends just call us Emma and Burk."

"Well, Burk," Trivnor picked up the bag of food and opened it for the young boy. "I guess we should put something in our bellies before we see if it's safe to move on."

After Burk took the biggest chunk of bread and dried meat he could hold in his hands, Jassan pulled a lump of cheese wrapped in a cloth from the bag. "So, what do we do now?" he asked Trivnor as he nibbled at the end of it. The others stared at Trivnor with anticipation as well.

"I really had hoped that we could get at least a few of you home, but as things stand, that's no longer possible," Trivnor said, looking into the youthful faces around him. "It seems we'll have to stick together for the foreseeable future, and I can use all your help anyway."

"Are you saying we can't go home?" Emma said.

The other dragons began to stir and sit up at these words. Jassan wondered if they'd been listening to the rest of the conversation too.

"Not as soon as you'd probably like, anyway," Trivnor answered. "Do we need to get messages to your families?"

Emma shook her head. "Our parents obviously know we won't be back soon," she said, "and they will certainly be in contact with everyone else's parents too."

"What about you, Jassan?" Burk said. "You haven't asked about going home even once. Won't your aunt be worried?"

"I doubt it," Jassan grumbled. "I come and go all the time. She'll only miss me if she has an errand that she can't do herself. She may not even notice I'm gone."

In the silence that followed, he thought about his aunt. He knew he couldn't be absolutely sure how she would be feeling in his absence. This had definitely become the longest amount of time he'd ever been gone. He thought she might notice but she wouldn't worry, at least not at first. Then again, he didn't really care that much whether she worried or not. All he cared about was that he was finally on an adventure and was with other creatures who needed him. He didn't feel any pull to return to his aunt any time soon.

"Why do you need our help, anyway?" Dasha asked Trivnor, sitting up and breaking the awkward silence.

"What can kids do that you can't?" Burk said.

"We're not children," Dasha shushed him, shaking her head.

Trivnor held up his hands to stave off any other questions. "First of all," he said, "as I said before, it is of utmost importance that I find the other keys. Second, you're not children, and you're certainly not ordinary, are you? Each of you is either part or full dragon, so you're much more mature and capable than full humans, centaurs or goblins. Third, if any of you go home, not only will you be in danger, but your families and friends will be in danger too."

"They already are," Emma said. "I don't even know if our father is okay."

Burk whimpered and curled back into his sister's dark blue scales.

"I'm sure your father will be fine," Trivnor consoled them. "They have enough dragons to either restrain the beasts or at least scare them away. But that won't put an end to it. The monster knows who you are. And I mean the real monster, Kelraz. I suspect that back when he left our home village as a young adult, he traveled across Avonoa and came to know the powerful people and families of all the different races. He saw you then and recognizes you now. And he's seen you with me, so he could well have assumed that I've told you everything about the keys and have enlisted your help to find the others. If you go back to your families now, he'll find you. All of you. Whether he'll be so desperate as to kidnap or torture you or your families remains to be seen."

"What about Taka?" Burk said. "We saw him turn into a black monster thing. What will happen to him?"

Jassan assumed Burk referred to the grey dragon who had risen from his ash as a monster after being killed in the fight at the castle. He agreed, it was a good question.

"I'm sorry, Burk," the faerieman said. "There's nothing to be done for Taka now. If someone is killed, Kelraz can corrupt their soul and seize control of them immediately, as you saw happen with Taka."

"But Taka isn't bad," Burk insisted.

"Neither was Milah," Lokna said with a scowl.

"They didn't have to be," Eleka said, breaking off a huge piece of bread and handing the rest to her sister. "Kelraz is controlling him with the one key in his possession."

"The Sky Key," Trivnor said, "yes."

After a silence only interrupted by thunder, Dasha asked, "What do you need us to do?"

Trivnor nodded. "I need help getting the rest of the keys back."

"Where are they?" Emma asked.

"I don't know." Trivnor sat down in front of the dragons. "I'll have to travel across Avonoa to find them. Like I said, I scattered them to the farthest reaches. I have no idea who has them now or which ones anyone might have. The only one I traced is the one Jassan has now."

"How are we supposed to help with that?" Gizi asked. "We don't know where they are either, other than Jassan's."

"What are you looking at me for?" Jassan said when all eyes turned to him. "I don't know where they are either!"

"Actually," Trivnor said, "you and I might be able to find them with the aid of the ones we already have. When one key is being used, anyone who holds another key will be drawn to the ones being used. The keys literally pull toward each other and that pull gets stronger the closer it gets to a key being used. The keys want to be used together, not apart."

"That's how the monster found us," Lokna said, "because Jassan used the power in the key."

"Not on purpose," Jassan muttered.

"And," Trivnor continued, "if neither of us uses our keys but other key holders do use theirs, their keys will hopefully draw Kelraz away from us. Their keys will also draw us in so we will be able to find them. And hopefully before Kelraz does."

"So where do we start?" Tyla said, jumping to her feet.

"Wait a second," Emma said, waving one of her claws. "Maybe we should stop and think about this. We can't just jump headfirst into helping some mad faerie without a plan. It might take some time to organize, but I'm pretty sure my uncle's army would protect all of us, no questions asked."

"Unfortunately," Trivnor sighed, "time isn't going to help us, nor is any living being. Your friends and family will demand answers just as you have and your wyrd prohibits explanation. But time is even more demanding." He turned to stare out into the drizzling rain. "The gate to the World of Souls is weakest in the fall. The sun burns strongest in the upcoming spring and shores up its defenses."

"I told you fall was the best time to try a summons," Lokna muttered to Gizi.

Jassan wondered if summoning Lokna's uncle in any of the other seasons would have given them a better outcome. The snow falling in winter might open the gates slightly, but autumn breezes, spring growth and summer sunshine would enhance the gates' strength, providing little to no chance for someone to access the World of Souls without powerful majik. Named for the sky falling, the rainy season of fall, when Avonoa got drenched for three months after winter out of the fifteen-month year, would supply the best opportunity for majik to open the gates.

"It's true," Trivnor continued, "but with the keys to the gate lost and separated and not functioning together, the gate is crumbling. The barrier between the World of Souls and the world of the living is breaking down. I fear if the gate is not repaired and restored to its full strength by the last day of fall, it will fully disintegrate and, barring another act of the gods…it will never be whole again."

"Two weeks," Lokna growled.

"You mean we have just two weeks to find these keys?" Emma said.

"And reunite them," Trivnor said.

"What happens if spring comes early this year?" Burk asked.

"He's right," Eleka said. "There's no way to predict exactly when the rain will stop. It could be two weeks. It could be two days."

"Can't centaurs read the stars or something?" the orange dragon muttered. "Can't you predict when the rain will stop?"

Tyla rolled her head at Gizi before stopping it to scowl. "Not when we can't see the *sky!*" she said pointing to the rain with an exaggerated roll of her arm.

Trivnor shook his head. "It's for these reasons I could use some help. I could take Jassan with me and you could all hold up in the Noble castle while we search, but…"

"But finding them would be easier and faster with all of us along to help," Emma said.

"Yeah," Dasha smacked her claw on the ground. "I'm in."

"What about my parents?" Burk asked worriedly.

"You heard the faerie," Lokna said. "They'll be fine."

Gizi shook her head at him. Emma shot him a scathing look.

Trivnor stood. "I'm afraid he's right," he said. "Both you and your families will be safer if you come with me. Your mother trusted me with your safety. I think she could sense that the monsters would follow us. Kelraz knows Jassan has the key and will try to hunt him down using the monsters to get it.

"As for where to start our search," he continued, "we should find a replacement for the key that got destroyed in my altercation with Kelraz. Perhaps we'll find other keys along the way."

"You had a fight with Kelraz?" Burk asked.

"After he attacked their village?" Gizi said with a pitying look to Burk.

"Yeah," Tyla said to the younger boy as well, "I bet they had quite the row. At least, we would if he had done it to me."

Trivnor took a deep breath. Jassan assumed he was remembering the dead, but he refocused quickly. "It all happened in the moment the keys were to be passed along to the new gatekeeper.

"The former gatekeeper chooses who they feel is best to take over for them," Trivnor explained.

"And he chose you?" Eleka asked.

Trivnor shook his head. "No," he said, still not meeting anyone's eye, "but I was among the very few chosen to be part of the Passing Ceremony held in the gatekeeper's chamber. Through special circumstance, Kelraz was allowed to be part of it too, but when, at the beginning of the ceremony, the gatekeeper announced that it was not to be him but another who would receive the keys, Kelraz flew out of the room in a fury.

"We all knew he was upset and assumed he would cool down, so we proceeded with the ceremony. After only a few minutes we heard commotion outside that came from beyond the gate to our village entrance. I ran out to the gate just as Kelraz, still in a rage, pushed it open with me behind it. He didn't know I was there, and he ran past me brandishing a long blade.

"Once he'd disappeared back into the ceremony, I looked around the gate doors into the remnants of our home. I couldn't think. I couldn't move. Hundreds of homes and structures crumbled into piles of char. Remains of bodies littered the ground and paths. Trees and structures and even the dirt on the ground were covered in a glistening black haze. I'm still not even sure how he made that happen unless he used dark and dangerous majik that he must have researched and practiced in secret for a long time.

"When I realized that Kelraz likely caused this damage, I ran back into the ceremony and found him standing behind the gatekeeper, his sword dripping with blood. The other faeries were all dead at his feet.

"I can only surmise that he interrupted the ceremony at the point of passing along the keys because the keys hovered in the air in front of the old gatekeeper. When I entered, Kelraz stabbed his sword through the gatekeeper's back. She had only the strength to hold her hand out to me before she fell.

"I don't know what came over me. I saw Kelraz step toward the keys. Had he reached them, they would have implanted in him and he would have received the full power of all the gods. Without thinking, I reached down and picked up a blade from one of the fallen faerie guards and attacked Kelraz.

"I don't know what happened in the fight, exactly. My anger took over. All I could concentrate on was not allowing Kelraz anywhere near those keys. I knew in my soul that he couldn't have them. It would mean the same destruction for the entire world as my home had just experienced.

"Kelraz probably got desperate because at one point he abandoned his blade and reached out to the keys to try to attain them. I slapped his hand away with my sword but he got one gem and my sword split another one at the same time. I believe he was momentarily overcome with the sensation of the key he had gained and distracted by its abilities. He hesitated and I made an attempt to get the rest of the keys. When I reached for them, I connected to the Cloud Key first and in that moment I knew what I must do. He made another attempt and I tried at the same time. We both clasped our hands over the keys and we each connected to the other's key.

"I instantly saw the soul you all were summoning. I believe that with the connection of our keys Kelraz saw it too. I used the Cloud Key to send the rest of the keys out to the far corners of Avonoa, well outside of Kelraz's reach, but I couldn't know where they scattered or else Kelraz would know too. Still using the key, in my mind I connected to the place where I had seen your uncle's soul appear. I released Kelraz and came to you. I'm not sure when he corrupted your uncle's soul, but when I left him behind, he must have figured out that he could use the soul to get to me and all of you."

Silence fell over the group. The pouring rain outside made Jassan feel like someone had smothered him in a cold, wet blanket. He couldn't breathe. The wicked faerieman hunting him had killed hundreds of majikal beings. All at the same time. People he knew. Faeries he had grown up with. Gone, in one powerfully evil majikal moment. He had destroyed an entire civilization made up of his friends and family. What might he do to Jassan when he found him? Because Jassan knew he would eventually find him.

"I have no explanations for his actions. Only the conjecture that he is mad for the power that is just beyond his reach. He must be filled with hatred toward those who keep it from him," Trivnor finished with a crack in his voice.

Everyone stayed quiet for a moment, with thoughts of respecting the dead. Jassan saw the purple skin around Trivnor's eyes darken, but no tears leaked out. The next moment, the faerieman sighed and straightened his shoulders.

"The Wind Key was destroyed in the fight. I'll have to replace it," Trivnor said.

"The Wind Key?" Tyla asked.

"Snap it!" Emma hissed at her. She sat staring at Trivnor. Jassan could tell that she was trying to allow Trivnor to grieve. She always seemed to know what to do in a difficult moment.

"So how many keys are there?" Gizi said into the silence.

"Gizi," Emma hissed again.

"What?" the orange dragon grumbled back. "I'm trying to lighten the mood and keep him from being sad."

Trivnor held up his hand out to stop any pushback from Emma. "It's alright," he said. "There will be time to mourn later." Then he turned to Gizi. "Seven keys in total, one for each of the high gods," he said. "Kelraz has the Sky Key for Tartaku. Then there's the Sun Key for Shurka. The Star Key for Khurta. The Air Key for Tarka. The Wind Key for Tarsa, that's the one that was destroyed. I have the Cloud Key for Kruh and Jassan holds the Moon Key for Shurta."

Jassan looked down at the mirrored gem on his arm. It wasn't just a powerful key, it was a key touched by the goddess Shurta. Shurta was the goddess of the moons.

Although he couldn't see them behind the clouds of fall, Jassan remembered the clear sky of summer nights when he loved staring up at the three moons of Avonoa and imagining flying past them as they glowed their silvery essence in the sky. Now he held the one key which the goddess Shurta had empowered. A thrill ran through him as if he had been personally chosen for such a magnificent responsibility, and not just received it accidentally. Then he turned his hand over to see the reflection of his pale blue faerie skin and the triumphant feeling vanished like a leaf on the wind.

"And the Sky Key for Tartaku?" Eleka said. "The one Kelraz holds?"

"Yes, Kelraz holds the Sky Key," Trivnor confirmed.

"Tartaku is just," Eleka said. "She would be the one to corrupt or…"

"Purify," Trivnor finished. "The Sky Key purifies souls, but you are correct, in the wrong hands, it can corrupt and control them."

"How could Tartaku allow such a thing?" Eleka murmured.

"The gods don't *allow* anything," Trivnor said. "They imbued the gems with powers and trust the keepers to use them wisely, the way they were intended to be used."

"But how can you make sure they're used right?" Lokna said. "You've got a little boy faerie that doesn't know how to use the one he has and won't give it up. Who knows what he would do with such power?"

Trivnor sighed again. "The village where I was raised has a very specific purpose. That is to raise the succeeding generations of gatekeepers. Yes, we learn reading and numbers like all children do. But our goal and purpose in life is to be worthy of being the next gatekeeper. Or to support the current gatekeeper and rear the future generation.

"Kelraz was arrogant and greedy. He thought, that of all the young villagers in training, only he had what it took to be the next gatekeeper. Then he thought only he should have power over all the living species, which became the idea that he should be all-powerful and rule over the living *and* the dead." He paused to reflect. "To have power over death is a common desire. Kelraz succumbed to the temptation the keys offered and was, at one point, banished from the village, not unlike others before him. But Kelraz willingly left to pursue and learn the majik he would need to come back and seize the power he craved. When he returned from his banishment, he tricked us all, making everyone believe he had changed and now understood the true purpose of the keys and the mission of the gatekeeper and respected them for it. His ruse took in everyone involved, especially the current gatekeeper who agreed to allow him to participate in the Passing Ceremony."

Trivnor closed his eyes and swallowed hard. He sniffed and opened his eyes again. "I'm the only one left now to gather the keys and use them to guard the gates to the World of Souls. The way they were intended to be used."

"What do we do if something happens to you?" Jassan asked, remembering the one key he held.

Trivnor turned and stared at him in silence. Jassan dropped his head. His hopes of using the key to fly on dragon wings faded away. He didn't want the weight of the World of Souls on his shoulders with this key in his possession. But if he gave up the key, dreams of flying beside Emma in a warm summer sky would be forever gone. He knew no one else would want him to keep the key and gain the others to become the new gatekeeper. The dragons around him would never accept him even if he were a dragon, let alone if he had so much supposed power over them. To make his point, Lokna spoke up.

"You can't be serious!" the brown dragon barked at Jassan before he turned to Trivnor. "He's not worthy of holding the key he already has, let alone any others!"

"Maybe," Trivnor said, making Jassan's heart contract a little. "Maybe not. Maybe one of you would be the better keyholder to take my place should anything happen. Growing up in my village, the gatekeeper would choose who they wanted to have the keys when they retired because they had known us from birth and knew who would do the best. I was only third or fourth in line, but that was much closer and more worthy of keeping the keys than Kelraz was in his position. I can't be certain what changed her mind about his intentions after he returned, but the former gatekeeper could see the evil in his heart when she banished him."

Trivnor continued. "I don't know any of you well enough right now to judge for myself who should be my successor, if that should become necessary. Previous gatekeepers had decades and even centuries to get to know the next generations and decide for themselves who was worthy and who would do the job properly. For now, I'll let Jassan keep the key he has and I'll humbly ask all of you to help me find the others. Perhaps we'll discover a different path along the way."

"I have a different path for you," Lokna said. "Make Jassan give me the key he has. I'm sure I would do better with it than he would."

"Lokna," Emma tried to hush him. "Be nice."

"Yeah," Burk said, "Jassan is my friend."

"You said," Eleka spoke up over Lokna's grumbling complaints, "that we need to get a replacement for the Wind Key. How do we do that?"

"Yeah," Gizi said. "We don't know of any super powerful majikal god keys just lying around somewhere."

"What does the Wind Key do?" Eleka asked, ignoring Gizi's remark.

"The wind whispers…" Trivnor said, seeming to anticipate Eleka being able to figure it out for herself.

Eleka's eyes lit up. "We *can* get you a gem like that!"

"What?" Emma said. "From where?"

"The goblins," Eleka said. "Dasha, didn't you say that the goblins have gemstones that can communicate your thoughts to one another?"

"Yes," Dasha nodded. "But those are kept under tight guard…in the heart of the palace… surrounded by guards… and more guards… Only the king and the royal majishun jewelers are allowed in… And did I mention all the guards?"

"Well," Eleka said with a shrug, "I didn't say it would be easy."

8

TO HUNT

"I still don't understand how all the keys work," Jassan said as the group slogged through another forest the next day. Trivnor hadn't said anything about the jeweler's vault in the goblin palace but some of them thought that should be their destination.

The group had come out of hiding much drier, but still somewhat hungry and grouchy. Those who could change into dragons had taken care of most of their discomfort by doing so. Trivnor insisted that they walk instead of fly at least until they could get far enough away from the Noble Kingdom to escape the monsters. Everyone agreed, but complained so loudly about the mud on their feet and cloaks or the cold water dripping down their backs that Jassan thought they might get caught anyway.

Both Gizi and Lokna had recently eaten so they could easily go a few days without eating again. For the others, being in their dragon forms could stave off hunger and other needs for a time. Their dragon stomachs were larger and burned stronger, which filled their bellies and made emptying the waste more efficient. Even Burk reluctantly handed his cloak to Emma and scampered into the woods to change in private and return as a human again. When he returned, he seemed a little happier. Most of them chose to remain in their dragon forms, but they all had to change back into their smaller forms occasionally to share the small amounts of bread, cheese, dried fruit and dried meat that Trivnor had acquired.

"I'm not sure what I can tell you," Trivnor answered.

"Why not?" Jassan pressed. "You come from the place that has all this knowledge and you have a key and I need answers. How do I use it? What all can the keys do? How did they get their powers? What will we do when we find a new one?" The questions tumbled out of Jassan faster than he could control them. The curiosity pressing inside his head was almost more than he could handle. It almost made him forget about his growling stomach and his squelching shoes.

"Please understand," Trivnor said with a sigh, "I'm still learning myself. Half of these questions you're asking aren't answered until someone becomes the gatekeeper. I'm trying to figure much of this out as I go."

"That's not yet our top priority anyway, Jassan," Tyla said from behind them. "What we need to figure out first is how we're going to steal a highly guarded gem from super-warrior goblins."

"No," Emma said from in front of Jassan, "we need to focus on where we're going to sleep next and how to get more food. *Without* stealing it," she emphasized the last part for Trivnor's benefit.

"We'll do what we have to do," Trivnor said.

That was pretty much all he had said about their quest the entire time they'd been together. He would point them in a direction and tell them to keep going, but never give them a reason why or say where they would arrive and what they would do when they did. Jassan knew he must have a plan in his head, but for some reason he wouldn't share it with them. Or maybe he was uncertain himself about where they should head, either for safety or to find the keys.

"You need to tell us what to do if something happens to you," Jassan said, surprising himself at his boldness.

Everyone stopped walking, even Trivnor. Lokna gave Jassan a look that said the dragon wished he had been the one who pushed the faerie for that answer.

"Yeah," Dasha said. "What are we supposed to do if something happens to you? We don't know where you're leading us or what we're supposed to do when we get there. And we're going to have to work together, aren't we?"

"Yes," Trivnor said and began to walk again. "Don't worry about me, I'll be fine. And we can discuss things better when we get where we're going for now."

Jassan refused to move. "You said you were the only one who can stop Kelraz," he said. "What do we do if something goes wrong? What if we get split up? Or worse? We should decide this before we take another step. Do you think we could just go back to our normal lives knowing that something deadly is chasing us and Kelraz is going to take over the world?"

Trivnor stopped again. "It won't come to that."

"How do you know that?" Lokna growled.

"You can't possibly," Emma said.

Trivnor sighed. "Fine," he said, turning to face them. "There's an old goblin settlement a few hours' flight by dragon to the west." He pointed in the direction they had been tromping for hours. "If we can get there by nightfall, we can eat, sleep, dry and…discuss plans. The only problem is…"

"Goblins have been resettling," Dasha interrupted. "After our people came out of hiding during the dragon war, many decided to reclaim our lands on the surface. Goblins might be living there again."

"…And goblins are very powerful with the gems they mine," Trivnor continued.

"Yeah, right," Lokna said. "I've heard the same thing. They may be able to take on a full-grown faerie, but there's no way they're stronger than a dragon. You faeries will just have to fend for yourselves."

"Hey!" Dasha shouted back at him. "My dad tells me the story all the time of how Auntie Shvika dropped Hiro to his knees. He was practically crying. No offense, Emma."

"It's fine," Emma said. "My dad tells me the same story, but it's a story of caution for the same reason."

Dasha gave Lokna a smug grin.

"I don't believe it," Lokna said, waving off the comment.

"I wouldn't be so sure," Trivnor said. "The goblins mine gems that have very similar qualities to the gate keys. That's been a source of concern for my people for some time now. The goblins are getting too powerful."

"Says the faerie with more secrets and power than a tree has leaves," Gizi said. She glanced up at the stark trees overhead, then amended her statement. "Or at least, branches."

"Wait a second," Eleka spoke up. "You said that goblin village is only a few hours by 'dragon' flight…"

Dasha pursed her lips at Trivnor. Lokna bared his fangs and growled, "I'm not carrying anyone. Least of all a lying, deceiving, untrustworthy faerie." He turned to show his fangs to Jassan.

Trivnor shrugged. "Then you'll just have to slow down and wait for us. Faeries don't fly as fast as dragons. Our wings are much smaller."

"I say we walk," Tyla said.

"I'll carry Trivnor," Eleka said.

"What?" Tyla spun on her sister. "Why would you—?"

"—My hooves hurt!" Eleka shouted. "I need to stretch my wings! And I want to get there tonight!"

"Ugh!" Tyla grumbled and trotted away from her sister. "If we weren't twins, I would swear we weren't related. I would rather die than carry anyone, for any reason, in *any* form!"

Eleka just waved away her sister's drama. Jassan assumed she was used to those kinds of comments from her twin because she didn't react.

"Fine," Trivnor said. "That only leaves Jassan."

No one made eye contact with him except Lokna. When Jassan met his eyes the dragon said, "Don't even ask."

Jassan tried to meet Emma's eyes next. She was the only one who tolerated being around him, other than Burk. She'd heard him but her eyes were locked with Burk's.

"I would carry you," she said, "but I think Burk probably wants to…"

"No," Burk said, "I'll fly myself." He glanced up at Jassan for only a moment before he looked down at the forest floor again and pulled his cloak from his shoulders. "Just don't laugh," he said quietly. Jassan blinked and the young boy turned into a small, dark teal dragon in front of him.

The small dragon stood almost as tall as Trivnor. His dark scales were greenish-blue with black tips. A small ridge of spikes, no more than bumps really, ran down his back and a couple of dark horns grew from his head.

"Why would I laugh?" Jassan asked. He leaned in closer and said in a conspiratorial tone, "At least you're a dragon. If anyone laughs at you, you can just rip their leg off and hit them with it."

"That's what I've told him," Emma said, now in her dark blue dragon form and tucking her cloak under the scales that were wrappings for her human form.

The young dragon chuckled. "I would carry you," he said, "but I think you're still too big for me."

"I'll carry you," Emma finally said to Jassan. "I'm used to carrying Burk and you're not much bigger than he is."

Jassan's stomach jumped and he had to fight a smile. With difficulty, he simply nodded.

"Fine. Great, everyone's happy. The faeries are coming too. Yay," Lokna said, dripping with sarcasm. "Can we get going? I'll show you faeries how to really fly!"

Trivnor flew above the trees to make sure the coast was clear before the dragons could all lift off. He hovered for a moment with the musical hum of faerie wings. He circled above the trees around the immediate area then announced to the others that they could follow.

When Eleka got into the air, Trivnor flew with her for a moment before she reached out and grabbed him with her claw. Her claw barely fit around his waist, so he kept his wings on the outside of it and used them to keep himself upright.

"Um," Jassan heard Emma behind him, "how do you want to do this? Should I—" She reached her claw out to him.

"Oh, I can—" Jassan pointed to the sky where the others were already flying away.

"Maybe, if you—" she mimed him sitting down, but it looked more like lying down.

"Just get on her back," Burk said. "It's more comfortable. Plus, if you fall off, you can fly anyway."

Jassan nodded as Emma stooped to the forest floor, but he used his wings to spring onto her back. He straddled her spine with his legs, thankful she didn't have spikes on her back, only behind her wing joints. And he was glad he had worn pants and a tunic, rather than the traditional faerie robes his aunt usually insisted he wear.

As they lifted above the trees, the others rushed ahead and they hurried to catch up. Jassan gripped Emma's wings outside his legs to keep himself on. He couldn't be sure if it was her heat that warmed him or the rush of going faster than he ever had before. Either way, a small grin lit his face as they flew.

Jassan's fingers almost immediately began to go numb in the frigid rain. Everyone assumed that the waters of fall were meant to melt the snow from winter and make way for spring. But Jassan couldn't imagine the freezing rain melting anything.

When his hands began to ache from the cold he decided to try to distract himself. "Burk," he said, then cleared his throat as his voice shook. He hoped the shaking was just from the cold and Emma didn't think he was scared. "Why didn't you want to change into a dragon?" He leaned against Emma's scales and realized how warm they were, so he stayed there.

Burk, flying next to him, shrugged a shoulder. "I don't know," he said. "It's kind of embarrassing."

"Burk thinks he shouldn't have 'girl-colored' scales," Emma said. "But mine are practically boy-colored, if you're going to look at it that way."

"I don't know," Burk shrugged again. Jassan noticed the young dragon had a difficult time meeting his eye. "I like the color and all, but girls are supposed to be the colorful ones. I just feel weird when other people see me."

"What about Dasha?" Jassan said, his body giving a strong shake in the cold rain. "Her scales are greyish-blue. That's kind of boy-colored, but it doesn't seem to bother her."

"Yeah, but she's a goblin," Burk said. "She's used to being grey."

"What about our horns?" Emma said. "Dames are allegedly supposed to be smooth, with no horns or spikes or anything. These days you can't find a younger dame without some kind of ridges or spikes, even if just on their tails."

"But every dragon has spikes or something," Burk said. "They're all the same."

"My aunt says," Jassan said, "the world is changing. She says it can be seen in the plants, the stars and creatures. Maybe that's what she means. Dragons are changing too. It might be gradual, but you're one of the first ones. Like your parents were the first humans to transform into dragons and change back. You're just ahead of everyone else."

Jassan pulled his head up from her warm scales when he felt Emma curve her neck around to look at him. He shook a little more from the cold rush of air but saw the small smile on her lips, and Burk lifted his head a little higher as he flew.

Unfortunately, his body decided to give a powerful tremble and he felt better putting his head back down against her warmth, away from the wind.

"Are you going to be ok?" Emma asked before she turned back to watch her way ahead.

"I'll be fine," Jassan lied as he hid from the pelting raindrops.

"Can't we fly above the clouds?" they heard Eleka ask Trivnor as they caught up. "We could get out of the rain."

Jassan felt himself shaking more violently. He thought getting out of the rain would be better too, but he had stopped feeling the piercing of the raindrops. Either he was numb to that by now or the cold was just getting worse.

"Not wise," Trivnor said. "We could try, but the boundary to the World of Souls is riddled with holes right now. There's no way to know if we would get above the clouds and stay in this world, or slip through into the World of Souls. Without all the keys, I can't be sure we would make it back."

Eleka's eyes widened and swung to the clouds above her. She dipped a little lower to continue on her way. Jassan felt Emma do the same and the heat from her scales cooled underneath him when he was pulled away by her movements. In that second, his body shook the longest yet, but calmed when he dropped back down to meet her scales again.

As they flew, Jassan noticed a black shadow in the distance drop from the rain clouds and disappear into the horizon to the south.

"What was that?" he asked Trivnor, pointing a shaking finger. He hoped the faerieman wouldn't say it was the monster coming to find them again.

"It was a soul," Trivnor answered, and Jassan wasn't sure if he really wanted to know any more. "Like I said, the boundary to the World of Souls is weak. Souls are leaking into the mortal world."

"But it was black," Emma said. "Has Kelraz corrupted all the souls?"

"I'm not sure how it works exactly," Trivnor replied. Jassan shook and closed his eyes, suddenly exhausted, and listened to Trivnor through a haze of fog he was in. "He might be able to call forth souls. Either that or with his key he can sense them slipping through to the mortal world and corrupts them as they do. Or both."

"Why would he do that?" Eleka asked. "You never explained why Milah's soul spoke like Kelraz."

Trivnor sighed and wiped beaded water from his brow. "He can control them," he said. "He can see through their eyes and speak through their lips. The key he has isn't omni-powerful but it is the most powerful of the seven. It allows him into their minds. Normally what would purify, Kelraz can use to corrupt. What would guide, he forces. What he's doing is not just evil. It goes against the very fabric of existence. Against nature. Against the gods." His voice trailed off as Jassan spun in his own fog with his eyes closed, uncertain if he was hearing things correctly.

"What can be done about it?" Jassan asked, quietly. His mind felt fuzzy. His eyes wouldn't open against the chill of the air. He thought his lashes might be frozen together.

He could just hear Trivnor say, "We must get those keys. All of them."

"There it is!" Eleka saw their destination first. It was no secret that centaur dragons had better vision than any other dragon or creature. Their centaur vision was already majikally enhanced to see the stars better, then to add dragon vision gave the centaurs an advantage that no one could have foreseen before they were able to transform too.

She pointed ahead of them, but Jassan had to fight to open his eyes at all. He could barely lift his head, let alone look for anything. He kept his body pressed against Emma's. Though he might have been embarrassed to be so bold any other time, the cold and wet seeping into his clothes and skin inhibited any propriety.

"Trivnor," Emma said, "we need to get there quickly. I'm worried about Jassan."

"What's wrong?"

"I'm fine," Jassan mumbled. "Just cold."

"He's shaking," Emma said. "A lot."

"No, I'm not," Jassan said with his eyes closed. "I stopped shaking. I'm just tired."

He kept one cheek pressed against Emma's warm scales. But he felt her put on a little more speed. In better circumstances that would have sent a thrill up Jassan's spine, instead he felt the fierce sting of rain pummel his fingers locked on her wing joints. He would have moved them, but he hadn't tried to since he felt himself start to shake and wasn't sure if he could. He knew even through his fog that if he did move his hands, he would never get them back into place. So they remained locked where they were, and he could feel needles repeatedly jabbing them.

Finally, Jassan felt his stomach drop. He recognized the familiar sensation of descent, although when it was unexpected, his stomach fluttered. He had stopped shaking. He didn't have the strength to anymore. He wondered if the key was giving him power to be immune to the cold because he really didn't feel it anymore. He only felt the stabbing pain in his fingers. Was the key doing that?

He felt the flutter in his belly again. Someone was saying something, but he couldn't make out the words. That must be because of the thunder. Or was that roaring in his ears? Maybe he had turned into a real dragon and that's how they heard things all the time? He'd heard that other beings transform into dragons when they fall in love. Did he change now because he was so close to Emma? He couldn't lift his eyelids to find out.

"Watch out!" he heard in the distance.

"There's three of them!" someone added. Jassan didn't recognize that voice at all.

Jassan heard screams. Then he felt someone pull him from Emma's warmth. He wanted to protest, but he could only groan. He felt sure they had understood him though. He tried to get his feet under him, but the muscles pulled his legs in the wrong direction. He shook again hund his feet completely gave out. Where were they? Weren't they supposed to be flying? He heard Burk shouting for Trivnor, but his voice sounded like it came from under water. Or maybe Jassan was, he couldn't be sure over the noise of the rain.

"Lay him down," Trivnor warbled nearby.

Jassan could hear other voices and someone roaring. Lokna was probably complaining again. Yep, he could hear the dragon roaring now. Then Trivnor said, "Restrain them. You can't harm them."

'*Restrain them?*' Jassan thought. Was Trivnor telling someone to restrain the others? Had he led them into a trap? Had he betrayed them after all? Had Lokna been right all along? Stupid dragon. Lokna would probably insist that Jassan give him the key now. So much for his dream of being a dragon.

He tried to speak but he felt like he couldn't breathe. He had to stop Trivnor. Or was it Kelraz? Who was the bad guy again? It was Lokna. That was it, yes, the bad guy was definitely Lokna.

Jassan couldn't understand why his body wouldn't work for him because he didn't feel cold anymore. He figured they'd made it to the goblin town and Emma had taken him into a nice dry building to warm up. Or maybe he was just too exhausted to move. Yes, that must be it. He was just too tired. And he must have heard things wrong. He decided that they had all made it to the goblin town and Trivnor had promised they could sleep, so he would take him up on that promise now. He allowed himself to drift off.

9

THE KEYS

Jassan wished his dreams could have been better. He liked the ones where he turned into a dragon and flew away with Emma. He didn't like the ones where an ugly, grey-skinned old man with white hair sticking out of his nose hovered over him, yelling, "What have you done to him?" And, while pulling at his clothes, "You should have known better!"

The dreams got better, but they were still weird. He felt gentle hands on his face and something warm wriggling down his throat. Wait…down his throat?!

Jassan sat bolt upright as thunder rattled around him. Everything was dark. He felt a soft mattress under him and a soft, warm blanket over his legs. His bare legs. When lightning split the sky outside the window across from him, he caught a brief glimpse of the small room with a bed in which he had slept.

Confused, knowing he wasn't in his usual sleeping room at home, he pulled his feet over the edge of the bed. His thin leather boots were no longer on his feet. That was probably best because he knew they had been soaked through from rain and caked in mud. He touched the floor with his feet and felt the coolness of the stone through a soft covering. Exposing his feet and legs reminded him of the violent shakes he had experienced from being so cold as they flew. Or had that all been a dream? If it was, where was he now and why was he here? He glanced down at his forearm. The gem was still attached to him. That was not a dream. He felt cool air on his bare shoulders, so he pulled the blanket from the bed and wrapped it around himself.

As he stood up to walk to the door, his legs wobbled slightly. Taking a moment to steady himself and fight for control of his legs, he saw an orange glow appear beneath the door. He stood still for a moment, watching the glow flicker and fill more of the space under the door. Then the glow under the door went out, but Jassan could hear something moving around in the darkness of the sleeping room.

Suddenly, a flame burst from the ground in front of him. Jassan let out a yell and fell back to the bed when a small snake popped into existence, its head surrounded by fire. The snake couldn't have been long enough to wrap around his wrist twice, but its fiery aura was plenty to light the soft floor cover on fire.

"Whoa!" Jassan yelled again, wondering if he should try to stomp out the fire, but he remembered he wasn't wearing his boots. Then the door swung open and he saw Trivnor there, stooping over and holding a candle in his fist. With the candle lighting the room, soon the little snake's fire went out.

Another man rushed into the room behind Trivnor. Jassan recognized the grey-skinned old man with hair coming out of his nose, a goblin, from his weird dream.

"I told you to stop coming in here," the withered-looking old goblin said to the little serpent. He shooed the snake and stomped out the fire on the floor cover.

"You're awake," Trivnor said.

"I should have known he was awake when Bubbles disappeared," the old goblin said.

"How are you feeling?" Trivnor asked, sitting down on the bed beside Jassan.

Jassan took in the situation and tried to assess himself, and how much he should say. "I'm ok," he said. "I think. At least I thought I was until that snake tried to light me on fire."

"Ha!" the old goblin chuckled. "Bubbles didn't try to light you on fire; she came to check on you. But she couldn't see anything in the darkness, so she used her fire for light."

Bubbles slithered up the foot of the bed toward Jassan. He pulled back a little, not wanting to be sitting on a bed in flames next. She hesitated slightly, then slid up to Jassan's side and curled up next to him. In the faint light of the candle Trivnor still held, Jassan couldn't tell what color she was, but he thought he saw small specks of light dancing down her spine.

"She likes you," the old man said. "She hasn't left your side since you arrived, even camping outside your door *when I told her not to come in here.*" He raised his voice to add the admonishment. Bubbles turned her neck to face away from him.

"If you're feeling up to it, Jassan," Trivnor said, "you can get dressed and come out and get something to eat. I know our hostess is eager to feed you."

"Look who finally decided to wake up," Lokna said with a growl when Jassan had followed Trivnor and the old goblin down the hall to the main room in a house he didn't recognize, even though he knew everyone in it. Jassan noticed Lokna's voice held less malice than it had previously.

"Yeah, sorry to make you wait," Jassan mumbled back, remembering the urgency of their mission. "How long was I asleep?"

"Just last night," Emma said. Jassan noticed her eyes drooping, seemingly from lack of sleep.

He looked at Burk next. The younger boy seemed almost as tired as Emma looked. "Didn't the rest of you sleep too?"

"Not very well," Burk said. "We were worried about you."

"You and the idea that those monsters could burst through the door at any moment," Tyla said. When her sister glared at her, she said, "What? That's what kept me awake!"

Jassan helped himself to a stool near a small table. Bubbles hadn't let him leave his room without her. The old goblin had laid his dry clothes at the foot of the bed and Bubbles waited for him to dress before slithering up his arm to drape herself around the back of his neck. When he joined the others in the main room and sat down, she moved back down his arm to rest in his lap. In the light of the room, Jassan could see her lavender scales with gold specks down her back that had reflected the little light in the sleeping room. Once curled on his lap she stared up at him as if to make sure he would be staying put. Jassan knew snakes didn't have eyelids like most other creatures, but this little one appeared to blink like a dragon before she let her head rest and fell asleep in his lap.

"What is she?" Jassan asked, holding his legs together so the little snake didn't slip to the floor.

"She's a fire worm," the old goblin said. "We found her mother living in the hearth when we settled here. We didn't have the heart to kick her out because she had little ones with her. They live in the fire box and don't get in the way, so we leave them be. We've kind of taken to them, but now it seems she's taken to you."

"Why do you call her 'Bubbles'?" Jassan asked. The goblin opened his mouth to answer, but at that moment, Bubbles chose to sit up and light her head on fire. As Jassan watched, she lightly blew her fire above her head and the resulting bubble floated up a tiny bit before bursting in a puff of smoke. She did this a few more times until Jassan finally said, "Oh."

The room they had entered was laid out with windows and a door leading outside on one wall. Along that wall sat couches which Emma, Burk and Dasha had already claimed in their human and goblin forms, and the old goblin and Trivnor took the adjacent cushy chairs. An inviting fire blazed in a hearth on one side of the room, opposite the hallway that led to the sleeping room. On the side of the room opposite the door was a broad opening, large enough for the two full dragons to stick their heads through from behind to join the conversation, but also to pull them back into the larger room beyond, where they'd slept. Tyla and Eleka lay on the floor as centaurs between Gizi and Lokna. The large opening to the outside behind them was covered with a waterproof fabric and allowed larger creatures access into and out of the goblin home.

Jassan felt tall in the rooms. The ceiling was the right height for the goblins, but just high enough for a young human or faerie. Even Emma, who was tall for her age, could easily stand up in the room. However, a full-grown faerie like Trivnor had to hunch over, and the chair he sat in required that he fold his knees up closer to his chest.

A small goblin woman bustled into the room from around the corner to the hallway holding a plate piled with food and a cup of water. She and the goblin man resembled each other closely, with pointed ears, the same grey skin and pure white hair. The hair on the man's head stuck up around his ears, but the woman wore hers pulled back with a tie. "Poor dear," the old woman said, placing the food in front of Jassan, "you must be starving. Eat this and there's more where that came from. Everyone else, your cloaks are just about done, dears."

Jassan dove into the steaming vegetables, covered in a sauce thick enough to be its own meal. "What happened?" he asked between mouthfuls. He hadn't realized just how hungry he had been.

Trivnor pointed to the goblin man and woman. "These are our hosts, Arden and Val. They've been gracious enough to bring us into their home, and Arden saved your life."

Jassan swallowed a scalding chunk of wissop, but didn't know what to say to that. Is 'thank you' enough when someone saves your life?

"It wasn't nothing," Arden said. "You lost too much heat is all. Once we had those other... strange monsters taken care of, we brought you here to warm up. I had a few herbs to spare that healed you."

"Monsters?" Jassan asked, wondering what he had missed.

"You missed everything!" Burk chirped. "Three monsters dropped out of the sky just when we were landing. They looked like humans but they were black and shadowy and all skeletal and they attacked everyone almost immediately. They tried to rip out Gizi's throat with their bare hands! But the goblins jumped on them. The goblins tried to kill them, but they couldn't even hurt them. Five goblins were injured pretty bad before they realized it. So Trivnor convinced the goblins to bind them. Once they were bound, the goblins threw them into some kind of dungeon. That's when Emma told Trivnor she thought you were almost dead."

"What? Dead?" Jassan shot a look at Trivnor. "I was almost dead?"

"That's usually the state you're in when someone has to save your life," Gizi muttered.

"Close to," Trivnor said. "We were lucky to find these goblins willing to help a faerie."

"He's just a boy," Arden shook his head. "I wasn't going to let him die."

"We thank you very kindly, just the same," Trivnor said.

Jassan turned back to his food, but the wissop didn't sit as well in his stomach. He knew the goblin had only helped a faerie grudgingly. If he had been a dragon, the goblins wouldn't have hesitated. Of course, if he had been a dragon he would create his own heat.

"Yes, well," Arden said, "we'll be sending young Jassan with a cloak this time. I know the other goblins in town won't take to you faeries staying here much longer now that you're healed."

"Agreed," Trivnor answered. "We should be getting on our way."

"Where are we going?" Dasha said, casting a glance at Arden. Jassan knew she wanted to ask if and how they were still going to try to steal any of the goblins' gems, but she couldn't blurt that out in front of their hosts.

"Arden has been kind enough to give me directions to a very old shaman that might be able to help us," Trivnor said before slowly explaining to Jassan what they had told the goblin. "I told Arden how we were separated from Emma and Burk's parents by the same monsters that attacked their village, and I explained to him that we're trying to find our way back." Trivnor said it pointedly so Jassan wouldn't give away anything about what they were really doing this far from home, trying to find the gatekeeper's keys. Jassan thought Trivnor must have already instructed the others to do the same because they all nodded in agreement.

"Yes," Jassan said, "but will a goblin shaman help us get home?"

Arden shook his head. "No such thing as a goblin shaman, boy," he said. "I only know of one shaman anywhere near here. She's a faerie so she'll be more than willing to help you, but be warned, she isn't known for being predictable."

"Where is she?" Jassan asked. "Who is she? Maybe I know her?"

"She's several hours dragon flight south of here," Arden said. "Which is why I'm sending a cloak with you, so you won't catch your death in the cold and rain again. Just don't tell her I'm the one who sent you. She has a nasty temper, that one, and she's crazy to boot. Her name is Sha Ogalala Carpoo Shampeter. Goes by Shampy if she likes you."

"Before we go," Jassan heard Trivnor say to Arden as the goblin pulled Bubbles out of Jassan's bag... again, "would you be willing to take me to the place where you're keeping those black monsters? I'd like to see them before we go."

"Why would you want to see those creatures again?" Arden sneered up at him. With his back turned away and distracted, Jassan caught Bubbles before she could slip inside his bag another time. Instead, she slithered up his arm and twisted herself comfortably around his elbow.

"I just want to make sure they're contained," Trivnor said. "That's all."

"Well," Arden turned back to button up Jassan's bag for him. "I'll point you in their direction, but I can't say I wish to see them again myself." He picked up the bag and draped it over Jassan's arm while Jassan tried to wriggle his fingers under Bubbles's belly. She shifted slightly, then suddenly unwrapped herself and slipped over to circle Jassan's other wrist. "You might as well take her with you," Arden said with his hands on his hips. "She'll probably follow you anyway and if I try to make her stay here, she'll burn the place down. And this time she'll do it on purpose."

"I don't know how to take care of her," Jassan resisted.

"Don't need to," Arden said. "She's practically a wild fire worm. She can take care of herself. It's time that she leaves the nest anyway." He looked around at the others. Val had packed bags of food and returned cleaned cloaks and wrappings to their owners. "If everyone is ready to go, I'll show you through town to the way out."

The group tromped out into the drizzle of rain. Arden and Trivnor took the lead, with Emma and Burk and Jassan close behind. The two centaurs followed and Dasha, and Lokna and Gizi took up the rear.

As they passed through the goblin town, Jassan took in what he hadn't seen when they arrived. The small town seemed to have been in ruins and was in the midst of rebuilding. Many building roofs had caved in and were in different stages of repair, and doors and windows were wide open. But a few buildings standing had boards neatly placed over the windows as if to protect the indoors from the outside elements. When the rain abated slightly, Jassan could see four or five goblins sitting atop a roof, smearing mud and pounding nails. They stopped their work to stare at the strangers going by. But they didn't stare at the dragons.

Jassan could feel the onlookers' eyes specifically on him and Trivnor, but the older faerie didn't seem to notice or care.

"Why are they staring at you?" Burk mumbled to Jassan.

Jassan shrugged but Tyla, walking behind him, replied for him. "Because he's a faerie," she said, watching the workers. "They may suspect he's the reason the monsters attacked." She waved to one of them with a smile before turning to glare down at Jassan. "And they're probably right."

Jassan felt his ears get hot and likely turn bright purple. Although the rain had eased considerably, he lifted the hood of the waterproof cloak to cover his head, turning away from Burk's gaze. Before the little human could say anything, the group came to a stop.

"Through there," Arden said, gesturing, "and around the left corner. You won't miss it. I would suggest you don't stay long, though."

After accepting many thanks, Arden trudged away through the muddy streets. To avoid any more patronizing remarks, Jassan pushed toward Trivnor as he moved in the direction Arden had indicated.

"What are we here for?" Jassan asked him, knowing what awaited them. "Can't we just leave?"

"I'm with him," Emma said, appearing at Jassan's side. "I don't want to see those creatures again."

Trivnor stopped at the corner before turning it. "You can wait here," he said. "But there's something I must do."

As he slipped around the corner, Jassan realized he didn't want to be left behind, especially under the accusing stares of the goblins, and darted around the corner too.

Ahead of them two goblins stood under an awning and a dark hole behind them beckoned, gaping from the wall that was set down at a lower level from the street. As they got closer, Jassan could see the dark bars running across the hole and large, shadowy figures moving behind them.

"What do you plan to do with them?" Trivnor asked by way of greetings.

The goblins glanced at each other, then one of them returned the address. "Not sure yet," he said. "We're getting word of them back to the goblin king and we'll see what he says to do."

"You can't kill them," Trivnor said. To Jassan it sounded more like a directive than a question.

"No," the goblin answered through narrowed eyes. "As you informed us last night."

Trivnor nodded without taking his eyes off the shadow monsters. Jassan hadn't let his eyes rest on them for more than a couple of seconds. "I would highly recommend building an enclosure for them," Trivnor said. "Using one of the larger empty buildings, perhaps?"

"Why?" the second goblin asked.

"Because those creatures were just humans," he said. "But many more may be coming that aren't."

10

RUNAWAY

"Wait, you know her?" Lokna said, not masking his surprise as they flew over the Black Forest.

"I know *of* her," Jassan clarified. "I've never actually met her. Every faerie knows *of* her. Especially those who practice majik."

Bubbles seemed content curled up between Emma's back and Jassan's chest, keeping him warmer than he'd been for some time. Every time he looked down at her, she seemed to smile up at him and blink her eyes contentedly.

They all flew quietly together over the forest with orders from Arden to make sure they landed often in order to warm Jassan, because he couldn't warm himself like a dragon could. As if he needed any more reasons pointed out that he was a hindrance and generally useless to the group. But this was the first time Lokna had spoken to Jassan without insulting him.

"Every shaman has either been trained by her at some point or knows someone who was trained by her," Jassan said from Emma's back. The goblin had been right, the new cloak kept most of the rain off and held the heat from Emma and Bubbles in to keep him warmer. His feet still got chilled, but he could pull them under the edges of the cloak and actually feel them dry out a little.

"She's come to the castle a few times," Emma said, flying closer to Lokna, since he had all the questions and she knew most of the answers. "But mother and father try to keep her away from us."

"Yeah," Burk said on Emma's other side. "I'm glad they do, 'cause she's nuts."

"Have you met her invisible kangaroo?" Gizi asked. "My dromdan says that thing is the worst part about having her around. But he won't talk about anything else that happened when he met her."

"Why are we going to see her, anyway?" Dasha asked, carrying Trivnor in her fist. "She lives in the other direction from the portal to the goblin city. I thought we needed to get the gem?"

"We do," Trivnor said. "But we can use all the help we can get. Besides, I think she knows more than she's willing to tell almost anyone. She's been around too long not to."

Trivnor eyed the forest below them and motioned for everyone to land.

"Are we lost?" Dasha grumbled.

"No," Trivnor grumbled back. Jassan thought he sounded an awful lot like a dragon when he answered her. "I just can't receive memories with directions the way you can. I have to remember things the hard way."

Trivnor led them into the forest on foot and advised everyone to be on the lookout for the old shaman's hut.

They were looking through a forest just outside of the Black Forest. Trivnor said the old shaman was supposed to be in the area, but they couldn't find her little hut. He was mostly relying on Tyla's and Eleka's exceptional vision to find it tucked in somewhere among the rocks and trees.

"I say we fly over," Tyla said. "We could see much more, much faster if we fly."

"No," Trivnor said. "We're much too close to the Noble Kingdom to do that."

"Why does that matter?" Eleka asked.

"For the same reason no one here can go home," he replied to her. "Kelraz has had too long to bring out more souls and search for us through their eyes. He could be watching you and your homes from anywhere, deducing where we will go, and he's most certainly closer to finding the other keys than we are. I can only hope he doesn't—"

Trivnor's voice cut off so suddenly that everyone turned to watch him. He stood still, staring into the dark forest. The rain had held off for most of the day, but the persistent clouds made the forest even darker as it approached dusk.

"Eleka," Trivnor finally said. Without another word, Eleka trotted to Trivnor's side.

She stood a few steps closer to the shadows and stared into the dark forest in front of them. A light breeze rustled the branches and sparse vegetation. Eleka finally shook her head. "I don't see anything," she said.

"Me neither," Tyla said from slightly behind her.

Suddenly, Bubbles, who had been curled around Jassan's wrist, dropped to the ground. She slithered around his feet a moment, then burst into flame. Luckily, the wet forest floor had no kindling. Pausing a moment to taste the air, she zipped into the trees away from where Trivnor and the centaur twins had been searching, leaving a sputtering trail of flame behind her.

Jassan looked to Trivnor, debating whether he should follow the little snake away or continue the way Trivnor would choose.

Trivnor returned his look and waved his hand after Bubbles. "It's as good a way as any."

Jassan took off running after the little snake. He didn't know if she was just looking for something to eat or if she had some other base need that made her scoot away so quickly, but he felt responsible for her. Besides, he knew she had chosen to go with him, but he assumed she would stay a little longer than that. He didn't know if he'd be able to stop her, but this small creature had actually preferred to remain by his side and had chosen to be with him over everyone else. He didn't want to give up on the only being here who made him feel important, in her own small way.

As he darted through the trees following the burning trail, he stomped out the fires that he could, trusting the others to tamp down the rest or the falling sky to take revenge. Bubbles moved so fast that the trail grew longer and longer ahead of him as he ran. He had to cease stomping out fires so he could move faster and try to catch up. Then the rain came.

Jassan finally tossed the sides of his cloak aside and took to his wings as the rain began to drip through the canopy of branches overhead. He lifted into the air to see if he could find any sign of the little snake's fire. He caught a glimpse of light several dragon lengths through the trees ahead of him, but it disappeared so quickly he couldn't be sure it wasn't simply a trick of the light. He flew toward it anyway.

He flew so quickly he didn't realize at first that the rain had stopped. He hovered over the small clearing where he thought he had seen the last bit of flame, but couldn't see Bubbles anywhere. But as he searched the area, he noticed odd things.

Several logs and twisted branches that looked like hastily assembled chairs and benches dotted the area. Old scorch marks and flattened leaves in small depressions scattered on the ground around them. He noticed the lack of rocks, which brought his attention to the canopy. The tree branches had grown over and woven together so tightly as to create a roof, impervious to the rain dripping through it. So many trees had grown together overhead in this manner that he knew dozens of dragons could fit beneath it.

"Did you find her?" Emma asked as she caught up.

"Whoa," Burk said, looking around them. "What is this place?"

"Well, what do you know, Jassan," Lokna said, joining them under the canopy, "the only creature in Avonoa that likes you ran away from you!"

Emma huffed at the comment, but Jassan tried to ignore him, still searching the area for the snake.

Trivnor joined them under the canopy before Jassan could wallow too much in the same thoughts that Lokna had spoken aloud. "We must be close," the older faerieman said. "Those branches overhead don't look to have grown this way naturally."

"Not you again!" they heard a yell from off to the side of the heavy canopy. "Not this time! Get out, you little monster!"

Everyone's eyes jumped toward the noise to see a burst of light pop open in the trees. The shadow of a stooped faerie stood in the light. The faerie blinked at the group under the canopy, yelped, and slammed a door.

"I think we've found her," Trivnor said.

"Are you sure we want to?" Lokna asked, but no one answered.

Jassan saw movement on the ground in front of the door. The leaves on the ground rustled until they moved in front of him. Bubbles burst into flame at his feet.

"Agh!" Jassan shouted. "Bubbles, you have to stop doing that!"

The little snake slid out of the way to allow Jassan to stomp out the small blaze. Under this canopy the leaves were dry enough to spark the whole place. Unfortunately, Bubbles kept her fire burning and just lit a different part of the leaves each time she moved.

"You have to stop that burning," Jassan mumbled as he stomped out another fire.

The little snake looked down at her long body and finally put out her fire, but continued sliding back and forth between Jassan and the old faerie's hut. "I think she wants us to follow her," Jassan said.

"I think we must," Trivnor said.

The group slowly made their way toward the place where they'd seen the door. Bubbles slid up Jassan's leg to wrap around his knee as they approached.

"I can't even see it," Eleka said. "If she hadn't opened the door, I never would have seen it."

"Thanks to Bubbles," Trivnor said.

Jassan held out his hand to her and she slid up his arm to his shoulder. She lit just her head on fire and held it up like a candle.

"I think she's very proud of herself," Jassan said.

"As she should be," Emma said. "She found what we couldn't."

The hut wasn't entirely invisible, but the trees and rocks it was made from shifted in a way that made the hut almost an illusion. Jassan tried walking around it to see if it was all just good camouflage, and Trivnor did the same. As he stepped, Jassan thought he could see the rocks and branches move with his focus to make the building nearly invisible from any direction.

"Amazing," Trivnor said. "I've never seen majik like this. She must be incredibly powerful."

"Nope!" they heard from inside. "Just bored!"

Trivnor pursed his lips and knocked on the door.

The door burst open. "Don't have any!" the old faeriewoman yelled. She rapped three times on the lintel of the door and it slammed shut again.

"Have any what?" Emma asked.

Gizi snorted. "Sanity."

The door popped open again long enough for the old faerie to say, "And where are my cookies, huh?" Then slammed the door again.

Trivnor cleared his throat. "Shampy," he called, "we need your assistance."

"Everyone needs something," the old faerie called again. "And I no longer give it!"

"You're not willing to help some kids?" Tyla hollered.

"Even a faerie kid?" Lokna added.

"Nope," came the response from within. "I can't help anyone anymore. Shut up! You don't know anything!"

"What?"

"Who's she talking to?"

"We know we don't know anything!"

"That's why we're here, you crazy nifflehog!"

"Quiet!" Trivnor yelled over everyone's complaints. When they had silenced, he took a deep breath, then said to the closed door. "I come from the Lost Ruck."

After a moment of quiet the door opened a small crack, but the faeriewoman still wasn't visible. "It must be incredibly important for you to admit that."

"It is," Trivnor said.

"You risk much telling me," she said. "I know."

"I gave up everything telling you that," he answered her.

"No," she said, sighing, "you didn't."

11

SHA SHAMPY

The door opened wider to reveal a small, stooped faerie woman. She barely came up to Trivnor's chin, which meant she was a little taller than Jassan himself. A sheet of her stringy white hair hung over one shoulder. The other side of her head was shaved bare, with a glowing tattoo of a snake circling her ear and tracing down her neck to her shoulder. Her soft blue skin hung in wrinkles from her bony arms and legs. Her jowls hung down around a soft jawline, but her wide eyes pierced like a sharp blade.

"You!" Shampy snapped, pointing at Jassan. "You brought them here, didn't you?"

"I—I—" Jassan stammered, his hands beginning to shake. "How could—"

"Not you," Shampy barked at Jassan and pointed to his shoulder. "You. You're *her* little worm, aren't you?"

"Whose worm is she?" Jassan asked hesitantly.

Shampy's pinched eyes found him. "Her mother's, of course."

Jassan glanced at Bubbles on his shoulder. She perched there like a little snake-shaped candle, her head burning at the top. She gave the faerie shaman one quick bob of her head and flicked her tongue, although Jassan wasn't sure if that was meant to taste the air or to be rude.

"Well," Shampy sucked her teeth a moment, "I guess as long as you're with them. But NO lighting my house on fire just because you get stepped on! Just stay out of the way."

Shampy spun in a circle twice and kicked the stone wall next to the door. "You," she pointed to Trivnor and then to all the others, "wait in the tent."

Jassan caught a glimpse of a warm fire and cushy chairs inside the faerie's home before she retreated inside and slammed the door again.

"I guess we wait out here," Trivnor said, motioning to the dry forest floor under the canopy.

"Is this the tent?" Emma asked.

No one answered but Jassan assumed it had to be. No other structures could be seen from the door where the faerie had left them. None of the rest of her home could be seen either.

The group sat in a circle, waiting for the old faeriewoman to return. With everyone else still in their dragon forms, Jassan and Trivnor pulled two of the old chairs together and sat down. Jassan couldn't believe how wonderful it felt to sit comfortably in a chair made for a faerie! He allowed his head to tip back and felt the skinny piece of wood fit comfortably between the wing joints on his back. He relaxed his wings and shoulders and almost sighed aloud as Bubbles draped herself around his neck to warm him.

He could have fallen asleep right there, even with everyone else muttering about how "crazy" the faerie seemed and how they shouldn't be trusting another faerie, anyway. For the most part Trivnor ignored the comments.

Suddenly a thumping sound came from behind them. Everyone turned to see a little sled appear from around some trees, piled up with what looked like firewood and some other plants and branches. A little rope strap stood straight up into the air but was seemingly hooked to nothing. With each thump, the rope strap bounced and the sled moved forward a little farther.

Gizi's eyes lit. "Invisible kangaroo," she breathed.

WHACK!

"OW!"

The sight of the sled being pulled invisibly had distracted them to the point that Shampy had also come from the rocks and trees behind them without anyone noticing her. Everyone turned at the sounds to see Tyla rubbing her head and Shampy standing next to her, holding a bushel of bound leaves and branches the size of three brooms. One branch Jassan could see had long, sharp thorns protruding from it.

"Oh, I'm sorry, my dear," Shampy cooed. "What was your name again?"

"Tyla," she barked.

"Ah yes," Shampy backed a few steps. "Daughter of Ashel, correct? Twin to—"

WHACK! Shampy smacked Eleka, who sat next to her sister, without looking at her.

"Ow!" Eleka shrieked. "What was that for?"

"Cleansing!" Shampy said. "You are Eleka. The stripey one!" She swung her branches over her head and danced around the circle.

She ran to Dasha. WHACK! "You know my name," Shampy batted her eyes at the greyish-blue dragon, "but I don't know yours."

"I'm Dasha," she growled, "and if you hit me again…"

"Oh, no, no, no, I wouldn't dream of it." Shampy backed away from her but spun and hit Gizi on the nose.

"Ow!" Gizi yelped. "If you want to know our names, can't you just ask?"

"But I know your name, Giggles!" Shampy waved her branches in Gizi's face.

Gizi, very uncharacteristically, bared her fangs and crouched, appearing the most dangerous Jassan had ever seen her. "Don't. Ever. Call. Me. That," she growled.

"Ah," Shampy pointed at her with her branches, "prefers a faerie name, does she?"

Gizi eased herself back to the ground. "My father always said you were crazy. No. Correction. He said you were evil."

"Ah ha ha ha ha!" Shampy cackled as she moved toward Lokna. "Your father would know, child! He has seen things with those *toggling* eyes of his."

By then everyone knew what was coming. When she approached Lokna, he bared his fangs at her. "Don't even think about it, witch!" he growled.

He tried to snatch at the bundle in her fist, but the old faerie avoided him more deftly than Jassan thought she would. She only opened her wings for a moment to fly over his claw and smack him on the nose.

"Don't fight it," she said in a sing-song voice. "That will only make it worse." She began backing toward Emma, who was next in the circle, but she twirled a finger at Lokna.

Lokna narrowed his eyes at her. "Lokna," he mumbled.

Shampy straightened. Any joviality slid from her features. "Mitashio's son," she uttered.

"Yes," Lokna said. "What's wrong with that?"

"Nothing," she said, then smacked Emma next to her.

"Ow!" Emma yelped. "Is this really necessary?"

"'Fraid so," Shampy said. "But no need to introduce yourself, my dear. Your father and uncle are very good at keeping you and your brother away from me when I stop by the castle. Doesn't trust me, does he? Your father. Poor little Philip listens to every word your father says too. Ah, well. He never liked me either."

Next to Emma, Burk cringed but made no move to stop her when she came up to him, so she paused. "I'm sorry, dear," she cooed, then whacked him on the head too.

She ran to Jassan and he lifted his arms to fend her off. However, she simply scooped Bubbles from his shoulder and threw the little snake and the bundle of dried plants onto the pile of wood on the sled.

Everything erupted into an inferno of flame.

"Bubbles!" Jassan bounded from his chair.

Trivnor put a hand on his arm before he could run into the fire. "It's all right, my boy," he said. "She lives in fire, remember?"

Sure enough, when he looked into the fire, Bubbles had curled herself up into a little ball on a burning log. Jassan saw her sigh and close her eyes.

"Odd," Shampy said, watching the pair of them.

"You're calling *us* odd?" Gizi said, still rubbing her head.

"Not all of you," Shampy said. "Him."

Jassan looked away from Bubbles's sleeping form to see Shampy staring at him. "Who, me?" he said. He fought back the retort that passed through his mind, but heard his thought come from Lokna anyway.

"Everyone knows Jassan is odd," the brown dragon said indifferently. "Tell us why you hit us."

Shampy stepped closer to Jassan. "Fire worms only bond with dragons," she said. "So, either your fire worm is odd, or *you* are."

A thrill ran through Jassan's body and goosebumps prickled on his skin. Fire worms only bonded with dragons? That must mean he had the potential to become a dragon. He knew that for many years after the dragon war, all the races mingled and many male dragons found themselves falling in love with females of other species. When a male dragon's heart broke, as one's does when he falls in love, he would majikally change into a male of his beloved's race. Hence several part-dragons were created and more were born from those pairs. Eventually, species other than dragons who fell in love with dragons would likewise majikally transform into their beloved's race and become a dragon. However, love had never, not once in seventeen years, changed a faerie. No such thing as a part-faerie, part-dragon existed. No faerie dragons existed. And yet, here stood a faerie before him, implying that Jassan had the potential to be a dragon. Or she was just troll brains.

"Shampy," Trivnor said, "we need your help with something more important."

Shampy's eyes drifted to the key in Jassan's arm. "Apparently," she muttered. "So," she said much louder, "you need, what? A spell? Potion? Ingredients? Tonics? A poultice? A rhyme? Protection? Food? Shelter? Clothing?"

"A weapon," Trivnor stated.

"Ah," Shampy said. She pulled up another chair between Emma and Burk. Her light blue cloak waggled as she shuffled the chair closer. She spun and landed hard with her rump on the upright chair. The back two legs broke off the chair and she ended up tilting backwards. "Much better," she said, then crossed her legs. "You know what it is that chases you."

Trivnor nodded.

"What?" Tyla asked. "Trivnor hasn't told us anything. What is it?"

"He's said that we can't hurt it or kill it," Eleka said, "so what's the weapon for?"

"You're not going to hurt the goblins, are you?" Dasha said, with justified alarm in her voice.

"Goblins?!" Shampy barked. "What are you doing with the goblins?"

"Stealing from them, apparently," Gizi said.

"Stealing?!" Shampy launched into a fit of hysterical giggles. When she finally got control of herself, she laughed at them. "Stealing from goblins? I can see why you would need a good weapon for that."

"That's not what we need and you know it," Trivnor said.

"Hmmm," Shampy hedged with a lingering grin. She snapped her fingers and scratched at her chin.

"What?" Burk said.

"What is he talking about?" Emma asked.

"You're not using the weapon on the goblins, right?" Dasha said.

"Why did you hit us on the head?" Gizi growled, still smarting.

"—How do you put up with this?" Shampy cried over everyone's questions.

"It's been trying," Trivnor answered in agreement with her tone.

Shampy pursed her lips and looked around at everyone else in the circle. "Simmer down and let me speak and you'll find that I know more than you do," she said.

Everyone quieted down. Jassan wondered if she used majik to shut them up because it seemed many did so against their will.

"The dark creatures," she said, "are soul wraiths. And I hit you with the herbs to cleanse you of any curses or spells you might have picked up on your journey. There's nothing I hate more than catching a secondhand curse."

"Soul wraiths? What are—" Dasha began to ask more questions, but with one scathing look from Shampy, sealed her lips.

"Many kinds of wraiths can be conjured in the living world. The conjurer uses water, air, earth and fire for the basics, but they can use any combination of elements or other medium to majikally animate the new creature. Basically, a wraith is an animated creature of whatever medium the conjurer chooses. In the case of a soul wraith, the medium is a soul, whether conjured immediately when someone dies or from a soul pulled from the World of Souls."

"I thought souls didn't have substance," Eleka said. "How can it attack us? How can we touch it?"

"Good questions, you must be the smart one," Shampy said with an approving grin. "When someone dies and their soul passes into the World of Souls, their body stays behind. It still exists here physically, usually in the form of ash, like when a dragon dies or a human body decomposes. Which means it could conceivably coalesce again into a tangible creature. Whatever had remained here from the body clings to a soul. In order to kill anything, you must sever the connection between body and soul. But a soul wraith is not a *living* creature. That connection has already been destroyed. To create a soul wraith, one would have to summon a soul and majikally bind it to this world through dark majik as powerful as the gods themselves. Even I wouldn't know how to do it. Only the gatekeeper of the conjuror can decide to release it, which they usually do because any wraiths are notoriously difficult to control, especially soul wraiths since the person's soul would fight you so much.

"On the other hand, wraiths conjured from the elements in the living world can be killed fairly easily with the right ingredients and mixtures of those. I say 'killed', but you're really only uncreating an animated object. A collection of mud or fire or whatever it's made of, put together to do what the conjuror tells it to do. It doesn't have a soul."

"I bet a fire wraith is the hardest to kill," Tyla said.

"Not really," Shampy said, waving at something in the air that no one else could see. "A little water and they disappear in a poof of dust."

Tyla looked disappointed.

"No," Shampy continued, "a soul wraith can't be killed, destroyed or freed by anyone in this world other than the conjuror. I don't even know anyone in this world that's powerful enough to create one. When a corrupted soul crosses into the living world, or a soul somehow becomes corrupted before it moves to the World of Souls, it's up to the conjuror or the gatekeeper to return the soul to the World of Souls and allow them to be purified. A soul wraith in this world would crave other souls from the living world to join them there, so their only goal here is to kill living beings. In normal circumstances, if someone here were to conjure a soul wraith, the conjurer would be inextricably bound to that soul and would be forced to control it until the gatekeeper returned it to the World of Souls, unless they free it willingly. So they would have to have a really good reason to conjure one and be bound to it. They usually want it to do something for them and they keep it bound to them until they're done with it."

"Kelraz isn't bound to these wraiths in that way," Trivnor said. "He creates them when someone dies or slips through, but he can choose when or if he wants to control them."

Shampy sat up straight. "He has the Sky Key?"

Trivnor nodded.

"And the gatekeeper?"

Trivnor shook his head and dropped his eyes.

"Well," Shampy stood up, dusted off her butt and waved her arms at them, "you're hatched. Say goodbye to everyone and everything you love."

Jassan heard the murmuring around him immediately pick up. "What do we do now?" was the most repeated phrase. But Trivnor stood to stop Shampy from leaving.

"We have two of the keys," he told her. "And a plan to get a third."

Shampy glared at him. She sucked her teeth, scratched her butt, spun twice, stomped her foot three times, then sat back down. "What did you do?"

"I did what I had to do," Trivnor said. "I got the Cloud Key in a fight with Kelraz and sent most of the others away and now I have to get to them before he does."

"Never did like that boy," Shampy said with narrowed eyes. "But much good that'll do you if he can sense where you go."

"And Jassan has the Moon Key," Trivnor said.

Jassan withered under the crazy shaman's gaze. "Only puts him in more danger," she said, sucking her teeth again.

"Which is why we need your sword."

When they heard that, the entire circle hushed. Jassan realized that Trivnor had always known about the existence of the weapon he was after here. It seemed that Trivnor had told them very little about what he knew.

"Not much of a sword," Shampy said, then turned and shouted over her shoulder, "No, the bristle is NOT laughing at you!" She sighed and turned back to Trivnor. "You do realize what you're asking?"

Trivnor nodded.

"Well, *we* don't!" Lokna jumped to his feet. "We need to know if this faerie is putting us in more danger, or asking us for something dangerous or dragging us along somewhere to get killed! This has gone on far too long and someone needs to start answering our questions!"

"Now, look—" Trivnor started, but Shampy cut him off.

"Quiet," she snapped, "all three of you." She directed it at Trivnor and Lokna, but no one could tell who *else* she addressed. "This young dragon is correct. If you're asking them to risk their lives, they need to know why. They need to understand the repercussions of following you."

"I've told them about the keys," Trivnor said, "as well as the gateway, the keeper, everything."

"You should have let me tell them," Shampy muttered.

"Why?" Eleka shifted uncomfortably. "I'm sorry, but how do you know about all of this? I know you're very accomplished in majik—"

"I am a Sha, not just a Shaman, after all," Shampy interjected.

"Yes," Eleka continued, "but how do you know about the gatekeeper and what is the Lost Ruck? Unless..."

Shampy grinned. "Now she's onto it."

Shampy and Eleka nodded together, then Eleka whispered, "You're from the Lost Ruck too."

Shampy started to speak. "It's a—"

"Shampy," Trivnor said, suddenly, interrupting her. "Don't."

Shampy twisted her face at Trivnor, but Jassan couldn't tell if she was angry, confused or hungry. Finally, she slapped her thigh as if she had made up her mind.

"But you haven't told them about the weapon," Shampy said. She turned to squint at Lokna. "The sword he's asking for is the only one of its kind. Someone could make another, but there's a reason there's only one. Have you ever seen or heard of a blade with a majikal edge that allows a dragon's...pieces...to survive when cut off?"

Lokna recoiled. He had seen one, Jassan knew it. They had all seen it. They had used it in the circle to summon Milah's soul. It was the blade of the knife they had used to cut their claws and drip dragon blood into the fire in the circle. Jassan made a mental note to ask Lokna where he had gotten that knife.

"Uh-huh," Shampy nodded, "I can see you have. Well, these blades, and they're not extremely common, are dangerous to dragons, but not deadly, because they're very small. But, you see, if a dragon is somehow killed with one of these blades, I can't imagine how one would be, but if it happened, their body wouldn't turn to ash and their soul could not go on to the World of Souls. Don't ask me how I know this, all I can tell you is I've been around a very long time and have done my own experiments in evil.

"But that's why these blades are made small, so a dragon can't die after a strike from one. Unfortunately, in one of my many experiments, I was requested to create a short sword with a majikal blade. It would be just large enough to kill a dragon. I made it, honestly just to see if I could, but I refused to turn it over to the one who asked for it. I still have it."

"How does that help us?" Tyla asked. "We don't want to kill dragons anyway. Right, Trivnor?"

"Correct," Trivnor insisted. "But this sword does the one thing we need it to do."

"What's that?" Tyla asked. Everyone could hear the trepidation in her voice, the urge of wanting to hear the answer and at the same time, not hear it.

Shampy sighed, "It destroys souls."

Silence.

Then Lokna broke it. "We can't do that," he snapped, his voice rising with every word. "That's my uncle's soul we're talking about!"

Everyone immediately shouted to his aid.

"How can you consider such a thing?"

"It's because we're dragons, isn't it?"

"That's pure evil!"

"Kelraz might be the good guy after all!"

Jassan, who had been sitting quietly and just listening, allowed his eyes to drift to Burk. The young teal dragon lay curled into his sister's side with wide eyes. Jassan could see his claws shaking.

"We can't do that," Jassan whispered in agreement. "They're right," he said louder, somehow quieting the entire group from their arguments. "It's pure evil. How can you even consider something so evil? To destroy the soul of a dragon?"

"Lest you misunderstand," Shampy grinned, "this sword can destroy the soul of a living dragon, yes. But it will also destroy the soul of any being that is already dead, whether human, centaur, faerie, goblin or dragon. They won't be found again in the World of Souls or in the world of the living. They will cease to exist."

12

DRAGONS

"It's the only protection we would have," Trivnor explained. "Believe me, I don't want to use it any more than any of you would *want* me to use it. But if we have no other option… If it comes down to one of your lives over someone else's who is already dead…"

He couldn't finish the thought and Jassan didn't want to hear the rest of it anyway. No one in the circle could make eye contact with anyone else. Jassan knew they were all considering the consequences the same as he was. Jassan had never thought of taking another life, let alone another soul. He hadn't even considered fighting back when Milah's soul attacked them. Not just because the dark soul terrified him, but because Jassan never fought back. He never fought back when people picked on him. He never fought back when his aunt yelled at him. He never fought back when dragons berated him. He never even fought back when his own thoughts of his inadequacies assailed him.

Pulling his focus from his thoughts, he watched as Shampy reached under her chair. She lifted something off the ground that he couldn't see. It dragged a little, leaving a long trace in the dirt and leaves, but stayed invisible while she held out her hands as if to display it. She stood up, put both of her fists together and then slowly drew them apart while she stepped closer to the fire. She held one hand out with her fist pointing at the fire, and the tip of a sword appeared in the flame. The fire licked up the sides, revealing a medium-length, slightly curved blade with a curved guard and a single-handed grip.

"Don't worry," Trivnor said, standing to join Shampy at the fire. "None of you will have to worry about making the decision to use such a weapon, or about feeling guilty afterward."

Before Trivnor could take the sword from the shaman, Lokna jumped up. "No!" he said. "I don't trust you not to use it on a whim."

"Now, wait a moment—" Trivnor tried to protest, but Shampy cut him off.

"Perhaps you would like to carry it?" Shampy said, holding the burning blade out to the brown dragon.

"Me? No! I don't want it!" Lokna shied away.

"One of your friends, perhaps? Maybe you would trust them?" Shampy said, facing the members of the circle in turn.

After a moment of silence, in a low voice Lokna grumbled, "Jassan."

Shampy, wide-eyed, searched the dragon's eyes. When his finally met hers, he repeated it louder. "Give it to Jassan. He's the only one I would trust *not* to use it."

Shampy followed everyone's stare to see Jassan sitting with his head down. He knew Lokna was right, he would never use it. He was a coward. Lokna knew it and expected nothing more from him. A coward is the only person you can trust not to fight.

Suddenly the memory of the sight of Dasha, in her dragon form, with the shadowy monster of Milah on top of her, lifting a claw to kill her, entered his mind. Had it really been two days ago? The memory of the horror on Dasha's face felt fresh, as if it had only been moments ago. Before he had time to wonder about why the memory came to him, the image changed. He envisioned Emma instead of Dasha. Emma, her dark blue dragon form underneath Milah's dark shadow. Milah, poised to kill. Terror in Emma's eyes. Knowing she might be changed into the same kind of monster. Could he use the sword on Milah then? Would he have the courage? If only to save Emma? Could he destroy a soul? To save any of them?

Silently…slowly…Jassan stood from his seat. He noticed the way the faerie held the blade in front of him by only the grip. She still held the invisible sheath in her other hand and slowly slid the blade into it, quenching the flame from the fire, but allowing the glowing heat to keep the blade visible for a moment.

"Take off your cloak," Shampy said. "The harness goes around your shoulders to keep the sheath and sword on your back. It should nestle between your wing joints.

The hilt will stick out over your shoulder for easy access, but you can cover it with your hood."

As Jassan slipped his cloak from his shoulders, he glanced up at Lokna.

"Don't be so proud of yourself," Lokna grumbled sitting back on his haunches. "We can't let a crazy faerie keep it," Shampy snorted at that, "and the only thing I trust you to do with it is run away."

The old faeriewoman attached the invisible harness to Jassan with deft hands. The latch ends attached together snug and secure and the harness seemed to move with him and his clothing. Jassan worried that he would stab himself just trying to put the thing back in its sheath, should he ever pull it out. He pulled the blade out now, while it was entirely invisible to the naked eye. When he started to put it back in, the sheath seemed to draw the blade into it without any effort or guidance from him. At least that would prevent him from slicing himself in half with it. He figured he would practice removing and replacing it when no one was around, but he hoped he could otherwise just avoid ever taking it out of the sheath, for any reason.

"Wait," Eleka said, "isn't it illegal to use invisibility majik? My uncle Rylan told me that invisibility spells were banned a long time ago. How are you able to have an invisible sword and an invisible kangaroo?"

Shampy pursed her lips, then tapped them. "Well, now," she said, "the sword was made before that law was…um…"

"And the law was made because of the kangaroo," Trivnor said. "Isn't that right?"

"Maybe," Shampy said, "but he never did anything to that poor village. Not that they can prove, anyway."

"Of course not," Eleka said, "because he's invisible."

Shampy shrugged with a mischievous grin.

"Great," Dasha said, "we have an invisible sword none of us wants to use and no more answers than when we got here."

"Answers?" Shampy said pulling her cloak tight around her against a cold breeze. "Kelraz bad. Find keys. Stop apocalypse. What other answers do you want? Oh, and avoid being turned into soul wraiths yourselves."

"I want to know what we're supposed to do against Kelraz, without using that sword to destroy all his wraiths," Dasha said. "How are we supposed to stop him from turning everyone into wraiths?"

"Well," Trivnor said, "we get the keys. If we have the keys, we should be able to overpower him and his wraiths."

"By destroying his soul from existence?" Emma said.

"Of course not," Trivnor said. "We can trap him or restrain him. The sword is only for an emergency."

"Besides, the blade doesn't destroy souls of the living," Shampy said. "Against the living it acts like any invisible sword, if there are any other invisible swords. They're not easy to make. Enchanting them after they're made is even more difficult. It took me years to enchant this one and that was only after a very unfortunate series of events that ended with a large scar on my—"

"What was that?" Dasha twisted her neck around to stare up into the darkening night sky.

"What?"

"Did you—?"

"Quiet!" Dasha hissed loud enough for everyone to hear.

The entire group stood still, staring into the trees around them. No one spoke. The sword on Jassan's back suddenly felt heavier. Was he going to be expected to use it? So soon after receiving it?

A low growl emanated from the darkness around them.

Bubbles must have sensed something too. She slithered out of the fire and shot up Jassan's leg. He felt her pulling at his shirt and wrapping around the hilt of the sword behind his head.

"You need to go," Shampy muttered in a low voice. She grabbed Trivnor's arm and shoved him in the opposite direction of her illusory hut. "Take your little ruck and go."

"But—"

Without another word, the group pulled closer together on the far side of the fire. Before they could say or do anything else, Shampy ran into her hut.

"Oh, she's very helpful," Dasha said. "Why did we come here again?"

"To get a weapon none of us can use," Gizi grumbled.

A second growl rumbled through the trees, this one louder and coming from a different direction.

"Two of them," Emma breathed.

"Are you going to transport us or what?" Gizi asked Trivnor. "Your little witch abandoned us."

"I did NOT!" They heard Shampy's gravelly voice echo from the direction of her hut. When Jassan turned, he saw the door of her hut fly open. The little faeriewoman looked a strange combination of fierce and crazy. The tattoo around her ear glowed red. She had smeared a black substance sloppily over her face and neck. She was barefoot and held a long, thin whip in one hand and a bunch of puffy flowers in the other, which she tucked into a belt around her waist.

"Go!" she yelled to Trivnor. "I'll hold them off."

"What about you?"

The only response he got was a cackle as she darted into the cold, dark forest.

13

THE KRUSIBLE

Trivnor directed the group to go in the opposite direction the faeriewoman had gone, but a dark shadow form of a dragon jumped down in front of them from the woven branches overhead. The wraith swiped at Dasha, who dodged. Then it turned and swiped at Emma.

Jassan paused, wanting to help her, but Emma grabbed Burk and pushed them both away from the black wraith. Jassan could tell that this wraith was a different being. It wasn't Milah. It might have been Taka, the dragon Burk had mourned over, but Jassan hadn't known him and couldn't identify him. With Burk and Emma out of its reach, the black wraith ran and launched itself at Lokna.

Lokna batted the gigantic dragon with both claws, but one of the wraith's claws grabbed his front leg. He wailed as its talons sliced down his scales, finding purchase under a couple.

Tyla, in her spotted red dragon form, pounced on top of the wraith. She grabbed it by the head, digging her claws into the dripping black substance, but the wraith simply pulled her from its neck and threw her against a tree. Had it been a living being, Tyla most assuredly would have taken chunks of the beast's neck in her claws when she was thrown. However, her claws only retained a trail of the shadowy drips, which dissipated into smoke.

Eleka ran to her sister's side as Gizi and Dasha attacked the wraith from both sides. Lokna cradled his punctured front leg close to his body and used his other three good legs to run and latch onto the wraith's tail. As the wraith tried to rear back and claw at the others, Lokna repeatedly jerked on its tail as hard as possible, unbalancing the creature long enough to delay its attack.

Shampy could be seen on the other side of the shelter when the large wraith she was fighting swiped both massive claws, attempting to clap her between them. She ducked and rolled away, appearing more agile than many faeries half her age. She rolled onto her feet and snapped her whip out. The whip caught Milah by the horns on his head. When she pulled on it, Milah's head jerked to the side. As he began to topple, his claws lashed out and tore at the woven branches overhead.

"Time to redecorate!" Shampy whooped. She unwrapped the whip from Milah's head and snapped up one of the fluffy bulbs from her bunch of flowers. She ran under the shelter with Milah's wraith in pursuit. Once under the canopy, she glanced over her shoulder and tossed the flower up at the branches. They exploded over her head, but she continued running and the debris fell on top of the wraith.

"Go!" she shouted again to Trivnor.

Trivnor ran to Eleka's and Tyla's side. "Run!" he yelled to them, pointing into the forest away from the creatures. "We'll catch up!"

Having slowed one wraith, Shampy ran up to the other being contained by Gizi, Dasha and Lokna. She let her whip fly. It cracked around the wraith's neck. Shampy didn't stop running. Holding the other end of the whip, she slid under the wraith's belly and popped up next to Lokna, who was still holding its tail.

"Wrap this around it, will ya?" She handed the whip to Lokna, pulling the wraith's head under its own body.

With a grin, Lokna strapped the whip handle around its tail and jumped back as it struggled to untangle itself.

Behind them, the shadowy Milah had freed itself from the branches. Jassan froze as it jumped into the air, aiming for Lokna.

"Watch out!" Jassan called, pointing feebly to the airborne menace.

Lokna turned, but the monster had spread its wings and Jassan knew it would follow the brown dragon.

Suddenly, a dragon Jassan hadn't ever seen met Milah's wraith in midair. A fully grown, dark grey dragon, with a light grey belly and light grey wing membranes, tumbled to the ground with the wraith. They both roared, rolling with their claws locked onto each other. Milah's wraith used his back claws to kick the new dragon off. It slammed into the part of the shelter that was still solid, then dropped onto the ground just as hard.

Shampy ran up to the pair and launched another exploding flower at the wraith. "You'll have to transport!" she cried, getting between the wraith and the new dragon.

"I know!" the dark grey dragon said.

It took Jassan a moment to process the reality of what had happened and who this was in front of him. He turned back to the others, who stood staring at the big grey dragon in equal shock.

"Liar!" Tyla shouted.

"And take the boy with you!" Shampy said, continuing toward the recovering wraith.

"You made me carry you," Eleka said with more of a grumble.

"Jassan," the dark grey dragon said, gently cupping Jassan's arm and shoulder with a huge claw. A claw, Jassan noticed, with an embedded gem with swirling clouds in it. "We have to go."

Gone in a churn of vapor, Jassan found himself and the grey dragon form of Trivnor standing in a humongous open space as round and smooth as a stone bowl.

"What?!" Jassan stuttered. "Where? What?"

"Stay here," is all Trivnor would respond before disappearing again.

Jassan searched his surroundings. The enormous open space was a massive stone bowl shape, attached to the side of a mountain. The grey clouds overhead, very similar in color to Trivnor's dragon scales, looked like a blanket ready to smother Jassan into the hard stone beneath him. The rains of fall had accumulated in the bottom of the massive pit. A vast black opening, darker than the night sky around them, gawked at the newcomer from the far side of the depression. A wall of sharp boulders lined the boundary between the bowl and the mountain that towered up through the clouds. As he watched, a small black figure in the distance slid from the clouds to tumble down the mountain.

"Uh," Jassan began as Trivnor's dragon form suddenly reappeared with Dasha's dragon form.

"Stay hidden," the older dragon hissed before disappearing again.

"Good idea," Jassan said. He waved to Dasha to follow him, pointing to the boulders at the edge of the bowl.

"What are you…" Dasha's voice trailed off as her eyes darted to the black figure creeping down the mountain and she ran to join Jassan. Dasha shrunk into her grey-skinned goblin form and the two huddled against the boulders, trying to hide from view of the mountain.

Trivnor reappeared first with Burk then with Emma. Dasha waved them over, shushing any questions. They both changed to their human forms, smaller and easier to hide.

Trivnor brought Lokna next. "Wonderful," the young dragon said wryly. "The Krusible. Why didn't you bring us here in the first place? We can go to my parents, they'll help us."

The Krusible. Jassan had heard of it. The massive stone bowl attached to the largest mountain, called the Inner Mountain, was used in the old days to test young dragons, but since the dragon war ended here, it had only been used for gatherings. The Inner Mountain was surrounded by the floating mountains of the Rock Clouds. The Rock Cloud Ruck lived in these mountains, including Lokna's family. And many other dangerous dragons who remembered well that the faeries were to blame for the dragon war. Jassan swallowed hard, realizing that he sat in the most dangerous place in Avonoa for a faerie.

The group huddling against the boulders waved Lokna toward them. "What are you doing?" he called, comfortably close to home here and much too loud for Jassan's liking.

Dasha ran to him and pointed at the cloud, appearing to drip with three more smaller black figures falling down the mountain.

"Are those—" Lokna began, but Dasha jerked his arm toward the edge of the bowl to hide with the rest of them.

"—more wraiths?" Lokna finished in a low voice as he joined them.

"Trivnor said the clouds were letting souls through," Emma whispered. "The peak of the Inner Mountain is probably keeping a giant hole open between here and the World of Souls."

"How can we trust anything Trivnor has told us?" Lokna whispered back. "He never even told us he was a dragon!"

"How would knowing that have helped?" Jassan asked before he could stop himself. All the surrounding eyes glared at him.

No one said anything else as Trivnor reappeared next with Eleka, then Tyla, then Gizi. Without a word, the huddled group waved the newcomers over to join them.

"We can't stay here long," Trivnor said, joining everyone against the wall. "I'm guessing the Rock Clouds are overrun with wraiths."

"But my parents—" Lokna began before Trivnor interrupted him.

"Are most definitely gone from here. They're either hiding from the beasts or are busy restraining them in some way." Trivnor peeked over the edge of the boulders. "They're certainly smart enough not to stay here."

Lokna seemed to realize that Trivnor was paying both him and his parents a compliment and turned away. Jassan noticed a hint of a crease on his brow and realized that the brash dragon was probably worried for his parents just as much as Emma and Burk were for theirs.

"Why did you bring us here? Where are we supposed to go?" Jassan asked quietly. He didn't want to remain anywhere near the dragons still living in the Rock Clouds longer than absolutely necessary. Especially if they hated faeries as much as he thought the ones huddled around him did. Though now even he would have to trust a faerie that had lied to all of them, including him.

"Through the portal," Trivnor said. "It's the best one I know of to get us to the goblin city."

"Won't Kelraz be able to track us, now that you used the Cloud Key again?" Eleka asked.

"Yes, he will," Trivnor confirmed. "Which is why we need to leave quickly. And why I think it's Jassan's turn to transform into a dragon."

A tingle ran up Jassan's spine and made his chest burn at the same time. When all the dragons turned to look at him again, he tried desperately not to seem too excited, but he couldn't help the grin spreading on his face.

"Won't that give away where we are too?" Eleka asked.

"No more than I already have," Trivnor said. "When I use the Cloud Key, it pulls the other keys to two different places; the place I've been and the place I end up. If Jassan and I both used our keys at the same time in the same proximity, the pull for the others would be even stronger. I'm done now, so if Jassan uses his key to become a dragon, we can use the portal, get to the goblin city and hope that the goblin defenses will protect us from Kelraz and his wraiths until we get the gemstone we need to recreate the broken key."

Jassan's stomach jumped with excitement.

"Why does he have to be a dragon?" Lokna asked. "He shouldn't be using the key anyway."

Trivnor pursed his dragon lips at Lokna. "Do you really think the goblins will let a faerie into the goblin city under these circumstances? We haven't seen anyplace untouched by the wraiths." He turned to Dasha, who shook her head.

"Doesn't matter how young or vulnerable he looks," the goblin said. "They would leave him to the wraiths, no question."

Trivnor turned back to Lokna, who shrugged, resigned.

"What do we do once we're inside? Shouldn't we come up with a plan first?" Dasha asked.

Trivnor looked toward the looming Inner Mountain. "Not with more wraiths coming," he said. "If Kelraz uses one of these wraiths, he'll sense us and be on us in a moment."

"We'll get through the portal and plan the rest once we get to the goblin city," Emma told Dasha.

As rain began to drip again, Trivnor placed his hand on Jassan's shoulder. "I'm sorry to thrust this upon you," he said. "But I'll help you figure out how to use that key, and quickly."

Jassan nodded and stared at the key attached to his arm. "What do I do?" He hoped he sounded more confident than he felt. Bubbles dropped from his back onto the ground with a soft thud and turned to watch him expectantly.

"Look into the key," Trivnor said. Everyone around them seemed to hold their breath. "Imagine seeing yourself as a dragon in that mirror."

Jassan did as he was told, staring into the key, but he could only see his blue-skinned, freckled face. His dripping black hair, his pointed ears. He had no idea what he might look like as a dragon and nothing changed.

"I don't—" he began. He looked up at his friends to see a wraith of a dragon much larger than any of them flying over the treetops and the mountain in the distance. If he was going to do this, he had to do it quickly.

He looked at Burk, then Emma. Their dragons were dark-colored. Emma's deep blue was almost black, like her father. Her father's scales were smooth and two gently curving horns graced his head. Burk's small dragon self had several short horns on his head and ridges on his back. Jassan knew those would continue to grow and would be much more intimidating when he got older than the two curved horns on his father's head.

Jassan looked back into the key. Suddenly it struck him. He had no idea what kind of dragon he would have been had he been born part dragon, but he knew exactly what kind of dragon he wanted to be now, if he could use the key to make his wish come true. A dragon with the capability to not only fly high over the clouds, but to also strike fear in any other species, even in other dragons. He wanted to be the most fearsome dragon on the ground and in the sky but nothing happened.

"It's not working," Jassan muttered.

Trivnor turned to him. "When I use my key," he said. "I get a feeling in my chest."

His attention was abruptly pulled away, but Jassan had a good sense of what to do.

He focused on the tiny pinch he had felt in his chest when he wanted to disappear and accidentally turned into a tree. He felt the little pinch and imagined his face changing first. His mouth and nose elongated into a sharp, triangular snout. He imagined scaly ridges over his eyes and an angled jaw as he felt them tug on his face. He looked up, excited that his hopes were coming true before him, but Trivnor only glanced over at him once and then back to the dark skies.

"It's a good start," Trivnor said.

"Ok," Jassan muttered to himself, savoring the first changes. He stared into the key again. He imagined his eyes turning bright golden with slit pupils. Before they appeared he saw in his mind the twisting horns on his head. He imagined his long fangs and forked tongue. By the time he was done, his fully adorned blue dragon head stared back at him.

"You're going to need more than a big head," Lokna said.

"Why?" Gizi sniped. "You don't."

Jassan looked again to Trivnor for approval, but the older faerie dragon's head was still turned, watching the wraiths.

"What about my clothes?" Jassan asked.

Two more roars and a scream got closer.

"You won't need them," Dasha said. "Hurry up."

"They'll change with you," Trivnor said. "Whatever you imagine will happen." They all heard another roar in the distance and he glanced back to Jassan. "Hurry, Jassan," Trivnor whispered. "The rest of you, head for the portal to the goblin city. Dasha, lead the way."

As the others changed back to their dragon forms in order to gain speed and ran for the portal on the far side of the Krusible, Trivnor told Jassan again with growing urgency, "Hurry!"

Jassan looked into the Moon Key again. This time he imagined generous, wicked spikes running down his back. He envisioned a long, sinewy neck stretching out. He looked at his hands briefly and when he imagined them changing into sharp claws, they did so.

The roar echoed closer, pulling Jassan's attention away for a moment.

"Almost there," Trivnor said.

Jassan nodded and looked into the Moon Key one last time. The reflection became disorienting as he could see all his body changes just as he had imagined them. He saw strong back haunches, greater and stronger than Lokna's. He imagined the spikes running down his back onto a strong tail that whipped from side to side once he felt it stretch from his back end. Long, sharp spikes tipped the end of his tail.

Jassan took the briefest of moments to admire his reflection, and couldn't help but wonder what Emma would think of him now. Then, the transformation complete, Jassan looked to Trivnor again, but the older dragon grabbed him by his scaly front leg, his eyes still on the sky. "Run!" he shouted.

Bubbles sparkled as she slithered up Jassan's dragon leg and onto his back while he took off running. He felt her wrap and settle around the sword hilt in the harness still attached to his back, confident that no one else could see it. Jassan had started running on only his back legs, but his claws soon dropped to the ground and it immediately felt natural to run on all fours. He turned to look over his tail and saw a wraith flying swiftly down the mountain in their direction.

The two faerie dragons ran side by side toward the portal, tails lashing, claws digging at the rock beneath them to gain speed, but the wraith flew faster than they could run. Even with the threat of Kelraz's wraith behind them, Jassan couldn't help but feel elated as he ran faster than he could fly as a faerie. He ran hard, not just to escape but to feel the power in his dragon legs. Still, the wraith gained on them.

The wraith screamed as the two dragons dove into the black portal together. It being only the second time in his life to use a portal, Jassan felt quite brave diving into it. He tumbled to the ground on the other side at the bottom of the Inner Mountain.

"Keep going!" Trivnor hollered from ahead of him, continuing his stride without missing a step.

Jassan thought the portal had meant safety for them, but Trivnor's actions made him realize that the wraith had followed them through the portal. He picked himself off the ground as the wraith flew over his head.

Trivnor turned at the sound of a commotion behind him to see Jassan stopped and the wraith between them overhead. The wraith slowed its flight. It snaked its long neck around the look at Jassan on his own, and dropped one wing to spin in mid-air. The black, shadowy creature bared its fangs and dove with all four claws at Jassan.

Jassan's eyes widened and he froze with fear. He immediately felt gratitude that at least he'd gotten the opportunity to be a dragon once in his life before he died. Maybe that had always been Trivnor's goal, to give Jassan the one thing he wanted most in this living world as a parting gift.

The wraith landed on top of Jassan. He felt the creature's sharp claws, regrettably longer than he had made his own, scratching at his neck and shoulders trying to find purchase. Jassan instinctively flinched away from the knives of pain digging into his front right leg. He screamed and tried to bat away the creature like he would have swatted at a vicious bird in his faerie form.

The claws he had imagined for himself found the monster's belly. Though the wraith wouldn't die, apparently it could feel pain. Or, he hoped, Kelraz was feeling the pain. Either way, the wraith pulled away slightly from Jassan.

Jassan took advantage. He pulled out of the wraith's grip, but not without receiving a long gash along his shoulder. The pain shook him and he fell to the ground.

Before Jassan could react, the wraith tumbled onto its side with the bulky grey dragon on top of it. Trivnor clawed at the wraith's face. "RUN!" he yelled to Jassan as he scratched at the wraith's face and head.

Jassan jumped up and ran in the direction that Trivnor had been running when suddenly Trivnor and the wraith disappeared in a swirl of clouds over his head. Jassan's dragon claws pounded on the rock beneath him, making the pain in his shoulder pulse with every clawfall.

"Come on!" Trivnor shouted, reappearing back at Jassan's side still in dragon form. "I took the wraith far away, but Kelraz knows we're here. He probably already has more wraiths on the way."

As if in answer, the two heard several roars behind them. Jassan forgot the pain and ran hard again beside Trivnor.

14

KIRLIK

After just a few dragon lengths, the pair of dragons ran up to a sweeping arrangement of four portals sprawled against the mountainside. Each opening had room across for a few dragons. A banner hung vertically at the side of each entrance, with painted yellow writing indicating the destination.

The words were written in two languages. One was the language of the goblins, a language Jassan recognized but couldn't read or write. The other was the common tongue. Jassan read the titles of all four goblin destinations and noticed that the goblins didn't include the language of the faeries on the signage.

The pair found the banner reading "Kirlik, Goblin City of the King" and headed for the portal entrance next to it. The roars behind them grew closer. Trivnor turned toward the sounds but pointed at the portal. "Go," he told

Jassan, "the others have gone ahead. I'm right behind you."

Jassan ran toward the portal with all the strength he had in his dragon legs. This was the third darkened portal he had entered in as many days and he still had to prepare himself. Luckily he ducked his head and closed his eyes again this time because instead of going through the darkness he expected, he smashed directly into a solid black wall.

Coming to after a brief blackout, Jassan blinked his eyes to see Gizi and Dasha standing over him, giggling. "Need some help?"

"That's not funny!" Trivnor exclaimed, helping Jassan to his dragon feet.

"It's a little funny," Gizi said, leading the way back through the portal.

Jassan shook off his embarrassment and stepped through the portal. On the other side, the rest of the group waited ahead of him in a long, dark tunnel. His eyes adjusted quickly to the darkness due to the majikal cubes attached to the ceiling of the cave.

The others lay resting on the cold stone floor. Emma reclined with her arm around Burk. The centaur twins sat alert, wary and watching. Lokna cradled his front leg and smirked at Jassan to taunt the blue dragon about his clash with the sealed portal.

Standing next to the cave's opening, a grey-skinned goblin spoke with Trivnor, still in dragon form. "I'm sorry," he said to Trivnor, then turned to Dasha. "This is not the time for pranks, Dasha."

"Oh, they're fine, dad," Dasha rolled her eyes. "They'll live."

The older goblin stood just above Jassan's dragon knee. He thought the goblin's stubby orange hair would have come up to his faerie waist, but the sheer size of his shoulders and arms made Jassan want to do whatever he said. Glowing tattoos encircled his ample arms and a silver circlet adorned his head. The gems in the circlet were round, all the same size, in a few different colors and grouped on one side of his head.

"I can see the blue one is hurt," the grey-skinned goblin said to Trivnor. He turned his full attention on Jassan. "You should go with Dasha to get some medical attention."

"Are you staying here?" Dasha asked her father.

The other goblin nodded. "I'm on duty, Dasha. You know I can't leave. You know your way to the medics."

Trivnor turned to the goblin. "Thank you…er…"

"Keeahrspi," the goblin helped.

"Thank you, Keeahrspi," Trivnor said. "I'll make sure these young ones get to where they need to go. What will you do about the wraiths?"

"Wraiths?" Keeahrspi asked. "Is that what they are?"

As if to emphasize the question, they heard a rumble come from inside the portal and the stone wall shook where the portal entrance once was. Keeahrspi touched his hand to the wall and the solid rock seemed to reopen. Jassan and a few others gasped as they watched a wraith come into view just beyond the portal boundary and slam into the transparent wall covering the entrance before falling to the ground from the collision.

"Is that what I looked like?" Jassan asked Burk, but Gizi answered.

"You were much more graceful," she said with a grin.

"We're sealing up portals all over Avonoa this way," Keeahrspi said, watching the wraith scratch at the transparent wall. "And working on containing the ones already within the cities. More goblin troops are being called in to help, but we don't have the resources to go around to everywhere they're needed. Especially if they continue coming at this rate and turning everyone into one of these monsters."

"You've lost guards?" Trivnor asked.

"And others," Keeahrspi mumbled. He placed his hand on the transparent wall and its appearance changed back to one of a smooth stone surface.

"Resources?" Trivnor asked.

Keeahrspi tapped the silver circlet on his brow. "Do you know what this is?"

"An obruck, correct?"

Keeahrspi nodded. "These are only issued to high-ranking officers because of the rarity of the gems with power in them, and there's not enough of those to go around. But we're doing the best we can with what we have."

"And we thank you for it," Trivnor said.

Keeahrspi narrowed his eyes at Trivnor. "Not sure I've seen you before," he said. "Are you from the Rock Clouds? What's your name?"

"My name is Trivnor," he said, avoiding the first question. "I'm just trying to help these young ones get to safety. Do you know if many Rock Cloud dragons are here?"

It wasn't lost on Jassan that Trivnor's answers danced around his origin. Many faeries had the talent of mincing words when necessary and Trivnor definitely was not from the Rock Cloud Ruck.

"Several," the goblin rumbled. "Our city is full to bursting with refugees. We've been trying to find places for them to go, but these monsters have been showing up everywhere. I know many dragons like you are still out there, trying to help. That's why I stay here. To let in any help or refugees."

"Have you seen my parents?" Lokna asked with his brows drawn together.

Keeahrspi shook his head. "I'm sorry, Lokna," he said. "I haven't seen them come through. But they might have gone to one of the other portals or another dragon ruck."

"Where should we go?" Trivnor asked.

"I have an idea," Dasha spoke up. The goblin and grey dragon turned to look at her. "If the main housing areas are full, maybe we can rest in the barracks? I know our house isn't big enough for my friends here."

"Hmm," Keeahrspi seemed to consider it. "I don't know. Shvika wouldn't like it."

"But you know they're not all being used right now," Dasha persisted.

Keeahrspi pursed his lips a moment. "And you know she doesn't want anyone to learn the secrets of the goblins, especially the army's secrets." He turned to Trivnor. "Shvika is a dear friend that I have fought alongside for many years, but she can be very stuck in her ways."

"But these dragons are no threat, Dad," Dasha said. Keeahrspi paused and Jassan was sure he was going to refuse, but Dasha made one last push. "If we can't trust the dragons, who can we trust?"

The older goblin sighed and shook his head. "Fine," he said. "I'll talk to her. Go to the medics first and I'll send word when she gives permission."

Dasha smiled. "Thanks, Dad!" She spun to lead her friends down the tunnel.

"Don't take them to the barracks until you hear from me!" he called after her, but Jassan was pretty sure she either hadn't heard him or wasn't listening.

"Thank you," Trivnor said, while the others ambled down the tunnel after Dasha.

Keeahrspi nodded and turned back to the portal entrance. He placed a hand on the wall and the stone dissolved to show a second wraith landing next to the first. The two massive dragon wraiths looked at each other. Without a word or acknowledgement between them, they both turned and sprinted at the portal. Their bodies bashed against the unseen barrier, making a loud THUNK.

Keeahrspi mumbled to Trivnor without taking his eyes from the wraiths, "Feels like this is just the beginning."

The group walked down a long stone tunnel that would take them to the underground goblin city of Kirlik. As Jassan limped along, Lokna sidled up to him. He noticed that Lokna walked gingerly too, but made a point to ignore the gash on the brown dragon's leg.

"Nice disguise," Lokna said quietly to the blue dragon, so any goblins wouldn't hear. "You look ridiculous."

Jassan limped along, confused. He thought he'd made himself into a fine dragon. Had his dragon form changed? He looked down at his claws, clacking against the stone. "What's wrong with it?"

Lokna scoffed. "Blue? Isn't that a girl color?"

Burk turned sharply in front of them to glare at Lokna. When Lokna noticed, he said, "His is a little more noticeable than yours. Especially with the little spots."

"And what's wrong with spots?" Tyla turned on him. Her tail snapped threateningly behind her.

Lokna sighed. "I didn't mean spots. Look at him. He's freckled. Have you ever seen a freckled dragon? And his color says 'faerie' more than 'dragon'."

Tyla turned her back on him with a low growl and kept walking. Lokna lumbered after her, but stopped when Jassan didn't move.

"No, he's right." Jassan turned the Moon Key to face him so he could study the problem. He could see his scales clearly in the light of the majikal glowing cubes along the tunnel pathway. The scales were the exact freckled blue color of his faerie skin. No other dragons were freckled. Even Tyla's dragon spots were bigger, encompassing more of her scales.

With a brief glance down the tunnel to make sure no one else could see him, Jassan imagined what he wanted his scales to look like. The spots, he could live with but he didn't want any part of him to be blue. He didn't want anything on him that resembled a faerie feature. Then he remembered how Emma's father appeared. Even without all the extra horns and spikes, her father was terrifying, if only because he was pure black.

As he thought about the older midnight-black dragon, Jassan imagined his image in the Moon Key the same way. Immediately, all his scales turned almost as black as the color of a wraith.

Pleased, Jassan searched Lokna's face. The brown dragon nodded.

Resuming their pace, Gizi said from behind them, "Jassan, why don't you just make yourself the same color as Lokna if you're so eager to please him."

"I don't want to be the same as him," Jassan said, afraid that would only irritate Lokna. "Then you wouldn't be able to tell us apart."

"Yes, they would," Lokna said. "I'm the handsome one."

As they entered Kirlik, Jassan expected to find safety and security with the goblin medics and somewhere quiet to rest. He wanted the opportunity to simply gaze at the wonder of the underground city and walk the streets of this secret place he'd only heard about in tales. What he didn't expect to find was another nightmare like the one they had just escaped.

The colossal cavern that held the city was easily massive enough for dragons, considering it did provide quarters for several part-dragon families who lived there. Although made of solid stone, the sky of the cavern was enchanted so that it mirrored the sky beyond its surface; however, the clouded night sky outside now was obscured with smoke.

Jassan had studied other races and cultures with his aunt. She had told him about the sprawling city of the goblins, but it seemed to Jassan that the place before him had grown larger and taller than she had described. Several immense buildings reached toward the inner sky to rival that of the grandest and innermost structure, the goblin king's palace. Jassan noticed that many major structures' walls had crumbled or burned. Homes had been smashed to cinders. Walls and roofs displayed gaping holes. Jassan could make out small groups of goblins running through the streets.

In the distance he could see a gathering of goblins and dragons surrounding a wraith. Although, from so far away Jassan couldn't be sure what kind of wraith it was, it appeared to be larger than a goblin but smaller than a dragon. He hoped it wasn't a faerie wraith.

The home of the goblin king connected to the city below it and the sky above it. Paintings and artistry adorned the outside walls, along with windows and balconies. However, disrupting the intrigue of the beautiful palace, Jassan could hear the windowpanes reverberating with occasional screams or roars. He could see plentiful gashes in one of the colorful exterior murals, and soot blackened part of the walls.

"What happened here?" Eleka asked in a low voice.

"What do you think?" Lokna muttered.

"Wraiths," Dasha spat.

"But how did they get into the city?" Emma said.

Trivnor had rejoined the group and now stepped up, surveying the destruction. "The same way everyone else has," the grey dragon said. "It would be easy enough for Kelraz to send whatever wraiths he wanted through the portals and into the city. If the goblins weren't prepared, the wraiths would get through and kill them, giving Kelraz more souls to work with. We're lucky they can shut down the portals now like they're doing."

"Lucky?" Dasha turned on him. "Lucky? You call any of this lucky?"

Trivnor sighed. "I call it lucky that the goblins are the best equipped race to deal with these creatures."

Jassan stifled a gasp as a burning pain throbbed in his shoulder again, but Trivnor must have sensed his discomfort. He circled Jassan to get a better view of the injury. As Trivnor inspected the wound, Jassan felt a fresh wave of pain tear through the flesh. He felt as if the gash had opened even further.

"We have to get Jassan to the medics," he told Dasha.

"No, don't worry about anyone else," Gizi snapped, pointing a claw at Lokna's wound.

"Yes, I see that," Trivnor nodded. "But Lokna's injury might not affect him in the same way."

"Why? What's wrong with me?" Jassan asked. He snaked his long neck around to peer at his injuries. The burning seemed to dig deeper into his body. He let out a hiss as the pain spread.

Three long gashes burned in his scales and hide. He thought about trying to cover the wounds with the power of the key, but he wasn't sure he could concentrate enough to attempt it with the pain that was bothering him. The top gash on his shoulder was the deepest. The smaller gashes appeared to be normal flesh wounds, but the top one was tinged with black around its edges. Jassan wondered if the blackness had come from his new black scales, but looking closer at it he could see dark speckles embedded in the reddish-pink flesh.

"This way," Dasha said, seeing the concern on Trivnor's and Jassan's faces.

"What does it mean?" Jassan asked Trivnor about the dark speckles as the group limped over soot-stained cobblestone roads.

"I'll tell you when we get there," Trivnor said.

Fortunately for Jassan, they soon reached the oversized red building with a strange symbol painted in yellow over the door. Dasha and Trivnor, still in his dragon form, helped Jassan through the sizeable open door. The rest stayed outside.

"Hello!" Dasha called. "We need some help!"

She and Trivnor pulled Jassan into the building. The tall room held several small goblin beds taken up by occupants with a variety of burns and bandages. In the back of the room, two giant areas with bedding on the floor were empty.

"What happened?" a diminutive goblin came shuffling into the room. The stark white hair on his head stood straight up, and his pointed ears drooped from age.

He wore all yellow—pants, shirt and even his soft, leather boots.

"He was injured by a wraith," Dasha told the yellow-garbed goblin. "We have more injured outside."

The goblin medic shook his head. "Too many of those these days." He snapped his fingers and another goblin dressed in yellow came from another room. The white-haired goblin medic pointed to the door and the other goblin ran outside.

The medic indicated for Jassan to lay down on one of the two bedding areas in the back. Appreciating their roominess, Jassan figured they must have been added and/or designed specifically for dragons. But just as he started lowering himself to the ground, the strength in Jassan's good arm gave out and he landed on his side with a thump and a groan. Luckily, Emma wasn't there to witness his awkwardness. The medic inspected Jassan's shoulder much the same as Trivnor had done, but poked at the scales around the edges. Jassan tried to growl low as the goblin prodded him, but again the sound came out as only a groan.

"I'll need a lot more tonic," the medic muttered, then hurried through a doorway adjoining the greater room. They heard glass clinking and soon the goblin scuttled back in with a vial almost as big as his head in one fist and a cloth in the other.

"Diluted flarote," the medic said, shaking the fiery red liquid in the container. "This should do the trick. But don't use it with dragon fire." He splashed a generous amount of the liquid on the cloth, then slapped the cloth onto Jassan's shoulder.

Jassan tried to roar, but it came out as only a shout. He wondered why he didn't sound more like a dragon, but his thoughts returned pretty quickly to the pain.

"Apply as much as you can," the goblin told Trivnor, when two goblins ran into the room shouting for help. "If it starts feeling cold, apply more, then let it sit. I'll get more for your friends."

He handed the bottle and cloth over to Trivnor and hurried out of the building with the others.

"Cold?" Jassan asked as Trivnor dabbed the wounds again.

Trivnor nodded. "Pain feels cold to a dragon," he said low so the other recuperating goblins wouldn't hear. "But faeries feel pain as a burning sensation."

"What about you?" Jassan asked. "How do you feel pain?"

He hadn't meant his question to come out with such malice, but the pain he was already managing made it hard to hide the betrayal he felt after Trivnor's sudden unexplained transformation into a dragon.

"As a dragon, if it's a bad pain, it feels cold," Trivnor answered without acknowledging Jassan's spite. "As a faerie, it burns."

Jassan gritted his teeth as Trivnor applied the tonic, then relaxed enough to spit out, "You're a dragon," with as much venom as he could muster. He was calling Trivnor on his lie.

Trivnor closed his scaly eyes a moment and his chin dipped toward his chest.

"Of course," Dasha breathed. "A ruck is a group of dragons. And if you're from the Lost Ruck—"

"Yes," Trivnor said, wanting to take accountability before he could be accused. "All of us are part faerie and part dragon; it's been that way for thousands of years."

"Why didn't you tell us?"

"Faerie dragons," Trivnor said so low that both Dasha and Jassan had to lean a little closer to hear, "cannot exist outside of the Lost Ruck without consequence. But…"

"The world is changing," Jassan finished for him.

Trivnor's eyes darted to see if anyone had overheard them, then returned to Jassan. "Yes," he said, "and the Lost Ruck isn't sure what to do about it. Or even if we should do anything."

"A bigger problem for much, much later," Dasha interrupted. "Will that stuff even help him?" she asked, pointing at the bottle.

"Why wouldn't it?" Jassan said.

"Flarote heals animals and dragons," Trivnor said.

"Yeah," Jassan replied, "and I'm a dragon."

"No," Dasha said, pointedly. "You're not."

"She's right," Trivnor sighed, inspecting the wound further. "You only look like a dragon right now."

"Is that why I can't roar properly?" Jassan said, pinching his eyes together from the pain.

"Maybe," Trivnor said. "But remember how you imagined the rest of your dragon form? You should be able to figure out a roar the same way."

"What do you mean?"

"Do you really want to discuss this right now?" Dasha said, throwing her eyes over her shoulder at the other goblins.

Jassan cringed and pulled away from the cloth again. "As a distraction?" he said. "Yes."

"Ok," Trivnor continued blotting at Jassan's wounds as he spoke. "I don't know how much you've been around dragons, but many of them will tell you that they each have their own distinctive voice and hence, roars and growls. You can use the key to imagine your own distinctive sound, kind of like giving yourself actual dragon vocal chords, but without having to dissect yourself to do it."

"So," Jassan took a deep breath before continuing, "if I focus I can make my own roar."

"And growl. And hiss. And whatever other sounds a dragon makes that a faerie can't, yes. At least, I believe the key can help you with that." Trivnor pulled the cloth away and let the red liquid sit on his injuries. "How does it feel now?"

Jassan wrinkled his snout. "It burns," he said. He looked at the injury to see more black spots crowding the pink flesh. "It's getting worse, isn't it?"

"I was worried about this," Trivnor said, consternation in his eyes.

"Worried about what?" Dasha said, before Jassan could ask as well.

Trivnor took a deep breath. "I'm worried that any injury from a wraith will effect someone with a key differently than anyone else. It might be that Kelraz can corrupt or poison through the wraiths as well."

"And he'll definitely try that with anyone that holds a key, wouldn't he?" Dasha whispered.

Trivnor could only scrunch his eyebrows in response.

"What's going to happen to him?" Dasha asked. Jassan heard a hint of anxiety in her voice.

Trivnor shook his head. He had started to dab at the injury again when suddenly Jassan felt movement on his back. Bubbles slithered out from around the sword hilt and his shiny sharp spikes. He had forgotten all about her.

The little fire worm slid down Jassan's shoulder and circled the injuries. "Go away," Dasha said, shooing the little snake, but the snake paid her no mind.

She circled the wounds for a moment, then slid over them.

"I'll get her," Dasha said, reaching out for the snake.

"No," Trivnor put a claw out to stop her. "Let the snake try."

Jassan felt his little friend slide over his wounds as the small yellow flames licked her own scales. He thought the flame would cause him pain, but when it touched his wounds, they felt as if someone was rubbing a cool piece of ice over them. The burning simmered down.

"But the medic advised not to use fire," Dasha warned, watching Bubbles move back and forth.

"How does it feel now?" Trivnor asked.

"Better," Jassan said, sitting up. "She cooled it down."

"With fire?" Dasha said, aghast.

Trivnor shook his head at her quickly as the white-haired goblin returned. "How is he doing?" he asked, inspecting the deep slashes. "And what is *that* doing in here?" Jassan turned enough to see the goblin pointing to Bubbles.

"That's Bubbles," he said. Hearing her name, Bubbles blew a liberal fire bubble at the goblin. Jassan couldn't be sure if she'd done it in greeting or out of spite.

"Well, tell it to get out," the goblin waved a hand at Bubbles, who instead of moving, blew tiny, rapid-fire bubbles at the man. "This is no place for…one of those. This is a hospital, not a zoo."

"She's a fire worm," Trivnor said, and with a brief glance that warned the others not to contradict him, he added, "and she's helping. She's adding her fire to help him heal."

The medic narrowed his eyes at Trivnor. "I'm sure I don't have to tell you how dangerous it is to mix this substance with dragon fire."

"She's not a dragon," Dasha said.

"And he said it feels better," Trivnor added.

Bubbles ceased her bubble attack to swiftly slither back and forth over the three deep gouges. Jassan sighed with relief. He didn't care what the others thought. The pain finally felt like it was ebbing.

"Well," the little goblin squinted his eyes to peer closer at the wounds, "it doesn't look like she's doing much for these wounds. They aren't healing nearly as quickly as your friend's did outside. Strange."

The goblin jerked the vial out of Trivnor's hand, while the others exchanged glances. He swirled the contents and read the miniscule writing on the edge of the vial. Trivnor pursed his lips at Jassan and Jassan knew what he was thinking. They had to leave before this goblin figured out that he wasn't actually a dragon.

The medic sniffed the vial, then handed it back. "Very strange," he said, almost quietly enough to be talking to himself. "He should be healing better than this. All the other dragons are healing from it."

"Perhaps he just needs a little more," Trivnor said, splashing the tonic on the cloth again.

"Be careful," the goblin said. "Flarote with dragon fire creates dragon poison."

"Maybe Bubbles' fire has healing properties that we don't know about," Dasha added helpfully.

As Trivnor applied the tonic and Jassan winced again, another call came from the door.

"Turmin, we have more," the goblin who had gone outside to help came through the door, half-carrying another goblin. The injured goblin's purple hair had been burned off the side of his head and his arm dangled at his side at an unnatural angle.

"Do you need the tonic back?" Dasha asked with a note of concern.

The white-haired medic shook his head. "No," he said, "we should have plenty."

"We should go, anyway," Trivnor said, rising from next to the bed. "I'm sure you can use the space."

He started to hand the vial back to the medic, but the goblin shook his head and waved him off, running to help another injured goblin coming through the door with blood dripping down the side of his head. "Take it with you," he called. "Apply as necessary."

"Dasha," Trivnor turned to her and said quietly, "we need to get somewhere we can speak."

15

PLOTS

"The barracks? Are you crazy?" Tyla tried to whisper to Dasha as the group hurried through the blackened and littered streets.

"Why not?" she said back. "That's the only place that has enough space for all of us right now. And no one will be using them during the day. And there are several that no one uses at all."

"What about your dad?" Gizi said. "We haven't heard from him yet."

Dasha waved her hand at the comment. "It'll be fine," she said. "I'm sure Aunt Shvika will be ok with it. At least, I think she will be. I hope."

She led the group toward one of the tunnel entrances marked in blue rather than yellow. When they all reached the entrance Dasha ran headfirst into the banner hanging against the wall. Jassan flinched, remembering the pain of running into a solid wall, except Dasha didn't rebound, she disappeared.

Everyone stopped until Dasha popped her head back out from the middle of the hanging flag. "Come on!" she said. "Try not to let anyone see."

Tyla led the rest of them through.

They entered a long, dark hallway with doors leading off to either side. The hall was only wide enough for one dragon at a time to pass so they had to squeeze together. As they all entered, Dasha poked her head in each doorway. She would declare a negative, then move on to the next one.

"Who are you?" came a voice from farther ahead. A large goblin stepped out of one of the doorways. Although considerable by goblin size standards, he only came up to Jassan's dragon shoulder and he didn't seem at all bothered by the size of the dragons he faced behind Dasha.

"Uh," Dasha hesitated, "hi," she said. "I'm Dasha. And you are?"

"Aware that you're not supposed to be here," the goblin said.

"Actually," Dasha said, "my Aunt Shvika said I could bring these refugees to the barracks for somewhere to rest until we can find another safe place for them."

The goblin ground his teeth and peered at her when she said the name 'Shvika'. He scanned the group, then pushed past everyone. "We'll see about that," he said. He stopped briefly to inspect Jassan's injury, but continued past them. "They shouldn't be using the barracks for anyone but the army. We keep it hidden for good reasons."

Before Dasha could argue further, the goblin stormed out the way they had come.

"That's not good," Dasha muttered as the goblin disappeared through a doorway. "That sounds exactly like what Aunt Shvika would probably say."

Dasha watched him go, then turned to the next doorway. She poked her head into it and pulled it back out. "This one," she said. "Quickly."

"We'll have less time than I had hoped," Dasha said as the friends entered the barracks. "It's late and Aunt Shvika may be asleep, so both my father and that goblin might have to wait to bother her about it, but there's no way to know that for sure."

Although the beds were goblin-sized, like at the medic's building, the room was spacious enough for everyone to fit. The dragons pushed aside the beds and the boxes next to them to make space for each to sit down. Other than the beds, boxes for belongings and an exit on the other side of the room, there were no other adornments to show that anyone lived in these quarters.

"This is the best we can do and it was thanks to your quick thinking, Dasha," Trivnor praised her. "But you're right, we won't have as much time as we could use."

"Maybe not," Lokna said. "But Shvika knows Gizi and Emma and Burk and me. She might be ok with us resting here."

"No," Dasha said, "he's right. We shouldn't be in here and my aunt will probably be furious when she finds out. She might have made an exception had we waited for my father to get her permission, but when someone does something without asking, she digs in her heels. At the very least she'll make us go somewhere else. But we're closer to the palace jeweler here so the risk is worth it."

"Proximity to the jeweler is probably why they won't want us here," Trivnor said.

"Exactly," Dasha said, "but not only that. Primarily they don't want anyone to know where the army sleeps so they can't be attacked directly. Plus, this is where they keep all their weapons and it's directly attached to the palace of the goblin king."

Trivnor nodded toward the opposite door they had come through.

"Yes," Dasha said. "Although it doesn't go directly where we need, it gets us much, much closer."

"But we were so far from the palace when we came in here," Jassan said. He had a difficult time wrapping his mind around how the goblins worked and where all the different portals led.

"The portal in each barracks room leads to the same place in the palace," Dasha said.

Lokna shook his head. "I don't like the sound of this. We should find somewhere else. We shouldn't be here."

"No, we need to stay," Trivnor said. "We need to get a gem."

"Jassan needs rest," Emma said from his side. "He needs time to heal."

"We could all use some rest," Eleka said. "It's the middle of the night."

"And food," Burk said. "Maybe the rest of us dragons can last, but Jassan needs food to heal, no matter what he looks like."

"Ok," Trivnor held up his hands for quiet. "Lokna, Gizi, you've been here before. I need to talk to Dasha for a bit. Do you know where to get us some food?"

Gizi squirmed. "I might be able to find my way to Dasha's place. We can get some food there." Dasha nodded at Gizi and looked back to Trivnor.

"You two go," Trivnor said. "Dasha and I will plan how to get the jeweler's gem. The rest of you can rest."

"When do *we* rest?" Lokna grumbled.

"When you die," Tyla and Eleka said at the same time. Jassan assumed Lokna had heard that from them before, probably many times, because he waved the comment off.

"Or when you become a wraith," Gizi said, shoving Lokna toward the door. "I'm sure Kelraz wouldn't mind you taking a snooze."

The two disappeared through the doorway and Dasha and Trivnor huddled in conversation.

"Trivnor," Jassan said before the older faerie completely turned his attention away, "what happens if I change back into a faerie while I'm sleeping?"

"I don't think that will happen," Trivnor said. "You have to concentrate to cut the connection, yes? It should hold until you wake. But we'll wake you if something happens. Now, sleep."

As Dasha claimed Trivnor's attention to scratch out the directions of their plan, Emma sat down next to Jassan. Burk curled up on Emma's other side. Tyla and Eleka curled up together in a heap and almost immediately fell asleep. Even Burk's breathing seemed to ease.

Another ripple of pain burned through his shoulder as Jassan adjusted himself on the floor. Although he knew he would be extremely uncomfortable in this position as a faerie, it felt natural in dragon form. Bubbles must have felt him tremble because she immediately slid along his back onto his wounds and poured more cooling heat into them. As he settled down, he tilted his head to see Emma, who rested her head next to him. "Don't worry," she said, "we'll all keep watch over you."

Gizi and Lokna came back while Jassan slept, then fell asleep themselves. Sometime later Jassan woke to a massive snore coming from the corner of the room. His aunt had told him dragons snored, but he had never been around one when it did. Or he must have been tired enough then that he hadn't heard it. Lokna's snore rattled the room and a few more eyes peeked open. A few bodies shifted in the quietness.

On the floor next to Lokna was a bag about the size of his dragon's fist. Jassan could see it bulging with food inside. His stomach churned and he realized the last time he had eaten was when they were on their way to find Shampy's home in the forest. He must have taken off his bag of supplies when she put the sword and sheath on him and left it behind in the chaos to escape.

When he was startled and flinched from another of the brown dragon's resounding snorts, Jassan's shoulder began to burn again.

"How are you doing?" Emma said at his side.

Jassan shrugged his other shoulder. "It hurts," he said. He didn't want to sound weak, so he added, "but I think it's getting better. I slept a little."

"It doesn't look good," Emma said, her eyes skimming over his back.

Jassan snaked his neck around to look at the wound. It sported fewer black spots than it had at the medic's, but it still looked like he'd rolled it in fresh soil.

"Should I put more of this on it?" She held up the little bottle of liquid flarote and the cloth that Trivnor had given her.

He shrugged, unsure of how to respond. The liquid had given him some reprieve from the pain, along with Bubbles's ministrations, but he didn't want to be any more of a hindrance, especially to Emma. Emma removed the stopper from the bottle and began to dab at him without a direct answer. Jassan felt Bubbles, curled up on his back, lift her head and watch.

After a moment, Emma slowed and allowed Bubbles to work her own special majik on the wounds. But her eyes filled with tears.

"Is this what's happening to my father?" she wondered aloud. Her voice caught in her throat and Jassan realized he had forgotten all about the black dragon dragging himself away from the attack of Milah's wraith.

"I'm sure he's fine," he told her. "He's much bigger and stronger than I am."

Her eyes glistened as she looked up at him. "His wounds were also much worse."

"To a big dragon like that?" he said. "Nah, those were probably less to him than mine are to me. I'm sure he's more worried about you than you are about him."

"Another reason we should go home," Emma sighed.

"You can't," Jassan said, trying not to sound desperate. "Not yet. But maybe soon." He didn't want to admit that he knew he had to follow through with helping Trivnor, but he also knew he couldn't do it without Emma along to help him. He even needed Lokna's goading to motivate him to push on. He knew his role would be easier to do with friends by his side. Even if they didn't think of themselves as his friends.

Emma shook her head then turned it, searching their surroundings. "There's too many of us," she finally said. "We stand out and there's no good place to hide so many of us."

"Are you suggesting a few of us should try to go home?" Jassan's heart contracted. He immediately assumed the worst, that she wanted him to leave. He knew that of all of them, he would be of the least use. He still had to learn how to roar properly.

"I don't know," Emma said, unable to meet his eyes. "But I know there are too many of us. And all our families must be worried sick."

"Which is why we need to act sooner rather than later," Trivnor said. He lifted his head and Jassan couldn't tell if the faerie dragon had slept at all or just been listening to their conversation. Around them, the other dragons gradually lifted their heads or shifted their bodies to see Trivnor.

"I wouldn't be surprised if our parents have already been in contact with each other," Dasha said. "All of them." The twins rubbed their eyes and nodded. Tyla gave a massive yawn.

"What are we going to do?" Tyla said. "Do you have a plan yet?"

"Of sorts," Dasha said. "But we've only discussed it a little."

Trivnor nodded. "To start with, we're going to need a distraction before we can enter the palace."

"The wraiths aren't distraction enough?" Eleka said.

"The wraiths are certainly keeping everyone busy right now," Trivnor said. "But we need something serious enough to lure the goblins away from the king's jeweler's vault in the palace."

"The jeweler has the best guards and more than even the king himself has," Dasha said. "I know *about* where the vault is…"

"But," Trivnor picked up the statement, "we'll need time to search for it when we get there, if we get there."

"What kind of gem do we need?" Eleka asked.

"It will be a blue gem," Trivnor said. "Exactly seven and one fives in weight would be ideal."

"The same shape?" Eleka asked, pointing to the key in Jassan's arm.

Trivnor shook his head. "No, the key will reshape itself when we perform the enchantment. The weight is what matters."

"So, we have someone create a big disturbance in the city?" Tyla said. "Or somewhere in the palace tunnels close to the jeweler's vault so someone else can sneak in and get the gem?"

"The closer to the jeweler's vault inside the palace, the better," Trivnor said. "But that will only be one of them."

"One of what?" Emma asked.

"The distractions and deterrents," Dasha said.

"We'll have one crew go in and cause a disturbance, that will lead more of the guards away," Trivnor explained. "Then another crew will go in and trouble some of the guards at the jeweler's vault. That will hopefully take up all their attention and lead most of the rest of them away. Then the last crew will actually be able to get to the gem in the vault."

"But the vault will still have guards," Jassan said. He couldn't decide which of the teams he wanted to be part of; the safest, the most dangerous or the most likely to be caught.

Trivnor nodded. "Yes, the last team will have to somehow overcome and get past the last guards at the vault."

"Those guards will most certainly be the most skilled," Dasha added, not helping anyone's comfort level with the situation.

"I'll take them," Tyla said, standing up.

Eleka sighed, but didn't stand. "I suppose that means I'll go too."

"I'm not going to protect you," Tyla snipped.

"No," Eleka said, sounding almost bored. "I'll be the one making sure you don't do anything stupid."

"I'm not going to—"

"You never think—"

"You can't—"

"I have to—"

ROAR!

Trivnor burst at the twins before they could start fighting, quieting them. "Yes," he said after he got their attention. "I will need both of you on the last crew. Everyone else is too well known here. And I'll need you for your individual strengths."

"Wait a minute," Emma said. "You haven't said anything about anyone else yet. This is risky and I won't agree to let Burk be put in harm's way. I won't let you use him as a distraction."

Jassan saw Burk glance at Emma and give a little sigh, then hang his head in defeat and say nothing.

"He won't have to," Trivnor said. "We'll have Lokna and Gizi make the first attempt on the jeweler. I'll go behind them with Dasha and she'll lead the way."

"But won't Dasha get in trouble?" Emma said.

"Probably," Dasha said. "But only if we get caught. Other than that, we'll just look like some wild youth getting into trouble."

"Once I see the place," Trivnor said, "I'll come back and transport Eleka and Tyla and we'll force our way into the jeweler's. Eleka can help me find the gem we need. Tyla can watch our backs.

"However," he continued, "losing any of our number would be devastating. Getting caught and held captive would make finding us that much easier for Kelraz, so we must be absolutely certain about what we're doing."

"We should know the incantation for the gem, too," Eleka said.

Jassan considered what she'd just said. He knew Eleka was the smartest one of them. If she said they needed to do something, anyone would be a fool not to follow through.

Trivnor bit his lip in thought. "Alright," he finally said. "But I'll only say it once. Allowing the wrong beings to discover the incantation and how to use it could be catastrophic.

"It goes like this.
Shurka, Shurta, Khurta, Kruh
We come before to plead with you
Tarka, Tarsa, Tartaku
Bless this key with power true
Use the power deep in you
Bond the key and keeper through
Power to connect imbue
Seal the bond your will to do
Life or death to rend anew"

He finished with a knowing nod to Eleka. They all knew that she was the one who would retrieve the gem and would need to remember the really important information.

She thought for a moment about what she'd heard, then said, "'Connect', that's the word that will—"

"Yes," Trivnor said, not allowing her to finish the thought out loud. Jassan thought he knew why. He assumed that 'connect' was the word that would create the power to connect thoughts and minds across any distance and allow them to communicate.

"Then what word would …?" Eleka said. Her mind worked faster than anyone else's Jassan knew. The question formed in his mind after she said it. *What word would they use to enchant any other gems, if it came down to needing one?*

"Listen carefully," Trivnor said, as if talking to everyone, but keeping his eyes on Eleka. "Connect, transport, see hearts, give strength, reflect, see light, lift up."

Hopefully the string of words wouldn't make immediate sense to anyone who might be majikally listening or reading their minds. But Jassan began to wonder about what these words meant for the other keys. He knew which word belonged to his key: reflect. The Moon Key could reflect the thoughts of his mind and heart. And he certainly felt a bond with that word.

After a moment of silence among them in which Jassan could practically watch Eleka's mind continue working, Lokna whispered, "What if we find someone who has another key?"

Trivnor took a deep breath and sat up straighter. "Now, that is a good question," he said. "I can't say it all, but I can give you the incantation. 'My will is free, I give to thee, this sacred key,'" he said. He glanced down at the key in his palm. "If a keyholder says that three times, the key will lift from its bond and be free to pass to someone else."

"So, if we find someone who has a key," Lokna said, "we just have to persuade them to say that three times and let us take the key."

"Without telling them why they have to release it and why we need to take it," Gizi finished.

"…Or you could kill them," Trivnor said. "The key lifts free when its holder dies."

"Oh, sure, great. That would be easier," Gizi said, with a roll of her eyes.

"But wouldn't the key stay attached to their wraith?" Emma asked.

"No," Trivnor said. "Wraiths can transport a key like a regular stone, but it won't stay attached to a soul, only to a living being."

"So Kelraz could kill us," Lokna said, "and use our wraiths to take these two keys for himself."

"Exactly," Trivnor said. "But if we can obtain or recreate the Wind Key, it will allow us to speak to each other in our minds, no matter where or how far apart we are."

"Because that evens the playing field," Gizi grumbled.

Eleka nodded to Dasha. "Alright," Dasha said, apparently ready to move past the reminder of their obvious disadvantage. "I'll lead in Trivnor, Lokna and Gizi and try to draw away as many guards as we can. By the time we get far enough into the palace, hopefully we will have drawn away most of the guards. Then Trivnor will be far enough into the palace to use the Cloud Key to get Eleka and Tyla into the jeweler's vault to find the right gem. In the meantime, the rest of us will do whatever we can to keep the guards busy and away from the jewelers before we make our retreat."

"Burk and I will wait at Dasha's house until this fiasco is over," Emma said.

Jassan saw Burk sigh again. He watched the younger boy continue to inspect the ground, his jaw muscles working hard to hold back whatever it was he wanted to say.

"If everything goes to plan," Trivnor said, "we will all meet back at Dasha's parents' home with the gem we need."

"But most of us will have goblin guards on our tails," Tyla said.

"Or at least they'll know what we look like and be on the hunt," Eleka finished.

"I didn't say we wouldn't have to leave quickly once we meet up," Trivnor amended.

"I know!" Dasha suddenly exclaimed. "As long as we can all get back to my house ahead of any goblins, if they do come looking, Emma and Burk can claim they haven't seen us and don't know where we are. Just like they'd say if we weren't there."

"Won't they search the house?" Lokna asked.

Dasha shook her head. "They can't," she said with a smile. "They can only search a home if the owner is there to give permission. Emma can't give her consent for the homeowner unless my parents are actually there, which they shouldn't be. My mother is away on assignment and my father has his own guard work to do."

"And this is all only if they recognize Dasha among us," Trivnor said.

Everyone nodded in agreement. Jassan searched the faces around him. Some expressions were anxious, like

Emma's, some were excited, like Dasha's and Tyla's, and many were like Lokna's, determined.

"Sounds good," Jassan said, realizing he hadn't been selected for an assignment yet. "What's the initial distraction?"

"Well," Dasha said. "Jassan, you make a great dragon. Really, you do. But…"

Trivnor cleared his throat. "We're thinking you would make an even better wraith."

16

ATTACK

With visions of Lokna ripping through his flesh, Jassan's eyes bulged, and he scooted away from the group slightly.

"Not like that," Dasha said.

"But you can make yourself *look* like a wraith," Trivnor assured him.

After the initial shock of hearing their plan for him, Jassan thought he would make a pretty good wraith too. For the next while, as everyone else focused on eating, he used the Moon Key to practice turning himself into a wraith.

"Won't this draw Kelraz to us?" he asked Trivnor, taking a break to eat something.

"No more than you being a dragon already has," Trivnor replied. "He knows we're in Kirlik and he and his wraiths have been trying to get to us for a while. The only way we can truly prevent them from tracking us is if we don't use the keys at all. We need the keys' powers, so for now we'll just have to rely on our strategy and the goblin defenses as long as we're in their territory."

"And try to rob them at the same time," Gizi said, handing Jassan bread and a good chunk of salted pork.

So Jassan continued practicing. He was able to turn all black and shadowy quickly. He imagined the shiny black scales bleeding together into a soft, shadowy substance. Making the shadow appear to drip was a little more difficult. He imagined a blurry edge, but he couldn't make the shadow seem to fall from his body. He moved on, remembering the wraiths that had followed them and trying to emulate their snarls and groans and screeches. He eventually got the hang of the shadow falling off him when he pictured its drips swaying back and forth and then sagging from their weight, so they appeared to detach, but never actually did.

Jassan had been sitting on the floor in his dragon form and made his body smaller, holding up his front claw and changing it into the indistinct form of a wraith's. All that experimenting with one claw while trying to eat with the other claw. While he practiced and ate, Burk held Bubbles. She blew her fire bubbles and he popped them with a claw and giggled.

As Jassan worked, he was suddenly aware of Eleka and Tyla critiquing him. Eleka was nice enough to look away occasionally so it didn't seem like she was evaluating his every move. But Tyla glared openly while she watched him. After a moment, the bold centaur dragon seemed to come to a decision and she crawled closer to Jassan.

"What does it feel like?" she blurted.

"Tyla," Eleka said, "Leave him alone."

Tyla rolled her eyes at her sister. "Didn't you say we should have as much information as possible?" she retorted. "Well, this is me getting information."

"You aren't doing it tactfully," Eleka muttered.

Tyla waved off her sister's reproach. "Well?" she barked at Jassan.

"Well, what?" Jassan said. "What does what feel like?"

"What does it feel like to be an obnoxious, useless faerie?" Tyla sneered.

"Tyla!" Eleka said.

"I'm just kidding," Tyla said, although Jassan could tell she wasn't. "I mean, what does it feel like to use the key?"

"Oh," Jassan said, then he looked down at the Moon Key. He checked his reflection to see that he was still a large, black dragon, even if he didn't feel the least bit intimidating next to Tyla.

"How…do…you…use…it?" Tyla said slowly, enunciating every word as if speaking to a child.

"You don't need to know," Eleka said. "Just ignore her, Jassan."

"No, it's fine," he said. He knew he needed to make an effort to stand his ground with others. Even with the aggressive ones. Especially with the aggressive ones. "I look into the key and then I feel, well, it's like a pinch."

Tyla lifted one eyebrow. "A pinch?"

"Yeah," Jassan replied, trying not to wither under her stare. "I feel a pinch in my chest and then I focus on what I want to look like. When I want the changes to stop, I imagine the pinch going away."

"A pinch?" Eleka said. "Does it hurt?"

"No," Jassan said. "It's not a painful pinch, just kind of a squeeze."

"Then why didn't you say 'squeeze'?" Tyla said.

"I don't know," Jassan persisted. "Because it's more of a pinch."

"Interesting," Trivnor said. "Mine feels more like a turning of the stomach."

"You mean you get nauseous?" Tyla's face twisted.

"No," Trivnor shook his head with a chuckle. "It's more like something inside me is moving, rolling over or twisting. Not painful or uncomfortable, and barely enough to notice."

"Yeah," Jassan agreed. "It's not so much as to bother me, just enough for me to recognize what it feels like so I can repeat it."

"Who cares what it feels like?" Dasha interrupted them. "When are we going to get started?" she asked. "Should we wait until night?"

Trivnor shook his head. "We need to go as soon as possible. It's a miracle we were able to sleep and let Jassan practice. We can't push our luck much further."

"What?" Tyla said. "Go out in the middle of the day?"

"It's still morning, barely after breakfast," Eleka corrected her.

"Yes," Tyla growled at her sister, "and everyone will be up and alert. Everyone knows it's better to attack in the dead of night. You catch your enemy off-guard."

"The goblins are *not* our enemies," Dasha said.

"They are when we need to steal something from them," Tyla shot back.

"I think it's best we go now," Trivnor said. "Yes, during the day. The goblins will be out of the barracks—"

"Farther away from us," Eleka said.

"And spread out," Tyla added, narrowing her eyes at Trivnor. "Ok, that makes sense."

Trivnor nodded. "At this time of day, the designated guards should be at their posts, whether that's at the palace, or at the portal entrances or somewhere else."

"Wouldn't they have fewer guards on duty at night in the palace?" Emma asked.

Dasha shook her head. "The number of guards is always the same in the palace, no matter the time of day. He's right. The only numbers that go down at night are at the portal entrances and the ones stationed around Kirlik and the other cities. They and all the others are in the barracks sleeping at night. If we go now, they'll be gone from the barracks and be spread out and busy. Hopefully. If we go at night, numbers will be in the barracks and can easily swarm us when we try to leave."

"So," Lokna said, swinging his head to Jassan, "the hope of the living world rests upon the shoulders of an optical illusion and its faerie sidekick's pinch."

Jassan looked up at Lokna, who glared down on him with disdain. Jassan shook his head and looked down into the mirror-like key in his arm, then stomped his claw. Feeling the small pinch in his chest, he morphed into a terrifying monster like the ones that had been chasing them. Towering over Lokna, he grinned.

Lokna looked up at him and grinned back. "Just checking."

Jassan, back in his black-scaled dragon form, left the barracks through the door and hallway where they had first entered. The others would leave through the opposite door that led directly into the palace. Emma and Burk followed Jassan to head towards Dasha's house. They wouldn't see the others again until they all met up there, hopefully after a successful heist. Jassan, Emma and Burk had strict instructions from Trivnor to get there as soon as possible after Jassan's job and wait for the rest of them.

"Let's find Dasha's place first," Emma said. "That might help lead the guards away from the palace if we're seen."

Jassan nodded and they turned up a street away from the barracks that led past the king's palace.

"Why do they call him 'slave' when he lives in a royal residence like that?" Jassan wondered aloud, admiring the beauty of the palace.

"You know the king's titles?" Burk asked him.

"My aunt tutors me in reading, writing and math as well as histories, cultures and majik," Jassan said. "Although most species know little about the goblins, the faeries know even less."

"Well," Emma said. "I'm not sure I can answer that either. As far as I know, the king is called a 'slave' because he has to do what his subjects tell him to do. In that sense, the command hierarchy works both ways for them. But since he's the king, he lives in the palace. King Herdal won't reign forever; when a new king is chosen, King Herdal will move out and the new king will move in."

Jassan studied the massive edifice with windows and doors grand enough for a dragon and with seemingly no access to the inside from the ground. At least, he couldn't see any from where they stood. Obviously, the goblins had built the palace with dragon visitors in mind. Jassan would have loved to continue asking Emma his questions, but he knew he had to stay focused. He made a mental note to ask them of Dasha as soon as he could, and he might be able to take some impressive knowledge home to his aunt.

The three dragons made their way through the town with only disinterested glances. The goblins in the streets were cleaning up messes left behind from the wraiths' attacks. It appeared that the wraith attacks had eased, and along with them, the fires and chaos, which is why the three young dragons had to move quickly, before the goblins could focus their entire energies on the strangers.

"There it is," Burk said. He pointed to a substantial red dwelling down a couple more streets. Jassan tried to take note of where they were in the city as he would need to know how to get back to it from the palace.

"Ok," he said. He searched the area around them. They were standing at the corner of a spacious square. He assumed that on a normal day in Kirlik before the wraith attacks, the square would be crowded with goblins and their friends buying and selling wares. Now only a few goblins wandered into the square and they hurried out again as quickly as possible. The square itself was nondescript, with a few abandoned carts of goods. The doors and windows of the buildings facing the area were closed and covered. Jassan thought it would have made a good area for refugees to stay, but then he realized it would provide no protection should more wraiths attack.

Jassan stretched his dragon neck to look over the structures around the square. The buildings were taller than he was, so he raised himself up to stretch further by putting his front claws on the building next to him. Feeling a sharp pain in his shoulder, he pulled his right front leg back and leaned on his left side.

"Over there," he said to divert their attention away from him favoring his right shoulder. "There's a big statue of a flower in a park, next to a big yellow building. If you wait for me there, we can all go back to Dasha's and wait together."

"I see it," Emma said, stretching up next to Jassan the same way he had, but still barely able to see where he was pointing. "We'll hide in an alley over there and wait for you." Emma shrunk to her human form and Burk quickly did the same. "We'll be less noticeable as humans."

Emma nodded to Burk and the two set off in the direction of the yellow building.

"Wait," Jassan said when he felt a tickle down his spine. "Burk," Jassan reached behind his back with one of his claws and scooped up the little fire worm, "take Bubbles with you. I think she'll be safer."

"Are you sure she won't just follow you?" Burk said.

"Nah," Jassan slid Bubbles down his long claw into Burk's outstretched hand, "I think she likes you too."

Bubbles curled into Burk's hand but watched Jassan wide-eyed and didn't blink. When he stepped back, she cocked her head and slithered to wrap around Burk's wrist.

"You stay with Burk for now," Jassan told her. "You'll be safer with him."

Bubbles tilted her head the other direction but curled up in Burk's hand again.

"I'll keep her safe," Burk promised.

Jassan told them to get going, but Emma turned back and paused briefly. "Be careful," she said. Then the two humans flitted away down the street.

Jassan couldn't help the grin he felt spread slowly on his face. She was worried about him. Him. A faerie. An ugly faerie, too. A faerie no one showed any concern. The most beautiful, most clever, most kind part-human, part-dragon princess of the Noble Kingdom was worried about him, a stupid little faerie called Jassan. Jassan's grin spread but fell abruptly once he remembered what he had to do to be sure he could earn that affection.

Jassan waited. He tried to be small against a far wall in the street where Emma and Burk had left him, but the goblins glared at him and checked the streets around him before hurrying past. He wondered if he should have kept his blue freckles, thinking the goblins would see them but wouldn't have felt suspicious, they'd only have laughed and continued on their way. Jassan would have been used to that treatment and not being seen for who he really was.

He waited for the signal longer than he'd expected, but eventually it came. He saw a grey dragon rise in the air against the palace wall and circle once, then dive out of sight. For Jassan it was now or never.

It's time, Jassan thought to himself. *Time for me to show what kind of dragon I might have been.* He had dreamed of being a dragon so many times. He looked into the Moon Key, which reflected his black dragon façade.

This, he thought, *this is the kind of dragon I would have been. Braver than Tyla and Lokna put together. More strategic than Dasha. Smarter than Eleka.* He couldn't imagine anyone being better than Emma, so instead of comparing himself to anyone else, he turned his mind toward becoming a wraith.

He watched in the key as his visage turned darker, with blurred edges and shadows shrouding him, blackness fading into gloom, deeper and darker than any blackness should be. He gave himself longer fangs, longer claws, sharper and more serrated skeletal talons. He made sure the dark shadow would billow in runnels off him. Then he finished with hollow, empty, hungry eyes.

When the transformation was complete, he looked around in the street where he'd waited for the signal.

No one was there, the street was empty.

How was he supposed to cause panic and get attention if no one was there to see him? He lumbered into the street, then stood up on his back legs, spread his wings and began to roar. The sound started as a weak moan, but he focused on the terrifying sound of a massive, bellowing dragon coming from deep inside him. Then he added the sound of desperate rage to the clamor. He allowed the anger he had felt for all the teasing and bullying he'd experienced from the other faerie children to overflow into his deafening cry. The pain he felt seeing his aunt's disappointed scowl. The loneliness he felt spending so many days and nights wandering the woods alone. His mounting pain culminated in a pounding, thunderous roar. He thundered louder and longer than any roar he had ever heard.

Whimpers and screams issued from the buildings, and goblins peeked fearfully from behind their window coverings. He ran toward the goblin homes and roared again over their echoing screams. He knew they felt threatened but they made no moves to stop him and he needed to get the attention of the palace guards before he could back down.

He roared and scratched at the houses with the goblins in them. He roared and waited but still no guards came. Finally, he decided he had to make his presence and threat unavoidable.

Jassan connected with the key and imagined himself growing larger, more colossal than any dragon or wraith the goblins had ever seen. He saw more horns, greater and sharper, on his head, yet they were still shrouded in his wraith's dark, threatening shadow. He took a limping, running jump and spread his wings. The real night sky was beyond the underground world where he was, but it still filled him with elation to spread his dragon wings and soar through the air…until the arrows came at him.

He felt a small sting on his back leg, then finally saw some guards running from the area of the barracks he had left this morning.

That's not good, he thought to himself. He needed to see the guards coming from the palace. So, he headed through the sky closer to the mighty underground royal edifice. He brushed the tops of the buildings in front of the palace with the tips of his wings as he circled above them. The buildings seemed much smaller now than when Emma and Burk had left him standing against them.

Roaring, he landed on top of the buildings, just out of reach of the enormous palace. Almost immediately he heard boots pounding on the cobbled streets of the city. Several more guards poured from a gate on the ground level of the palace. An entrance he hadn't noticed from afar.

Finally, Jassan thought. He roared and tore at the roofs of the goblin homes where he'd perched. He tore off a chimney and smashed it against another building's wall. He jumped on its roof, pounding his heavy claws and screeching the way he had heard the wraiths do when they were in chase. He ran from rooftop to rooftop, using his wings to jump across distances. All the while, keeping the flower statue and the yellow building harboring Emma and Burk in his directional mind.

The sting of another arrow interrupted his fun. The first strike hadn't disturbed him, but the second must have been a bolt. It dug into his rear leg joint. He glanced down at it, remembering that pain didn't bother a wraith. But he had firsthand knowledge that the wraiths could indeed be distracted, if only for a moment.

He turned to see a barrage of arrows loosed in his direction. Jassan spread his wings and pumped them, pulling his legs out of the way just in time. He was prepared to either run or fly away, but he wasn't yet convinced that the guards were ready to pursue him. He knew there was only one way to ensure they would. He dove at them.

17

INTRUDER

Surprising himself, Jassan survived. He rose back up and dove again at the guards just as they were preparing another round of arrows. He wanted to avoid hurting them, but he had to execute his moves to make sure they would follow him away. He swiped at the group of maybe twenty goblins, all miniscule creatures next to his enormous wraith. He slammed his claw on the ground just aside of the goblins and in time for them to leap out of the way. Then he swept his claw across the ground underneath them to knock them down or push them into each other. Some of them were thrown farther than he'd intended, but that ensured they wouldn't be getting up too soon.

He roared at them and felt another sting from behind. Turning, he saw a group of goblins coming from the direction of the barracks. They had hit him with another bolt. Jassan realized their strategy a little late. They would hit him with the bolt to get him to turn around and face them, then loose the arrows to find as many marks as they could in his face and head. A clever game plan when fighting a dragon.

He dodged away, but an arrow struck his shoulder where the injury from a real wraith still burned. He roared and flicked his enormous tail at the newcomers. By this time, the first group had righted themselves and readied their bows as well.

As they began to draw, Jassan saw the growing threat and knew he had to get out of there before they killed him. He flattened himself as much as he could to give them less of a target. Stretching out his wings and tail and neck, he swept himself around in a sharp circle, using his wings or tail to throw most of the goblins into the buildings on either side of them.

Jassan paused a moment. He instinctually wanted to make sure they were ok, but he remembered his purpose as a wraith and knew he had to go now or get caught. Before he had time to overthink it, another group of goblins ran around a corner. They carried heavy crossbows with bolts that were connected to lengths of glistening rope. Jassan could only picture what that rope might do when the bolt attached to him. He launched himself onto the nearest structure away from them to get his bearings.

He could see more goblins running at him from the other side of the palace, with more crossbows and lengths of glistening rope. He figured the goblins had learned they couldn't kill the wraiths, so they devised a plan to trap and contain them, the same thing Trivnor had told the goblins in the village to do. *In fact,* he thought, *that might be where they got their information.*

Great, he grumbled to himself. *Wish I had thought of that sooner.*

Jassan ran along the edge of the palace, hoping to coax out as many guards as were left inside. As he ran, he ripped out the projectiles that had made their mark. Along the way, he made sure to slip occasionally to keep his chasers close behind him, but not too close. Dodging between buildings and over rooftops, he could see the following he had gathered and he anticipated successfully completing his part of the mission by drawing out all the palace guards. When dozens of goblins with their weapons met up momentarily outside any view of him, he thought he might be able to turn his attention back to Emma and Burk, waiting for him elsewhere. He jumped over the tops of the buildings and ran in the direction of the park with the flower statue next to the yellow building.

With the guards back on his trail and in swift pursuit, Jassan jumped in the air and dove behind a building. As he landed, he glanced down at the Moon Key and made sure to sever the pinching connection and the key. He landed on two feet and caught a glimpse of his faerie reflection in a window. After smiling at his blue-freckled face for the first time ever, he turned to find the park with the flower statue.

He didn't have time to look through all the alleyways for a park beyond. He could hear the guards shouting orders only a few houses away.

"Jassan!" He heard Emma's voice from beside the yellow building. He darted into the space between a taller and the shorter building just as the guards invaded the park.

"Over there!" a goblin shouted. Several men ran to where Jassan huddled with Emma and Burk.

Emma pulled Jassan's hood tighter around his head and face, then pushed him behind her, next to Burk. Jassan put his arms around Burk and they tried to duck down together, Jassan keeping his head down and face covered. Emma stood protectively over them both to hide Jassan from sight.

As he leaned over Burk, Bubbles lurched from Burk's hand onto Jassan's. She wrapped herself around his wrist and squeezed, surprisingly strong to Jassan. Jassan couldn't help feeling that she might have actually missed him and worried about him. He knew he would find it difficult to leave her behind again.

"The monster!" Emma wailed at the guards before they could reach her. "It went that way! Toward the portals!"

"You kids get inside!" the guard instructed harshly as he and the rest ran off, away from the park and, more importantly, away from the palace.

"We've got to get to Dasha's," Emma said. She grabbed Burk by the hand. "You need to keep that hood up and your head down," she directed Jassan. As he used his injured hand to cinch the hood tighter around his pointed faerie ears, Emma grabbed his other hand. "And we need to stay together."

Jassan almost forgot about keeping his head down as she pulled him along in the streets. Her hand in his was warm and her firm grip comforted him. Only when he noticed someone else hurrying down the street did he finally tuck his chin and think about running.

Jassan ran hand in hand with Emma most of the way to Dasha's place. When they turned a corner with the big red house in view, Emma yanked both boys' hands to pull them up short. Jassan was about to ask why when he caught a flash of a small, red-haired goblin through one of the home's windows.

"Who was that?" Jassan asked as Emma pressed him and Burk against a wall, out of the house's sightline.

"That," Emma said, gulping for air, "was Shvika."

Burk gasped.

"So?" Jassan asked. "We can just tell her we're here to wait for Dasha."

Emma shook her head. She peeked around the corner then quickly pulled back again. "Shvika terrifies me. I would take a wraith over her any day."

"She can't be that bad," Jassan said. "She must care about Dasha. She's her aunt, right?"

"No, she isn't her aunt, Dasha only calls her that," Burk said. "Shvika is close friends with her dad."

"And she definitely cares about Dasha," Emma said. "She cares so much that she has continuously trained

Dasha to be a guard since she was a child. But anytime Dasha misses a session, Shvika gathers a squad of men and hunts her down. If she's even late for dinner, Shvika calls the guards. Shvika doesn't have children. She treats Keeahrspi's kids like they're her own, though she's overly protective and I can only imagine what she would be like as a mother."

"Once," Burk said, "I heard she had a boy arrested because he called her a mean name."

Jassan's eyes popped open. "But what would she do to us?" he asked. "If we just show up looking for Dasha and we genuinely don't know where Dasha is."

Emma chuckled without mirth. "Didn't you see the obruck on her head?"

Jassan hadn't thought about that during the brief glimpse of her he'd gotten, but now he recalled a gold circlet with gems that rested atop the short red hair on the goblin's head. "What about it?"

"Shvika," she whispered, "is high enough in rank to hold a gem that can read minds." Jassan's mouth fell open and Emma nodded. "Yeah, it's limited and yes, not many others know what all she can do with it, but I have a feeling she'll know exactly what we've been doing before we even get to the door."

"So, we can't go to Dasha's?" It was a rhetorical question because they knew the answer.

They all shook their heads.

"Not just us," Emma said. "Neither can anyone else."

"Where would they even be?" Jassan asked as Emma searched around another corner. They had decided to work their way back toward the palace to try to intercept the others before they could reach Dasha's house.

Emma waved for Jassan and Burk to follow her down the street. "If they're in their dragon forms, we can't miss them," she said.

"And if they're not?" Burk said.

Emma and Jassan shared a glance and Burk didn't ask again. They turned another corner and Emma stopped. She glanced back in the direction they had come and pursed her lips.

"What's wrong?" Jassan asked.

Emma shook her head. "I don't want to get too far from Dasha's. Just in case the others get past us."

"Good idea," Jassan said. "We know they'll head this way. Why don't we stop and wait for a few minutes?"

They eased into an alley between the next two buildings. Considering the direction the street ran, Jassan thought the others might have to cross it at some point on the way to Dasha's.

"Jassan," Emma said after they'd waited for a few minutes in silence, "how's your arm?"

Jassan shrugged. "I haven't felt any pain for a while," he said.

"Could that just be the fear from today taking over your brain?" Emma pondered absentmindedly, pulling back his cloak.

Jassan thought about the brief tenderness he felt from her, but could tell he didn't really have Emma's attention. Her eyes darted and she bit her lip. Jassan tried to think of something else she could focus her energy on.

"My legs were hit a couple of times when I was distracting the guards," he said. "Maybe we can check those spots."

Burk took watch at the edge of the building while Emma peeled back his pant leg where Jassan had been shot.

"I don't see anything," Emma said. "Are you sure you were hit? With arrows?"

"I ripped them out myself," Jassan said. "The first one was an arrow. The second was a crossbow bolt. Are you sure you don't see anything?"

Emma looked closer and ran her hand over Jassan's calf. "There's nothing here. Oh, wait!"

Jassan felt the tiniest of pricks as she pressed into the small muscle of his faerie leg. He turned his head toward her and she looked up at him. "Does that hurt?"

"Not really," Jassan said.

Emma shook her head. "It shouldn't," she pulled the cloth back down and stood up to face him. "It was the tiniest scratch I've ever seen. It looks the same as when I prick my finger while I'm embroidering. How can that be an arrow wound?"

Jassan thought about the moment he was hit. "My size must have made the difference," he said. "I was enormous. The goblin arrows felt like little pin pricks in my wraith legs."

"So that's all you felt?" Emma smiled.

Jassan chuckled at the different proportion too, seeing what little effect an arrow to his wraith leg had on his leg in faerie form. Unfortunately, his face contorted slightly as the pain in his shoulder flared.

Emma's grin disappeared, and she gently spun Jassan so she could see the wound she had tended before on his shoulder.

Jassan missed having his long dragon neck that enabled him to check the injury himself. He had to rely on Emma's report. "How is it?"

"You might be right about your size making a difference. Although it's not as big, it seems to cover more of your body. And your shirt is torn," she said. Then she pulled his cloak back over his shoulder and shook her head at him with a puzzled look on her face. "It doesn't look any different," she said. "I don't understand, shouldn't it be healing?"

"Faeries don't heal as quickly as dragons," Jassan said. "Maybe that potion is just helping it not hurt so it can heal over time."

"Maybe I should put more potion on it," she said.

Jassan heard the sadness in her voice. At first he thought it was out of concern for him, then he realized what the worry she felt was more likely about. As she patted the dampened cloth on his arm, he gritted his teeth against the burning.

"Is it ok?" she asked.

He relaxed his grimace before he turned to look at her face next to his. He almost wished her concern was only for him, but he knew better. "Your father will be fine," he said. "He's a lot stronger than I am and he has powerful majishuns working to heal him. He's going to be ok."

Her eyes finally met his and held them for a long moment. "Thank you," she murmured back.

Staring into her bright blue, almond-shaped eyes framed by her long, dark lashes surrounded by her soft, brown skin, Jassan's heart beat faster and his face burned hotter than the wound. He knew his cheeks had turned purple and he felt perspiration build on his brow.

"Do you guys hear that?" Burk's whisper pulled them out of whatever moment they were having.

Jassan listened for the sound Burk heard as Emma tucked away the bottle and cloth. They all heard it then, the unmistakable sound of boots and claws running on the cobbled streets.

18

BEING HUNTED

"Stop there!" a guard barked in the distance.

Heavy feet pounded on the cobblestones. Jassan, Emma and Burk peered from the corner of the building to see Gizi and Dasha running down the road in their dragon forms. They turned into a side street and revealed several goblins close at their heels. Before they reached the same street, the lead goblin pointed off in the direction the two dragons had gone and two from their numbers ran into an alleyway in the same direction.

"What do we do?" Burk muttered.

"They can't go back to Dasha's," Emma said.

"But they're probably trying to lose the guards," Jassan added.

"Can we do anything to help them?" Emma said. Jassan began to think, but when he turned to Emma, he saw her glance down at the Moon Key.

Jassan glid through the streets of Kirlik on his own two wings. While it felt good to fly with the simple ease of a faerie, he knew if he was caught he might be arrested for being blue. But throwing caution to Tarsa, he flew over a few rooftops anyway and saw the two dragons split up in an alley ahead of him. He flew in the direction of Dasha because she was closer.

He landed in a fenced area next to a house, but he stayed hidden and peeked over the fence until Dasha came into sight.

"Bubbles," Jassan said low enough that only the snake would hear him, "go get her."

Without another word, the little fire worm fell from Jassan's wrist and skated over the cobblestones toward Dasha. The greyish-blue dragon scanned the unfamiliar area until Bubbles lit herself on fire and the dragon recognized her. Dasha blinked and ran toward her.

"Over here!" Jassan whispered as loudly as he dared. Bubbles and Dasha joined Jassan on the protected side of the fence.

"We can't stay here," she said, panting. "I don't know how they're keeping up, but ..." She turned to peek over the fence.

But Jassan had already begun the transformation to match Dasha's own greyish-blue dragon form. Dasha jumped when she turned back to face herself.

"What the—?" she began.

"No time to explain," Jassan said as he climbed over the wall. "Other than you can't go to your house. Shvika is there."

"Oh, spit," Dasha muttered. "Wait, take these." She handed Jassan three broken gold rings with blue gems dangling from them. They looked fragile, like they might fall apart at any moment, but Jassan yanked them out of her claw and launched himself over the fence with the rings in his claw. Bubbles slid up his leg as he began to run.

"Find Emma," he hissed over his shoulder.

Sure enough, the goblins were already running down the alley. Jassan couldn't wait and he sprinted down the street opposite Dasha's hiding place.

Jassan ran for all he was worth. Somehow, almost miraculously, the goblins, even with their little legs a *very* different length than his own in dragon form, kept up. He knew they would be almost literally on his tail until he could find a park or open square and use his wings to fly ahead of them. But he also knew he was in trouble either way. If he flew he would be easier to track, and if he kept running he wouldn't be able to lose the goblins.

Clutching the gold rings in his claw slowed him as he ran, so he hurriedly shoved them up his arm. To his surprise the gold rings majikally grew as he slipped them over his claw, then shrank again to fit snugly around his scaly arm.

As he ran, he racked his brain for a way to escape his pursuers. Finally, a plan came to him. He would run as far and as fast as he could in the opposite direction of where he and his friends were supposed to meet. He would lead them away and then he would ditch them.

He ran. Away from the palace and away from the portals he had sent the other guards toward. He ran farther and faster and deeper into the underground city. He ran for so long he thought he'd almost reached the farthest side of Kirlik when he found a crack between two buildings where he could hide.

He looked around and down, desperately searching the area for inspiration, until he remembered when he'd accidentally turned into a tree. He couldn't disguise himself as a tree here, with no trees in the area, but he saw a couple of bugs on the ground that gave him an idea.

Two tiny black beetles with iridescent green wings scuttled along the edge of the wall.

There, he thought, *I need to be one of those.*

He stared at one of the little beetles, then looked into the Moon Key.

Nothing.

He groaned inwardly. He was going to be caught.

He imagined the pinch in his chest and thought about seeing himself as the beetle in the mirror.

Still nothing. He heard boots coming up the street.

Suddenly Bubbles slid to the ground and snapped one of the beetles into her mouth.

"Hey," Jassan whispered harshly, "I needed that."

Bubbles looked back and forth between Jassan and the other beetle still crouched on the ground. After a moment's hesitation she pulled away from it, but continued to glance between Jassan and the remaining bug.

Jassan heard the goblins shouting and the sound of them grew louder. He focused on the beetle, then gazed into the key and tried to ignore the guards closing in. He didn't notice everything around him getting larger as he focused on his own reflection in the key. He did recognize something like the beetle looking back at him, a small black creature with a green back.

He looked up at Bubbles towering over him. "Don't eat me!" he cried.

He went back to focusing on his image, watching the other bug and how it moved and crept along the wall. He thought he was looking pretty accurate, when suddenly he felt heavy, muscular scales wrapping around him.

"Bubbles?" he squeaked. He feared for a moment that she had decided to eat him anyway, but when he tried to push himself away, she scooped him up on the top of her head and quickly slithered to the wall just as the thunderous sound of pounding boots slamming against the cobbles reached the nearest corner.

The other beetle stared at him and Bubbles from its spot near the wall. The boots of the goblins turned the corner and all three of the small creatures pressed against the wall to avoid being squashed. The lead goblin stopped to scan her surroundings, but mostly focused on the roofs above her.

Jassan had to cover his tiny bug ears when she bellowed, "She must have taken to wing! You three, go that way; you others, come with me!"

Jassan realized she hadn't been screaming at the top of her lungs, he was just so small that the sound was amplified in his head more than a hundredfold.

He looked down at the other beetle from atop Bubble's head before he flew down by its side. "How do you stand it?" he said.

The beetle hissed at him.

"Bubbles," Jassan said, his eyes darting between the bug, the key and the snake, "come here."

Bubbles slid closer to him and Jassan placed one of his bug hands on her warm scales. He looked into the key and tried to change his wing color to the exact color of the other beetle's. Nothing happened. But then, keeping his gaze in the key's mirror, he took his hand away from the snake's back and his wing color immediately changed to match the other bug's.

"Huh," he said, gazing up at Bubbles. "I can't change myself if I'm touching someone else. You'll have to help me remember that."

"But," he thought back to his changes quickly, "I changed the color of my dragon scales while you were on my back."

Bubbles swung her head side to side then leaned forward and tapped Jassan's back with her snout. She bumped the hilt of the sword against him.

"Oh," he said, "You were on the sword. Clever little worm."

Jassan took a moment to really study the other beetle. As it circled him, probably trying to figure out what he was, he thought, Jassan changed his features to imitate the bug's. Bubbles watched, merely flicking her tongue occasionally. Checking his shape and size in the mirror, he completed his updated look in very little time. He sensed it was time they take off when the other beetle bristled at him and Bubbles began to hiss.

"Come on," he told the little snake that now towered over him. "I won't be able to give you a ride this time."

In response, Bubbles snapped the other little bug into her mouth and slid ahead of him.

"Just remember which one is me!" he said up at her. Jassan sprang into the air, nearly invisible to the bigger creatures now, and ready to fly.

It took them longer to get back to where he'd left Dasha than he anticipated. He realized within a few minutes of taking flight that beetles fly much slower than any other creatures do. But from his tiny vantage, he could follow and remain unseen by the guards that had been chasing Dasha. A stroke of luck.

As he neared his friends, he could see that Gizi had found Emma and Burk. The three of them huddled in an alleyway across from a fountain in the park with the flower statue. They were several streets over from where Dasha had found a hiding place behind a hefty cart in front of a store in the square. She had changed to her goblin form to be able to hide better. Jassan watched Bubbles slip between the cart's wheels and circle Dasha's feet until she noticed her. Jassan knew that Bubbles could lead Dasha to the others.

None of the others had guards around them, so Jassan thought they would be safe for the time being. He continued flying to look for Lokna, who should have been with Gizi and Dasha. As long as he was buzzing through the underground city, Jassan decided to check Dasha's house again.

Dropping down to house level, he flew in the window where they had seen the red-haired aunt. Jassan almost cried out when he saw Lokna lying flat on the floor in a massive room.

"Where is she?" Shvika yelled at the dragon. "I know you're her friend. Perhaps I will ask the king to be lenient in your sentencing if you tell me where she is."

Lokna didn't speak until Jassan noticed a white stone on Shvika's obruck glow. "Sentencing?" he asked. "I haven't done anything wrong! Is this how you treat all your dragon visitors?"

His mouth clamped shut as if an invisible rope had wrapped around his snout and tightened.

"Don't play the fool with me, dragon," Shvika growled. She tapped her headpiece. "I know more than you can possibly imagine. Wraiths chasing you. Hiding in the barracks, of all places! Where is she?"

Lokna's mouth sprang open. "I don't know!" he growled back through gritted teeth. And Jassan knew he was telling the truth. There was no way Lokna could know where Dasha was right now. The only thing he knew was that she was supposed to meet him at her house. But Jassan assumed that when Lokna saw Shvika there, he figured out that Dasha wasn't coming.

"Quiet!" Shvika said suddenly over Lokna's complaints. The white gem glowed again and Lokna's jaws slammed together. He grunted in annoyance, but Shvika was looking around the house. A light purple stone glowed in her headpiece as she searched with her eyes. "Who else is here?" she said. "Show yourself before I find you and I won't harm you!"

Jassan's wings almost stopped fluttering. He knew she would find him. He had to do something. He flew back out the window and around to the other side of the substantial red structure. A massive swinging door hung behind Lokna, roomy enough to allow dragons to enter the house. It appeared that Shvika had Lokna pinned to the ground majikally, so she wouldn't have been concerned that Lokna might escape. Jassan had to hope she also wouldn't expect anyone who might come charging inside to help him. Because he had an idea.

He didn't stop to land. Either his idea would work or it wouldn't. He circled Dasha's rooftop once. By the time he'd done a full loop he had transformed. He swooped down to go through the swinging door but slammed into it face first.

Jassan stopped his groan and roared instead to cover his mistake. Of course Shvika would have locked the doors. He roared, ran across the street and turned back to throw himself, uninjured shoulder first, into the large door. Luckily, it gave way in a splintered spray of shattered wood. Jassan ripped the door away and burst into the home in his wraith form.

19

FLIGHT OF THE BEETLE FAERIE

He had hoped to catch the distressing goblin off-guard. But she only flinched for a moment.

Lokna's eyes bulged for a second until it looked as if he recognized Jassan's wraith. Then his eyes seemed to plead to Jassan. Jassan saw them dart to Shvika and back to him again but he had no time to try to decipher what Lokna was trying to tell him.

Jassan roared. His bellow sounded much more intimidating when he was in his wraith form. He advanced without pause on Shvika and raised his claw.

"I am so…sick…of…these…MONSTERS!" She screamed each word, advancing on Jassan in tandem. But by the time the two met in the middle, Jassan still had no idea what he would do next. Shvika's resolve seemed the opposite.

She reached out one palm and a yellow gem in her obruck glowed. She slapped her hand on Jassan's claw and he felt a searing, white-hot pain tear through his body before it left a sizzling, allover burn in its wake. He felt his wraith form being thrown backwards, out into the street, but he was unable to either slow himself or scream in misery.

Landing in the street on his injured shoulder knocked down the white-hot overall pain slightly, although he still felt like he'd been charred on a grill. The agony in his shoulder was nothing compared to the blinding power the little goblin had used to control him. He wasn't sure what he could do against it.

He had hoped to scare her away with his threatening wraith embodiment. He had hoped to be the hero to the others. Then he felt the weight of her control pressing down on him.

"You will heel, dog," Shvika said, moving to stand over him. Her power forced his head flat on the ground. His legs unwillingly sprawled and his belly slammed flat to the ground. Even his massive, spiked tail could not respond to his thrashing effort and it stilled on the cobbled road.

"Shvika," Jassan heard Lokna calling to her from behind. "Wait!"

"Stay where you are," Shvika called back to Lokna, with her eyes deadlocked on Jassan. "I will deal with you once I have restrained this beast."

A blue gem glowed in her obruck. He knew she must be calling more guards to come and take his limp form away. He felt the crushing potency of Shvika's gems pressing him into the ground. His lungs deflated, pressing the air out of him.

"What?" Shvika said. "No!" She turned to Lokna. "Tell me you aren't part of this," she hissed.

"Aren't part of what?" he snipped in reply. Jassan could see the brown dragon standing behind her.

"They can't possibly..." Shvika said, obviously listening to what was being said at the other end of the blue communication gem.

But Jassan was losing focus on what she was saying. Pinned to the ground, he felt like a tiny beetle again with a massive boot over him, slowly smashing him into the floor. He wanted to scream, but he couldn't open his mouth. He tried to breathe, but the invisible weight holding him down kept his lungs from inflating.

Just as the edges of his vision began to swim in blackness, the weight on him let up. Jassan sucked air back into his lungs. He blinked the darkness away from his vision and took another deep breath.

"What do you think you're doing?" Shvika howled.

"I'm sorry!" Lokna called back.

Jassan rose up in time to see Shvika's headpiece roll away down the street. She stood in front of Lokna with her arms spread out. Jassan couldn't tell if she was trying to keep Lokna away from his wraith form or the other way around.

Jassan roared, demanding Shvika's attention. He lifted a claw and this time Shvika only crossed her arms in front of her face to protect herself. He batted her aside, sending her flying down the road toward her obruck. She slammed into a wall before she fell to the ground and lay still.

Lokna locked eyes with the wraith's. "Jassan?" he asked hesitantly.

Jassan nodded.

"Oh, good," Lokna sighed. "I was really hoping I hadn't just protected a real wraith from her."

"We have to go!"

The two ran off down the street together.

"Where is everyone?" Lokna asked as they ran. "We were supposed to meet there."

"We saw Shvika through the window before we got to Dasha's," Jassan explained. "We tried to intercept everyone."

"So you got to Dasha and Gizi?"

"Yes," Jassan said. "Then I went looking for you."

Lokna glanced away. "Thanks," he said quietly.

Jassan didn't respond. Caught off-guard, he wasn't sure what to say. The mighty Lokna was grateful.

"Hey," Lokna said, "did you really fly into that locked door?"

"Oh, snap it," Jassan shot back.

Lokna chuckled. "Stupid faerie." But the insult didn't have the familiar bite behind it.

"How did you get out of her grip?" Jassan finally asked.

"She can only control one being at a time," Lokna explained. "She has many of the most powerful gems, but each is limited. And can you do me a favor?" Jassan glanced at Lokna with confusion. "Can you change out of that creepy wraith thing?"

They turned a corner toward the fountain where the others waited. Jassan heard a scream issue from an alleyway.

"Told you!" Lokna said as he took off toward the sound. Jassan slowed so Lokna could approach first and the others would be alerted that the monster was actually him.

"Lokna," Emma sighed. "Thank Tartaku. What happened?"

"Shvika had me pinned," Lokna said. Jassan was surprised to hear him admit he'd been caught. "Where's Gizi?"

Emma shook her head. "She went to search for Dasha."

"Shvika knows what we're trying to do," Lokna said. "She knows someone is trying to steal a gem. But I'm not sure how much else she knows yet."

"Does that mean the others have been caught?" Burk squeaked.

No one answered.

"I'm going to find Gizi," Lokna said. But before he could turn away, Jassan's wraith claw grabbed his arm.

"No," Jassan said. "Shvika is already looking for you. You need to stay hidden. Bubbles is helping Dasha find her way back. Dasha and Gizi will find each other and Bubbles will lead them here."

Lokna ground his teeth, but nodded. "What are you going to do?"

Jassan swallowed. He didn't want to answer but he knew what he had to do. "I'm going after Trivnor."

"Are you crazy?" Lokna said.

"You'll get caught," Emma said.

"Even in your fancy wraith getup," Lokna said. "You can't go into the palace that way. You'll draw all the troops and make things even worse."

Jassan shook his head firmly. "I've got this."

He looked down at the Moon Key again. Remembering the pinch and his previous little companion, Jassan shrank back to the beetle form he had used to fly almost invisibly over the underground city. Emma had learned to expect sudden changes but Burk was entertained.

"If I see Dasha and Gizi along the way," he said. "I'll tell them where to find you."

"You sound funny," Burk giggled. Jassan felt the young boy's soft voice boom in his head but he smiled at the humor of it too, knowing Burk wasn't mocking him.

"We can't stay here," Emma said. "We're sitting dutguins."

"What about the others?" Lokna insisted.

"They'll be fine. This is Dasha's home. She'll know how to stay out of sight," Emma said. "We have to trust that they'll all be ok and will head for the park that has the flower statue."

"The what?"

"We'll look for them along the way," she finished. "But Lokna's right, we have to keep moving. And it's best if we travel in groups of as few as possible."

As they moved off again, Burk uttered, "There's too many of us."

Jassan flew as fast as his little beetle wings would take him. He swooped and dipped and dove looking for any sign of the others or the guards, either together or apart. Finally he saw Dasha and Gizi running down a side street together with Bubbles on Dasha's shoulder.

Jassan flew down and landed next to Bubbles. "Dasha!" he said, and the goblin stopped and spun in a circle.

"Who's there? Where are you?" Dasha asked up into the air.

Jassan buzzed in front of her and cut his connection to the key. Landing on his two feet in front of them, he explained where the others were.

Dasha agreed with Burk's assessment. "There are too many of us to gather and keep together in one place," she echoed. "Joining back up will only make us a bigger target and easier for Shvika to catch all of us."

"I have an idea," Gizi said.

Dasha turned to her with wide eyes. "Not just a snide comment?"

Gizi held up a claw. "Give it a minute. We'll head to the east portals," she continued without missing a beat.

"We'll hide there and wait as long as we can. If we have to leave, we have to leave."

"Understood," Jassan said, lifting into the air and changing back into his beetle form. "I'll find Trivnor and the others."

Bubbles slithered down Dasha's leg and squirmed in a figure eight beneath Jassan.

"Bubbles, I can't take you with me. I might need to change again," Jassan said. "Stay with Dasha and keep them all safe."

"Wait!" Dasha almost yelled, prompting a scathing look from Gizi. "The obrucks I gave you, where are they?"

Jassan had already forgotten about the broken bedazzled gold rings. He looked down at his tiny beetle arm. "They must have changed with me like my clothes do," he said.

"Well, change back," Dasha said. "We need those."

Jassan cut his connection with the Moon Key and appeared with the rings around his uninjured faerie arm. Pulling them off, he noticed that again the gold rings adjusted in size, allowing them to slide free.

"What are they?" he asked, handing all three rings to Dasha.

"These are the simple obrucks the lesser guards use for communication," she said, handing him one. "You keep one and we'll be able to speak to you."

"But they're broken," Gizi said. "They might as well be trash for all the use they are."

"They appear broken but they're still functional," Dasha said, lifting one that looked nearly intact.

"Ok," Gizi said. "How do we use them when they are in…shall we say…various states of repair?"

Dasha looked around her for something. She reached down and pulled up the bottom of her cloak. Using her teeth, she ripped a strip of cloth from it. "Here." She tied the cloth around the gem's setting so it held the stone in place. "The gem has to touch you, but the metal engages the gem and dictates which gems can communicate with which."

"Dasha thought we should steal something to make it seem like we had achieved our purpose," Gizi explained to Jassan.

"And we got something useful out of the deal," Dasha added. She handed the dubious obruck to Jassan. "Here. It goes on your head."

Jassan gently removed his hood and set the gold ring on his head. As the ring adjusted to fit the size of his head, the cloth holding it together moved at the same time to affix and adjust the gems in place. He could feel the blue gem touching the side of his forehead and he hurriedly pulled his hood back over his head.

"You couldn't wait to steal something," Gizi said mockingly.

"Not just anything," Dasha held up the other gold rings whose settings she also began fixing with more cloth strips she ripped from her cloak. "I've always wanted one of these!"

Gizi rolled her eyes. "Ok, but if your aunt finds out you took those, you won't get out of the dungeon until my grandkids are your age."

Dasha waved her off and adorned herself with one of the questionable obrucks with gentle reverence. The blue gem threatened to fall with every adjustment.

Can ... hear ... Jassan?

"What?" Jassan said. "Was that you?"

"Say it in your head!" Dasha said with a grin.

Was that you? he asked again.

Yes!

"They work!" Dasha shrieked.

"Shhhhhhhhh!" Gizi hissed. "Won't do us much good in the dungeon!"

"Ok, ok," Dasha dropped her voice but didn't lose the smile. "Get going. Now we can stay in communication!"

Dasha and Gizi wished Jassan luck and he flew on toward the palace.

At least he didn't have as much ground to cover on this beetle-winged flight. After he left the two girls, he recognized several groups of guards running back toward the palace so he joined them. As he sped on, Jassan's little bug innards twisted with fear at the idea that Trivnor and the centaurs might have been caught. They hadn't been heard from since Dasha, Gizi and Lokna had left them behind in the palace before the final assault on the jeweler's vault.

We all went...royal jewelers...split up...running for our lives, Dasha tried to communicate the whole story, but the integrity of the hacked obrucks made communicating over the gem difficult. Jassan listened quietly, trying to piece things together.

Where should I go to find them? Jassan asked Dasha as he flew into the palace through an upper story window.

…try…third   …portal   …tapestry…don't…throne room…

Jassan flew on his little bug wings into the massive palace. He knew it had been constructed with dragon visitors in mind, but even the hallways were much too large for the goblins.

How am I supposed to find anything in this place? he asked Dasha. *It's enormous!*

Find…passages…just…goblins, her broken message responded.

Jassan searched the area. A few small doorways led off the main hall. He buzzed upwards toward the third floor, where several tapestries adorned the walls.

This is going to take forever, Jassan thought.
What?

Nothing! I'm hurrying. He chided himself that he would have to remember to keep his own thoughts separate from sending them over the gem.

Jassan drifted behind the first tapestry and landed on the wall. He had to feel around to make sure he wouldn't miss anything, like the hidden portal to the barracks that he remembered was actually *through* a similar banner. That meant crisscrossing a path with his little beetle body up and down and back and forth over the wall behind the tapestry. After a detailed search with no luck, he moved on to the next tapestry.

A while later, as he flitted to search behind the fifth tapestry, the decorated cloth was abruptly flung aside and a very familiar goblin stepped out from the wall.

It was Shvika, her eyes ablaze like her blood red hair. Her lip was badly cut, she stepped with a limp, and she winced noticeably while holding her ribs. Behind her, a yellow-haired goblin guard backed out from the hidden opening. Shvika held the tapestry aside for the second guard to drag something heavy through the wall. Jassan caught his breath when the goblin revealed the unconscious faerie form of Trivnor.

20

WEIGHTY OPTIONS

Wh-what do I d-do? Jassan stuttered into the communication gem. *It's Trivnor. What do I do?*

What…you…hold the gem…head…what happened to Trivnor?

He's here. Jassan used a free limb to press the gem against his skin. Luckily, in his bug form the other legs kept him on the wall. *They have Trivnor captive and he's unconscious.*

Where are the twins? He thought Dasha must be pressing the gem against her head now too because her message was much clearer than before.

*I don't know, I only…*he stopped himself when he saw the goblins next drag an unconscious Tyla through the hidden doorway.

Oh, spit, Jassan cursed into the gem. *Oh, spit. They have Tyla too!* Jassan got no response from the other end. *Dasha!* he practically screamed in his head. *What do I do?*

Hold on, she finally responded. *I'm letting the others know. Do they have Eleka? Do you see her?*

Jassan watched as the guards, led by Shvika, replaced the tapestry against the wall and dragged their prisoners to an ornate set of double doors farther down the passageway.

No, he told Dasha, *I don't think they have Eleka. I don't see her.*

That's something, at least, she responded.

They're taking them to another room, Jassan said.

On the same level?

Yes.

Oh, spit, she said. *They're taking them into the throne room. King Herdal will have to pass judgement.*

Why can't we just tell him? Lokna had attained the last of Dasha's three obrucks and interjected the question. Jassan wondered if his gem was a little better placed in the obruck, or maybe it just worked better against a dragon's head, but his thoughts came through loud and clear. *King Herdal would help us, I know he would.*

We can't tell anyone, Dasha said. *I would have thought you, of all of us, would want to keep the oath we made not to tell anyone.*

But he's a king, Lokna said. *Your king. I would think you would want to tell him too and get his help. No, Dasha, wait!*

What? Jassan asked as he followed behind Shvika and the other guards. *What is Dasha doing?*

After a moment, Lokna growled. *She insists we go back to the barracks to see if Eleka is there. She might have tried to go back out the way they came in after Trivnor and Tyla were captured.*

It's not a bad idea, Jassan said, reluctant to upset Lokna.

Yes, Jassan was surprised to hear the dragon agree, *but it's dangerous under these circumstances.*

Emma's right, Dasha finally answered. *There are too many of us to stay together in one spot. I can go to the barracks to check for Eleka and then come back. Lokna and Gizi, stay with Emma and Burk. Jassan, keep going.*

Jassan's little beetle heart pounded in his head with worry as he sat on a window ledge watching the proceedings below. Eleka was missing. Dasha would be searching for her. Trivnor and Tyla had been captured and would most certainly be dragged to the dungeons soon. Lokna, Emma, Gizi and Burk waited in a park somewhere, unprotected. Now Shvika was giving the king her report below him and Jassan would report it back to the others.

Shvika wanted to find Dasha after Keeahrspi had sent her the message recently. He told her that Dasha had gone to the medics so Shvika went there first. When Shvika didn't find her there but heard about the most recent wraith attack (mine!), Shvika panicked and went straight to Keeahrspi's home to make sure Dasha was safe.

"Who's the centaur?" King Herdal asked. He sat on his bare stone throne with a look of consternation. Jassan noticed the mighty goblin king, the most powerful being in all of Avonoa, wore clothes as plain as his own, not the embellished and fine materials Emma and Burk and other royals wore. His only adornment was the substantial, heavy crown of gems around his short, white hair. This was clearly no regular obruck, but a crown for a being powerful enough to rule a kingdom.

"She's one of the daughters of the leader of the warrior centaurs, Ashel, and her mate, the centaur dragon Prakyndar," Shvika said. "I know Ashel. She would never condone this action."

"Contact her immediately," King Herdal said. "No one knows the faerie?" When Shvika shook her head, Herdal nodded. "Contact the faerie council. See if anyone can identify him. But let both the faeries and the centaurs know that these two have committed an extremely serious crime against the goblins and will not be remanded to their own kind. They can council. They can visit. They can audience with myself, but they will not, in no uncertain terms, be allowed to remove the criminals from Kirlik."

"Yes, Sire," Shvika gave a nod and turned to the door.

King Herdal indicated the prisoners to the remaining guards, "Take them."

They're moving them, Jassan told the others in his gem. *And they're going to tell the centaurs and faeries everything.*

Stay with them, Dasha told him. *No matter what.*

"Wait." King Herdal stopped the guards abruptly after they began dragging the unconscious prisoners toward a wall behind the king's throne. As the guard moved Trivnor, his arm flopped to the side, revealing the swirling key in his palm. "What is that? Is that one of our stones?"

The guard shrugged. Herdal moved from his throne to slide his hand over the key. The king hesitated, then waved for the guards to continue. Eyeing the prisoners carefully, he waved at one of the guards at the door. "You two come with me," he said. "We need to check the jeweler's vault."

The king is going to the jeweler's vault, Jassan said, unable to keep the panic out of his thoughts.

Stay with Trivnor and Tyla, came Dasha's response.

Wait, Lokna said, *what if Eleka is still there?*

Why would she… Dasha started, then her voice faded. *Of course, Lokna, you're right. Trivnor probably told her to stay hidden in case he or Tyla were caught. Once she was sure everyone had made it out, she could continue the search for the gem.*

So, who do I follow? Jassan asked.

Silence.

Dasha? Lokna said.

Trivnor and Tyla can take care of themselves, Jassan thought. *He can transport himself and Tyla out when he wakes up.*

Go after the king, Lokna said. *Then at least Eleka might have you as a backup.*

Jassan flew as fast as his little beetle wings could go. He caught up with the king and his guards in the hallway in front of the tapestry where he'd seen Trivnor and Tyla pulled out. One of the guards went behind the tapestry and through the door first while the others waited. Jassan flew with him into a dark hallway lit by a small, majikal cube. At the other end of the hallway stood another guard.

Jassan flew ahead but found the guard at the end of the hallway standing in front of an empty wall.

Another illusion, Jassan thought to himself. *This place is full of them. I wonder how many doorways and entries I've passed without knowing it.*

Jassan didn't wait for the king and the other guards to enter and make their way down the hall. He flew behind the guard and into the bare wall. The solid wall was indeed an illusion and Jassan found he could fly straight through it.

He found himself in an extravagant foyer packed with guards. A grand chandelier intertwined with gold and silver hung overhead, with dozens of crystal orbs trickling down from it in glowing drops. Three sets of wooden double doors stood on the far side. Several guards huddled against one door off to the right.

"Let's try to push again," a guard with green-and-orange-striped hair said.

One guard who had been kneeling on the floor in front of the door got up and moved out of the way. The rest of the group huddled together again and began to push. They heaved three times against the door but it didn't budge.

"What's going on here?" the king bellowed, announcing his presence.

Two guards snapped to attention when the king approached, but the others went about inspecting the door they were trying to break through.

The goblin with the green-and-orange-striped hair stepped over to speak to the king. "We're not quite sure, Sire," he said. "We can't get the door open."

"Is this the room where you found the culprits?"

"No, Sire. We discovered we couldn't open this door when we were checking for them in all the rooms. We found the thieves in the next room, the armory."

"So they were trying to steal a weapon? Why would they be in the finishing room?" the king mused. "Those gems aren't yet ready to be of any use."

"We're not certain they or anyone else was in there before or even are in there now, Sire," the guard said. "But it's possible that the faerie used some sort of majik to make the other guards disappear, and he may have locked them in this room. For all we know they might be in there now and trying to keep us out, thinking they're still under attack. We just don't know the situation here. Only that we can't get this door open."

The king nodded and said he would move on and inspect the other rooms, but Jassan knew that he himself needed to get into this one with the blocked door.

I think I know where Eleka is, he said into the gem on his head.

No response.

Lokna? he said, pressing the gem forcefully against his little beetle head. *Dasha? Can you hear me?*

Nothing.

Frustration seeped into him. Where were they? Did the gems Dasha stole for these simple obrucks work or not? He thought she must have gotten them from the locked room. He knew he had to get in there.

He buzzed around the heads of the guards, searching to see if there was any way for him to breech the door in his current form. Maybe he could turn into a wraith, then scare the guards away and rip the door apart like he'd done at Dasha's house. In the back of his mind, he reminded himself to apologize to Dasha for that.

A guard swatted at Jassan, exclaiming, "Don't we have spells against insects?!"

Jassan ignored the goblin, flying deftly around his hand. He was much more agile than a normal beetle and certainly more so than a faerie. He would have flown through the lock on the door but several sharp, broken metal pieces inside blocked his way. So instead, he flew straight down to the crack between the bottom edge of the door and the smooth tile flooring.

He flew directly under the door and emerged inside another enormous room lit by majikal cubes. One wall displayed stacks of large drawers, the contents of which were labeled on the outside by a symbol written in gold. Boxes and tools were stacked along the top of the drawers. One long table stood nearly the length of the drawers in front of them, and an aisle ran down the center of the room. On the opposite side of the room from the drawer stacks were three long tables filled with tools of all sorts, organized by size. Wrapping around that side of the room were open shelves filled with even more tools, as well as numerous dragon scale bowls, each holding different colors and sizes of gems. Scattered around all the tables were obrucks of various metals with different colored stones set in them, all in varying stages of disrepair.

At one of those tables stood Eleka.

21

CAUGHT

"Eleka!" Jassan squeaked in his funny beetle voice.

Eleka jumped and spun away from what she was doing at the table. "Who is that?" she yelped.

Jassan focused a moment on cutting off his connection to the key in his arm and appeared in front of her in his faerie form.

"Jassan!" She ran to him and threw her arms around his body, picking him up off the floor. Jassan froze, never having received contact like that from anyone, much less a centaur. "How did you find me? Wait, how did you get in here?"

A moan sounded on the floor under the table. Eleka pursed her lips and clopped the guard in the head with her back hoof. He fell silent again. She released Jassan and he spun to face the door. Jassan only saw a yawning black hole.

"I went under the door," he said, searching for it. "I've been flying around the palace as a beetle looking for you. I followed the king here. They're trying to force their way in."

"I know," she said and turned back to the table. Jassan took the opportunity to look closely at what she was doing. A scale stood in front of her on the table, with two copious amounts of blue gems piled on either side. What caught his eye after he'd taken in the contents of the table was a silver obruck around her head that held three brightly glowing gems of purple, pink, and yellow.

"So far I've been able to keep them out," she said, "but I've been trapped in here since Trivnor and Tyla were captured."

"What have you been doing all this time?"

Eleka sighed and picked up a blue gem from the pile on the right. She set it on the scale's pan and stared at the scale as it settled. "I'm still trying to find the right gem," she said.

"You don't have it yet?" Jassan almost shouted in panic. He turned to look at the darkened doorway, hoping he hadn't given them away.

"Don't worry," Eleka said, "portals don't carry sound. They can't hear us. Trivnor gave me very specific instructions on our way here. I was able to stay hidden while the guards fought Trivnor and Tyla. I snagged one of the obrucks and I'm using it to lock the door from the inside…" She tapped the obruck on her head.

"You've been in here all this time trying to find a gem?"

"Not just any gem," she said, pointing at the blue gems. "Remember, Trivnor was very specific about the color and size of the gem that will work for the key. I have to measure each one."

The knocked-out guard under the table gave another moan. Eleka kicked him again and he fell silent.

They both bent down to watch the scale's oscillations slow to reveal the weight of the gem.

"Six and four fives," she said, tossing the too-small stone into the pile of gems at her left. "Almost there. After doing all these," she motioned to the pile on her left, "I'm getting better at guessing."

She picked up another gem from the pile on her right and compared it to the gem she had just weighed.

"Can't you just take one that's bigger than we need and let Trivnor cut it?" Jassan asked.

"I could, yes," she said, "and I have one that would work." She pulled a blue gem out of a pocket of the short cloak she wore around her shoulders. "But it takes special majik to cut one of these stones. Trivnor said I should keep a larger one, like you said, and he could work out the details later, but if I can find one just the right weight he could create the key without that extra step."

She set aside the one she had been weighing just as they heard a scrape of metal on stone. They turned toward the sound to see the tip of a sword protruding from the bottom of the black portal.

"Oh, spit," Jassan muttered. "That's the way I came; I probably showed them a way to get in."

Eleka didn't say anything and didn't seem upset about the intruders. She chose another stone to weigh and placed it on the scale's pan. More sword tips appeared under the door.

"Even if we find the right gem," Jassan said. "How will we get out of here?"

Another moan emitted from under the table.

Clop! Eleka's kicks were expert.

Eleka removed the gem from the scale and still said nothing. The swords behind them began to work their way up from the floor, slicing through the locked wooden door they were piercing on the other side of the portal. The glowing gems in Eleka's obruck began to flicker.

Jassan searched the room again with purpose. He saw no other exit. The room was brightly lit by light orbs embedded in the ceiling, with stone walls and the same smooth floor and ceiling tile as the hallway outside, which bounced and amplified the light.

"Can you change both of us into beetles with your Moon Key?" she finally asked him, switching gems again.

Jassan shook his head. "No," he said. "I don't think it allows me to change anyone other than myself." The head of an ax appeared with the sword tips behind them. The gems in Eleka's obruck flickered more.

Eleka sighed. "You can still get out with the gem," she said. One of the gems in her obruck stopped glowing.

"What?" Jassan shook his head. "I won't leave you here—"

"If you change into a beetle again with the gem in hand," she said, "can you change the objects on you? Your clothes? A sword?"

"Yes, but—"

"Then fly back out as a beetle. Get this gem to Trivnor."

Chunks of wood burst through the portal and skittered across the floor. Eleka picked up the gem sitting on the scale and held it out to Jassan. "It's the right size," she said. "Exactly seven and one fives. Take it. If I get caught with one of these on me, I'll be in even more trouble. Take it."

She handed it to Jassan, who took it reluctantly. Then she pulled the larger gem from her cloak again and laid it on the pile with the others on the table. She and Jassan stared at each other as great chunks of wood flew into the room behind them.

Jassan shook his head. "I could turn into a wraith and scare them away and we can make a run for it."

"They have the power to shock you and immobilize both of us."

"I could turn into a wall and hide us."

"Hiding doesn't get us or the key out."

"But," Jassan muttered, at a loss for more arguments, "we didn't plan for this. Nobody was supposed to get caught."

Moan.

Clop!

Eleka grinned and relaxed her shoulders. "But I trust you to rescue me."

Jassan felt several new emotions that he couldn't sort through in that moment. He thought his chest might explode with pride, fear, anxiety and guilt when he felt the pinch, but he forced himself to focus on taking the form of a beetle. The blue gem in his hand melted into his little beetle leg, although one of his actual hands squeezed around it to keep it in place. He watched Eleka throw her arms and hands in the air as wood from the door burst into the room. She grabbed the obruck from her long dark hair and threw it as goblins poured in and surrounded her. Jassan flew up to a nearby shelf and watched as the goblins used the power in their obrucks to press her body down against the cold, hard floor.

Eleka's face stayed serene and she said nothing. She allowed the goblins to restrain her. She stayed calm as they checked her cloak and patted her dragon wrappings to make sure she didn't have any of their precious gems or other weapons. She glanced up at the beetle on the shelf as the goblins dragged her stilled form from the room. Jassan followed on wing as they dragged a wordless Eleka out into the hallway to show the king.

"Ah, the twin," King Herdal said when he saw her. "Are you going to tell me what you and your friends were up to in there today?"

Eleka turned her eyes away from the king.

"Fine, then," he said. "Your mother has already been contacted. I'll get what I want to know eventually. For now, take her to the dungeon with her sister. The rest of you, see to the inventory, search all the rooms for any more hidden accomplices, and fix this door."

Jassan followed the goblins dragging Eleka out of the room but as soon as he buzzed back through the doorway into the hall, he jumped when he heard *Jassan!* reverberate in his head.

Lokna? he answered.

Thank Tartaku! came the response, and Jassan couldn't help but smile at the sound of Lokna's voice, which made him feel like the dragon was relieved and happy to hear from him. *What happened to you? Where did you go? Where is everyone?*

Eleka has been arrested, but I got the gem Trivnor needs before they got her, Jassan relayed quickly. *Where's Dasha? Is everyone else ok?*

I'm here too, Dasha said. *I think the use of gems and other majik is barred in certain areas of the palace. My gem was cut off when I went back to the barracks to search for Eleka and I assume yours was cut off too since this is the first we're hearing from you.*

Preventing them from using any majik made sense to Jassan but he was immediately struck by an awful thought. *What about Trivnor's key? Will he be able to use it when he wakes up?*

Is your key working now, Jassan? Lokna asked.

Yeah, it is, Jassan confirmed, *and it worked when I was with Eleka in the jeweler's vault.*

Good, Lokna replied. *Maybe the keys are more powerful than the goblins' majik gems.*

Keep that in mind though, Dasha said. *We don't know if the keys will continue to work wherever you go. So pay attention to any changes and be careful.*

I will, Jassan said.

Jassan watched then followed as the guards continued their route through the portal with Eleka pressed to the ground, sliding along between them. They didn't stop in the king's audience chamber with her the way they had with Trivnor and Tyla. They dragged her through the chamber to another hidden door at the back, unmarked in any way. A few more turns into unmarked hidden doorways and the hallways grew dim while the walls around them became rougher hewn. Eventually the guards escorting Eleka turned into a broad room with two new guards standing there.

"The accomplice," one of the new guards said, and handed the other one a brown gem.

Eleka's accompanying guard finally lifted her to stand, although she didn't allow the centaur freedom of movement. Still buzzing along nearby, Jassan noticed behind the guards an entrance to a long, narrow hallway with several small prisoner cells on each side. The first few cells on both sides had iron bars across the front; only one of those held a goblin. Farther down the hall, the cells were just small, three-sided spaces with open fronts. A couple of those cells held goblins, and then Jassan could see a few more cells at the far end. One guard proceeded down the row with Eleka and the first sign of struggle from her came when her captor stopped in front of her twin's cell.

"Eleka!" Tyla called out. "What happened? Are you ok?"

Eleka, on her feet but still restrained, looked at her sister with wide eyes as she slid along between the two guards. In Tyla's cell Jassan could see one end of a heavy chain attached to the wall and the other end holding her back leg. As they pushed Eleka into the cell next to her sister's, they clamped the same kind of chain on her leg. On the other side of the narrow passageway, the faerie Trivnor sat chained to the wall in his own three-sided cell with no door.

"Don't bother changing into your dragon form," the guard said. "As I'm sure your sister can tell you, the chain adjusts with you."

"Yeah," Tyla grumbled. "Good times."

After ensuring Eleka's chain would hold, the guard stepped out of the cell and pressed the brown gem in her hand against the wall to the side of the open doorway. Nothing appeared to happen, but she seemed satisfied, so she left to go back down the hall toward the other guards.

Eleka could finally move and as she showed signs of life, she stared at the shackle on her leg. "Jassan," she said, "please tell me you're still here."

"Jassan?" Tyla asked.

"Did Jassan come with you?" Trivnor said, standing up in his cell.

"I'm right here," Jassan said, dropping from the spot he'd taken on the ceiling.

"Where?" Trivnor asked, squinting his eyes against the dark.

Jassan flew in front of him. "Right here," he said quietly.

Tyla smiled. "You sneaky little faerie. How'd you do that?"

"The goblins were close on my tail and I had to disappear," Jassan said. "This was my best idea."

"A beetle was your best idea?" Tyla grinned.

"It was a great idea!" Eleka said. "He was able to get under the door of the jeweler's vault so he could help me."

"Where is everyone else?" Trivnor asked.

"Last I heard," Jassan whispered, making sure to keep an eye down the long, dark corridor, "They're waiting in a park near Dasha's house."

"Why aren't they at Dasha's?"

"Shvika was waiting for us there." When the centaurs gasped, he hurried on. "But it's ok. Lokna was already there and restrained but I got him away from her and she hasn't found the others. We were able to stop the others from going there but they're still waiting for us."

"Well, she made it back here in time to catch us," Trivnor said.

"I thought she seemed especially cross," Tyla muttered.

"So we need to get out of here and hope she hasn't caught anyone else?" Eleka said, her arms folded across her chest.

"I can check," Jassan tapped the obruck on his head, then remembering that they couldn't see it in his current beetle form, he said, "I have one of the communication gems."

"That won't work down here," Eleka said.

"Yeah," Tyla said. "They wouldn't allow prisoners to call for help, would they?"

"But my key still works, it's worked all along," Jassan said. "Trivnor, does your key work?"

Trivnor nodded. "I'm sure it does," he said. "The problem being that I'm currently bound to an enormous palace by a heavy chain and I cannot transport all that.

"I've also had to remain in my faerie form," he continued. "The goblins don't know I can transform like the rest of you and I need to keep it that way. If I did become a dragon, the shackle would snap my leg off."

"Might solve your transport problem, though, wouldn't it?" Tyla muttered.

Eleka spoke quickly. "Let's leave that option for a real emergency, shall we?"

"Besides," Tyla added. "These are not exactly dragon-friendly accommodations." She swept a finger around to indicate her tight quarters. "Guess how we figured that out," she growled.

"But couldn't you transform and, I don't know, just let your head stick out?" Jassan asked.

Tyla sighed. "Jassan," she said. "Come here."

She held out her hand, beckoning him to fly into her palm.

"Tyla," Trivnor started, but she waved her other hand at him.

"He asked," Tyla said to Trivnor.

Jassan shrugged and flew on his little beetle wings toward Tyla. But just as he reached the threshold of the cell, he slammed into the same kind of barrier he'd become all too familiar with. Luckily, his beetle flight was slower than the others he'd taken into the same kinds of invisible boundaries, but he still had to shake his head to reorient himself.

Rather than laugh, Tyla put her hands on her horse hips and raised an eyebrow at him. "Did you really think they would just leave our doors wide open?"

"You could have warned him," Eleka said.

"Why tell him?" Tyla said. "*We* had to figure it out the hard way."

"You always have to figure things out the hard way," her sister replied, rolling her eyes.

Jassan thought of Tyla's remark about the tight space inside a cell for a dragon. He imagined her dragon form crammed into the cell with an invisible boundary on one side and chuckled to himself.

"Keep laughing, beetle faerie," Tyla snapped. "You won't be laughing when I squash you with my hoof."

"Ok," Trivnor said. "Calm down. We need to figure this out and Jassan is here to help."

"What can I do?" Jassan asked Trivnor.

"To start with," he said, "you can speak with the others. Let them know where we are. In the meantime, we'll try to come up with a plan."

Jassan buzzed away down the dark hallway to the open area where the other goblin guards were sitting at a bench, tossing speckled gems on the floor. He clung to the ceiling and told the others with his obruck that he had found Trivnor and the twins.

Great! Dasha said. *Now come and save us too!*

22

SHIFTING

Wait, what? Jassan clung to the ceiling above the goblin guards. His heart pounded with dread.

I'll lead her away! Lokna shouted.

No! Dasha said. *She'll follow me! Get Emma and Burk to a portal. We have to get out of this city!*

What?! Jassan called to them. *Who? What's going on?*

Shvika found us, Lokna said. *We split up, but she called in more guards. I wish we had a wraith here to distract her!*

He could never get here in time! Dasha said. *Lokna, run! Get to a portal and get out of the city!*

Too lat—! Lokna yelled before his sudden silence spoke volumes.

Oh spit! Dasha cursed, then she too was gone.

Lokna? Dasha? Jassan called to them through the gem, pressing it harder and harder into his head. *Lokna! Dasha!*

Don't worry, little friend, came a very different voice. *I'll have you soon, too.*

Jassan let go of the gem in the obruck. He didn't hear anything more, but he didn't need to. He flew as fast as he could back to Trivnor's cell.

"They've been caught!" he squeaked to the older faerie. "They're all caught. All of them. We've failed! Shvika has them!"

"We haven't failed yet," Trivnor said. Jassan didn't know how he could stay so calm. Everyone had been caught except Jassan, and remembering Shvika's voice in his head, he could feel his turn was next.

"What we need is someone who can get us out of here," Tyla said.

"We have Jassan," Eleka said.

"We need someone who can actually *help* us," Tyla emphasized.

"Jassan can do—" Eleka started but Jassan interrupted.

"No, she's right," he said, hanging his beetle head. "What can I do now?"

"Jassan," Trivnor said, keeping his voice low, but firm. "You hold a very powerful key. A key that, when used with the other keys, gives the wielder the authority of the gods. When used without the other keys, it still contains the power of a god. You're more powerful than you think."

"What am I supposed to do?" Jassan said, trying not very successfully to keep the rising panic he felt from his voice.

"Should he go to the king?" Tyla said. "Maybe if Jassan tells King Herdal the truth about everything, he'll help us. Maybe even let us go?"

"No," Trivnor said, shutting her down. "I should have kept my mouth shut. I shouldn't have even told you about the gateway or the keys. If any Avonoan king knew about them, he would insist that power be in his hands. Then we would be no better off than with Kelraz alone. In fact, we would be much worse off. Much worse."

"Who else would be willing to help us?" Tyla said.

"Shvika," Eleka whispered.

"Shvika?" Tyla scoffed. "She's put us under a pile of troll dung this entire time! She's the reason we're sitting in this dungeon. You're talking about the same goblin that just arrested her beloved adopted niece! The same goblin that once arrested her for missing a day of school! The same goblin that hunted us down when we were barely late bringing Dasha home from the Annual Centaur Dash! The same goblin that—"

"Yes!" Eleka snapped to stop her sister's outburst and turned to stare at Jassan. "But I'm also talking about the very same goblin that is going to come down here, insist on dragging us all back to the king for interrogation and then might just fly us all out of here—as a wraith!"

Silence fell over them. Then all their eyes drifted to Jassan, who wished more than anything that he could change into a wall at that moment.

"Can't I just steal the gem that will let you out?" Jassan said.

"You could," Trivnor said.

"But how would that look to the guards?" Tyla said. "A gem floating away on top of a beetle?"

"Ok," Jassan relented, thinking of the opportunity to help them with the power in the Moon Key. "I'll try."

"Transform yourself in the cell on the end so the guards won't see you," Trivnor said.

As Jassan flew toward the last cell as a beetle, he remembered the hidden gem from the jeweler's vault clutched in his fist. He had almost forgotten it as the beetle limb that held it tightly hadn't felt at all uncomfortable.

"Here," he said, when he got back to Trivnor's cell. Jassan noticed that he'd been in and out of Trivnor's cell without hitting a barrier. "Take this." Trivnor held out his hand. Jassan fluttered over the faerie's hand and opened his fist that held the blue gem. The gem detached from his hand and fell into Trivnor's with a soft thump.

Then he flew to the last cell and released his connection to the Moon Key, but only momentarily to change first into his faerie self before he focused on the scary goblin female he needed to become. Not being seen by the others helped. Especially since on his first try he ended up looking like a lump of grey cheese with flaming red hair on top.

He tried to smooth her grey face more accurately and made his lips fuller, like hers. Thankfully his own pointed faerie ears were like a goblin's, but his nose had to be slimmer.

When he peeked out of the cell, Tyla's face twisted in grimace at first but then she grew thoughtful. "She was wearing a dark blue shirt and pants," she said helpfully, trying to cover her initial reaction.

"Um," Eleka hesitated, her lips pursed, "you have Trivnor's boots."

"And you'll have to be very careful about her sash, that you can't get wrong," Trivnor said. "I might be able to talk you through it."

"This isn't going to work," Jassan said, frustrated at all the directions he couldn't imagine himself.

"He might be right," Tyla added. "Shvika will have dragged the others down here by the time he figures it out."

"I'll have to go back up and find her," Jassan finally said. He stepped out of the cell cautiously, wary of the guards.

Trivnor nodded. "You won't sound like her," he said. "An illusion can't change that."

"But you told me how to change my voice," Jassan insisted. "I've been able to roar like a real dragon. I can even sound like a wraith."

"Those can all be distinctly yours," Trivnor reminded him. "In this case, you would have to know and be able to copy the sound of Shvika's voice perfectly. If you had all the keys, it would be much easier."

"Maybe you could act like you're sick," Eleka said. "She would sound very different that way."

"But he still doesn't look like her," Tyla said. "One problem at a time."

Jassan sighed. "I need to go find her. I'll be back as fast as I can." He changed back into his beetle form, which, for the cover it gave him, he was beginning to like more and more, and flew out of the dungeon.

Now, where to find her? Jassan found his way out of the dungeon with relative ease. He had never been much at navigation. Remembering the direction of the flower statue had been difficult enough, but the palace hallways followed an easy path leading out. However, he ended up at the grand main entrance instead of in the king's audience chamber like he had expected. Too late for why he needed to know now, he realized he should have been paying better attention to the turns going in and out.

Jassan thought about flying around the outside of the palace to see if Shvika was anywhere nearby. Then he remembered that she'd already caught the others, and would probably be at Dasha's with them, so he buzzed out the palace door.

Once he got his bearings and knew which way to head for Dasha's house, he changed into a dragon to fly faster. That form came easy to him. He had imagined the shape he would take as a dragon since he had seen his first dragon when he was small.

Yes, the first dragon he saw had flown overhead and he watched it until it flew out of sight. Even from a distance it appeared deep black, which was probably why he had always wanted to be a black dragon. Then he'd seen Emma's father. He appeared especially fierce, and seeing him made Jassan want to be a powerful and mighty black dragon even more. He might have gone overboard with the horns and spikes and barbels, but he wanted to look terrifying, and he thought they did the trick. He certainly seemed to get more respect from the others after he had transformed from a faerie into a dragon.

BOOM! A thundering rattle shook the underground city. The majikal sky seemed to be pouring, but the rain didn't fall in the city since it was still a mountain that loomed over them. Jassan inspected the sky, but saw no sign of wraith attacks and the smoke from fires even seemed to be clearing.

He spotted Dasha's home and changed back into his beetle image. Flying down, he found the one scene he had hoped to see and yet hoped not to see.

Debris from the destroyed swinging door had been pushed aside. Shvika stood in the ruins of the large room where he'd first seen Lokna laid out. Now she stood in front of the others with her hands on her hips. Jassan fluttered down to sit on a windowsill and watch the others while he memorized Shvika's appearance and voice.

Dasha sat front and center in her goblin form. She held a squishy blue bag on her forehead, that was something Jassan recognized. He had had to use a cold bag like that many times due to his clumsy nature while foraging. Emma sat with Burk in their human forms, her arms protectively around him. However, Burk no longer seemed afraid. Instead, his brow furrowed and his mouth turned down at the corners in a scowl.

Lokna and Gizi lay nearby with smooth silver muzzles around their jaws and shackles clamping one each of their front and back claws together. Three guards watched over the dragons. Jassan saw only one gem glowing in Shvika's headpiece, but the guards watching over the dragons must have not needed anything more to control them.

Suddenly Burk jumped up, breaking free of Emma's arms. Jassan watched as he chased Bubbles across the room to the windowsill where he sat.

"Where are you going?" Shvika barked.

"I'm sorry," Burk said as he scrambled after Bubbles. "I don't know what she's doing. Bubbles, come back!"

Bubbles slithered up the wall to the windowsill and settled next to Jassan. Fear prickled up his tiny spine as he prayed she would remember his beetle form. He couldn't call out to her or Shvika would hear him. But he froze and watched as the corners of Bubbles's little mouth curled up at the edges. She flicked her tongue at him and blinked her yellow eyes.

Burk caught up with them and stared down at the little bug on the windowsill. His eyebrows scrunched together at the sight, so Jassan, momentarily hidden from Shvika's view, waved one of his front limbs and tapped the side of his head. He wasn't sure if Burk could see or understand his gesture until the young boy's mouth curved into a half grin.

"Get away from there," Shvika growled.

"Sorry," Burk said again. He simultaneously scooped up Bubbles and pushed Jassan to the other side of the open window and out of sight. "She saw a bug and she must be hungry." He composed his face again and turned back to Shvika with Bubbles in tow.

"Keep that creature under control," the strident goblin said through gritted teeth, "or I will dispose of it."

BOOM! The room shook as another thundering crash rattled all of Kirlik. Jassan listened from outside the window, only peeking over the sill occasionally.

"You need to tell me what under the mountain is going on," Shvika said.

"We were just goofing around," Dasha started.

"Goofing around?" Shvika growled very much like a dragon. "If you were just 'goofing around' why are you all so desperately trying to hide your thoughts from me?"

The others snatched glances at each other as Shvika grabbed her head. "Ugh," she groaned, then pointed to Gizi. "You!" she barked, "stop singing that song!"

"What song?" Dasha asked Gizi in a low tone.

"'The never-ending saga,'" Gizi chuckled before Shvika could stop her.

"Aagh!" Shvika bawled, and Jassan noticed the gem fizzle out. "What are you all hiding?"

"We all have secrets," Emma said.

"Secrets?" Shvika stood in front of Emma. "Like how to break into a palace, Princess?"

"We didn't mean any harm by it," Dasha muttered.

"'Didn't mean any harm'? Dasha, you were seen in the jeweler's vault! The barracks, I can understand, but the jeweler's vault?"

"I just wanted to show it to my friends," Dasha's voice got softer and softer.

"And these?" Shvika held up the two other golden obrucks with Dasha's telltale setting fixes. "You stole them, Dasha. No one can protect you from the punishment for that."

Dasha stared silently at the ground.

"I'll have to take you to the king," Shvika said. "He'll decide what to do with you."

Dasha shared a glance with Emma.

"But what I can't figure out is how you, Princess, and your little brother fit into the proceedings here," Shvika said, turning to Emma. "You weren't seen in the jeweler's vault or anywhere else in the palace, for that matter. Neither you nor your brother. But you were caught with the dragon who was in possession of one of the stolen obrucks. And you came into the city with everyone involved." She used one of the headpieces to point at Lokna.

"They haven't done anything wrong," Dasha uttered.

"And the twins?" Shvika shot back. "The centaur twins, Ashel's girls? Why would they fight me as hard as they did? What was so important? What are you kids up to here?"

"We're not children," Dasha said quietly, but defensively, still refusing to make eye contact with her aunt.

"You're certainly not acting like contributing members of society," Shvika spat. "Only grown adults do that."

"I've already applied to be in the guards, Aunt Shvika," Dasha said. "You know that."

"Well, you can wave goodbye to that dream," Shvika said. "You'll never be approved after this stunt."

Dasha closed her eyes and her shoulders drooped. Jassan felt a pang of guilt. If she hadn't been helping them in this complex and crazy quest, Shvika wouldn't be tormenting her and the goblin army would soon benefit from her strategic mind. But due to her given wyrd, she couldn't explain her heroic actions. Then he felt even worse remembering that Dasha was the one among them who had least questioned Trivnor's intentions before they accepted this risky endeavor. Yet she had lost the most.

BOOM! Another deafening quake shook the ground. The walls trembled. The guards looked to each other, but the tremor lasted only a moment and they turned back to their commanding officer.

"Now," Shvika said. "I'm taking all of you to the king. You need to think long and hard about what you're going to say to him. Dasha," she bent over to look at Dasha, who didn't meet her eyes, "perhaps if you tell the king about the faerie, you might get a lighter punishment. Who is he? Where did he come from? What was he doing in the palace with the centaurs? And what did he want in the armory?"

Dasha glanced at Emma again.

"Ah-ha!" Shvika said, standing up. She stood in front of Emma with her arms crossed. "So everyone knows the faerie?" After consideration, she pointed to Emma. "You need to come with me, Emma. No dragons," she pointed to Burk, "or you. We're just going to talk."

"Wait," Dasha perked up. "Why her?"

"Because she isn't as practiced as you are at countering my probing," Shvika said while pushing Emma away from the group.

"It's alright, Burk," Emma said. She peeled his hand from hers. "I'll be right back."

Shvika guided Emma into the adjoining kitchen area and closed the door behind them. Jassan flew to the next window to listen. Shvika pointed to a chair by the cold fireplace and Emma sat down.

"I know your parents very well," Shvika said, pacing in front of her. "And I've already spoken to the twins' mother, Ashel. She's aware that the twins are in our custody and will not be returning home anytime soon. They are on their way to Kirlik now to find out what's going on and what we will be doing about it, but they are cognizant of the seriousness of the twins' crimes. You know I can contact your parents as well. But like I said, Herdal might be more lenient with you and your brother, and might even let you go home if he gets what he needs from you. However…your brother is very young and could be somewhat impressionable."

Emma glared up at her. Shvika was a little shorter than Emma in height, but Emma was slouched in a goblin-sized chair. Emma's eyes burned as she looked up at the woman. "So that's the real reason you wanted to speak to me alone." Jassan had never seen Emma so angry. "You want to use my brother against me."

"I'm not threatening anyone," Shvika said. "I'm being very straightforward with you. If you tell me exactly what is going on here, I might be able to speak to the king for both you and your brother. But I can't make any promises for anyone else."

Emma dropped her eyes again. "Burk is stronger than he seems," she said.

"I'm sure he is," Shvika said. "But is he strong enough to stand up to a faerie?"

Emma didn't look up.

Shvika tapped the broken obrucks in her hand again. The blue gems jiggled in the makeshift setting from Dasha's cloak. Shvika inspected them closer.

"Three," she whispered. Emma's head came up slightly. "We didn't find a headpiece on the twins or the faerie." Shvika's eyes bored into the top of Emma's head. "There's still one more of you out there."

23

DISGUISE

Jassan knew he had to act. He couldn't bear to see Emma interrogated. Shvika knew Jassan was out there somewhere. She had spoken to him. He had to stop this before the sinister goblin gathered more intelligence or resources. He didn't know if he would ever get Shvika on her own again. The menacing goblin would probably rejoin the others and take the rest of his friends to the dungeons, and he would never be able to get them all out by himself.

Trying desperately not to think, Jassan leapt from the windowsill, cut off his connection with the key, grabbed a metal pot from a counter and slammed it into the head of the threatening goblin looming over Emma.

The pot clanged off the back of Shvika's head. Jassan couldn't see her face, but he watched as her body crumpled to the ground. Emma's eyes jumped to Jassan in utter shock.

"Everything alright in there, General?" came the voice of one of the guards from the next room.

Jassan and Emma stared at each other with gaping mouths. Quickly, Emma swallowed and answered, "We're fine," in a rough impression of Shvika.

"What are you doing?" Emma whispered, running to Jassan. She threw her arms around his neck and hugged him quickly before pulling away. "You're supposed to be with Trivnor and the others."

"Well," Jassan shrugged. "They had this crazy idea that I should find the rest of you and then go back and free them from the dungeon."

"How?"

Jassan scrunched his face, still not comfortable with the idea. "By…um…using the Moon Key to turn into…" he looked down at the still form of Shvika.

Emma covered her mouth with her hands. Her wide eyes mirrored the incredulity that Jassan still felt about the idea.

"I don't know if I can do it either," he said.

"No," Emma pulled her hands away, "that's a brilliant idea!"

Jassan shook his head. "It's a terrible idea."

Emma leaned over and pulled Shvika's much more elaborate and powerful obruck from her head. "You'll need this," she said, handing it to Jassan.

"Emma," he said, "I really don't think—" He couldn't finish.

"Yes, you can," she said, "and you'd better start trying. We don't have much time."

She ran to a cabinet in the kitchen and pulled out some meat string then set to work, wrapping it around Shvika's ankles.

Jassan glanced at the door and knew he had to move now whether he wanted to or not. He stared at Shvika with her obruck in his hand. "We're going to get in so much trouble for this."

Emma stood up next to Jassan. He worried that she hadn't finished tying up Shvika. But he looked back at Emma when her fingertips found his.

"We have to," she said. "I know this is important. I understand everything Trivnor has told us, and how dangerous and horrible… but, Jassan," she stared deep into his eyes. "Do this for me. Do this to help my father. Please."

Jassan couldn't think for a moment. He could only feel her fingers brushing against his.

BOOM! BOOM!

Emma let go of his hand to steady herself on the table. Jassan pressed against the wall.

"What is it?" Emma said, worry and fear evident in her creased brow.

"I think we already know," Jassan said.

"Kelraz," Emma breathed.

"He knows two of the keys are here," Jassan said. "And he's going to find a way in."

"We have to get out of here."

Emma went back to tying up Shvika. She found a kitchen towel to tie around her mouth. As she did so, Jassan studied every feature of the goblin. He checked the

Moon Key mirror a couple of times to get it right, but when Emma was done, so was he.

"Don't bother recreating the sash, just use hers," Emma said pulling the article from Shvika's shoulders. "It would have to be precise wording and we don't have time." She put the sash over Jassan, then turned to pick up the other two obrucks from where Shvika had placed them on the table. "Keep these as well," she said, handing them to Jassan. "We'll get them back once we're all free."

He took them and finished examining his reflection in the Moon Key.

"That is creepy," Emma said, glancing between Jassan and Shvika. She turned to lead him to the kitchen door, but stopped. "Wait," she said, "will you sound like her?"

Jassan shook his head and placed Shvika's bejeweled obruck on his blood-red hair. "No," he said, "but Eleka gave me an idea."

Jassan took Emma by the upper arm, guiding her through the door of the kitchen. They stepped into the main room of Dasha's home and the other guards turned to look at them.

"I'll—" Jassan caught himself and coughed. "I'll take—" he coughed again because that sounded terribly like himself and not Shvika. Then he coughed some more. Looking up at the guards he whispered loudly. "I'll take her to the palace now," he said. "Her and her brother."

"Are you alright?" one of the guards said.

"Fine," Jassan stage-whispered. "Been yelling a lot." He gave another dry cough to emphasize, then waved Burk over to join them.

Burk clung to Dasha and a guard stepped in front of him. "Shouldn't we wait for the other guards?"

Other guards? Of course, other guards were on their way. Shvika had probably been waiting for them so they could help transport the entire group together. Jassan shook his head. He couldn't wait until they were outnumbered and outpowered. "I'll just take these two."

"I can't let you do that," the guard said. "It's protocol. And these charges are too serious for a lapse. We're required to have at least one guard for each prisoner. More for the dragons. No exceptions."

Jassan huffed, considering forcing them to break regulations, but decided he shouldn't push it.

"Fine," he said, then whispered to cover his own voice. "I'll take her to the palace for now. Follow us as soon as you can."

Jassan pulled Emma toward the door but Burk called out for her.

"It's ok," Emma called back to him. "Stay with Dasha. And watch out for Bubbles."

Jassan tried not to be too rough, but he also needed to behave like Shvika would. He allowed Emma to answer Burk, but continued to push her toward the door before she could say anything more. Burk's scowl turned noticeably darker before they pushed past the guards and out into the street.

Jassan kept his hand on Emma's arm as they marched down the street. He glanced back a couple of times, but didn't remove his hand until they turned a corner. Both of them pressed their backs against the wall and took a deep breath. Emma checked around the corner to make sure they weren't being followed.

"I'm sorry," Jassan said, "I hope I wasn't too rough."

"No," Emma said, "it was perfect. We need to keep going, though."

"Which way?"

"We have to get to the palace," she said, pulling him to start down the street with her. "Stay next to me like you're escorting me."

"What do I do with these?" Jassan said, holding up the two obrucks they had retrieved from Shvika. The third remained on his head under the borrowed one from the general. "We need to get them back to the others."

Emma shrugged. "Put them on your head for now. That way you can conceal them with the power of the key and we won't lose them either."

Jassan nodded. He slowed slightly to check his Moon Key as he made the obrucks disappear on his head, then ran to catch up. "Why don't we just get out of here?"

"What?!?"

"We'll only get caught like all the others if we go to the palace."

Emma spun on him. "Where else would we go?"

"Away," he slowed again to reply somewhat wistfully. "Far, far, away."

"I know you'd never do that." Emma said, shaking her head. "You're going to take me to the dungeon, like you said."

"I didn't say that," Jassan argued. "I only said I was taking you to the palace."

"Well, you're going to take me to the dungeon," she said, and turned to keep walking. "Once we get the key to the cells, we can free Trivnor and he can transport us all out of here."

"What about Burk?"

Emma shook her head. "I've thought about that. He may be safer if we leave him here. In fact, they'll all be safer here if we can lead Kelraz away."

As if to emphasize her words, another resounding BOOM! BOOM! BOOM! filled the air. Emma and Jassan had to stop and steady themselves.

"There's too many of us here," she said. "Everyone agrees."

"But splitting up now isn't the right option," Jassan said. "I agree, we may have to split up if Kelraz closes in on us. But if we leave anyone here, they'll be easy targets for Kelraz even if we lead him out. He could just return to find them."

BOOM! BOOM!

"It's getting louder," he told Emma.

But Emma kept walking.

"He's going to get in," Jassan said. "We need to get all of us out of here."

Emma stopped. "I can't let him hurt my brother," she said.

Jassan put his hand on her shoulder, "He won't."

Emma shook her head and kept walking without looking back at Jassan. "No, he won't," she said. "Because

I won't let him. If you and Trivnor can get out of here, he'll follow you."

Jassan heard in her resolve that she might stay behind in Kirlik. He had to think fast. "And what if Trivnor was right about Kelraz?" Jassan said. "What if Trivnor transports us all to the outside and Kelraz eventually hunts down all of us in our homes? What if Burk *is* impressionable, like Shvika said, and Kelraz forces Burk to tell him where the keys are? What if—"

"My mother will protect him," Emma said. "If we get home, she'll know what to do."

"Your mother is protecting your father and the rest of your kingdom right now," Jassan said.

Emma stopped again and spun to look down on Jassan. He remembered that she was born a dragon, and a fierce one at that. "What are you saying?" she hissed at him. "That we should intentionally put him in harm's way and make the decision for him to risk his life?"

Jassan sighed. "Emma," he said gently, "I'm saying *he* made the choice to be on this journey as much as either of us did. Remember what you said to Shvika, that he's stronger than he seems."

Emma turned away from him, but stopped walking. After a moment, her shoulders shook.

He placed his hand on her back. "He'll be ok, Emma," he said again. "We have to do this."

BOOM!

Emma sniffed and lifted her chin. "Let's get Trivnor out," she said. "Then we'll figure out the rest." She stepped ahead of him off down the street and didn't look back.

They stopped in the shadow of a building in front of the palace.

BOOM! BOOM!

Pieces of rock fell from the enchanted ceiling. Emma ducked as a giant chunk landed nearby. "I keep forgetting we're inside a mountain."

Jassan inspected the artificial sky. "Do you know where we are?" he asked her. "I mean, physically? In Avonoa?"

She shrugged, "I think we're under the mountains near the Honorable Kingdom or near the Desert Ruck. I'm not sure. And Dasha won't say. But we need to focus on where you and I are going next."

"Still," Jassan said, "it would be good to know where we are in case we have to fly out of here under our own power."

BOOM! BOOM! BOOM!

The sound was as if a giant was pounding on the mountain, demanding entrance. Several more chunks of rock fell from the ceiling in the distance.

"We may have to prepare ourselves for that sooner rather than later," Emma said. They reached the street in front of the palace. "But for now, do you remember how to get into the dungeons?"

Jassan nodded, although he wasn't as sure as he would have liked to be.

He took Emma by the upper arm again, as if escorting a prisoner. They straightened themselves up before he lifted his chin and marched her straight up to the palace door in front of them.

24

FRAUD

The goblins had a majikal way to lift visitors up to the grand main entrance on the opposite side of the palace from where Jassan and Emma were. The main entrance was an opening cavernous enough to allow dragons to fly through it and high enough off the ground that the goblins would have plenty of time to bar the way from anyone at street level accessing the palace without approval.

The entrance Jassan and Emma stood in front of was close to ground level, with a short staircase made of stone leading up to it from the street as well as a second staircase leading down to another lower-level door. The two doorways could fit creatures no larger than the goblins. On his way out of the palace through the same door as a beetle, Jassan hadn't noticed the two guards standing in front of the staircase on either side of it.

"General," one of the goblin guards nodded to Jassan when he saw Shvika approach with Emma. "Your business? Although I think I can guess."

Jassan pulled Emma in a little closer. "Taking this," he coughed and tried to sound like Shvika had lost her voice. "Taking this prisoner to the dungeon," he said.

"Are you alright, General?" the first guard asked.

"Where are the others?" the second guard asked. "We were alerted to expect more."

"Coming soon enough," he loud-whispered. "I've been yelling all day and I've lost my voice. Now can I be done with this or do I need to yell some more?"

"Of course, General," the first guard said. Placing his hand on the wall behind him, a brown gem glowed in his headpiece and the door dissolved away rather than opening. Jassan wondered briefly how he had gotten out before, but assumed the barrier was there to prevent intruders from the outside rather than prevent anyone inside from leaving.

Jassan nodded curtly to the guards and escorted Emma up the stairs before pushing her through the small palace door. Once inside, they both looked around and saw no other guards. Jassan remembered the approximate location of the first hidden doorway inside the palace and pulled Emma through it.

Once on the other side, he found a more dimly lit hallway with walls that were rougher hewn, but this was a longer hall than the one he remembered. This one curved around, with several visible doors along the way.

"Which way?" Emma asked.

"Um," Jassan hesitated. "I don't remember any doors in this hallway."

"What do you mean?"

"I mean," he said. "The hallway to the dungeons looked like this, but our passage was through hidden doors. Walk along here with your hand on the wall and see if you can feel any hidden doors."

Emma pursed her lips a moment then moved to the opposite wall. Together they started along with their hands against the stone.

"Here," Jassan said, when a doorway gave way under his hand. He peeked his head inside. "Two more guards," he said quietly.

Emma held out her arm to him. "Don't engage them," she muttered. "Just continue your business unless they stop you."

Jassan nodded. Pulling her through the doorway, he walked briskly past the guards without looking at them. He pulled Emma down the hallway until it curved away from the guards' view. Luckily, the guards didn't ask for an explanation.

"Do you remember this at all?" Emma asked, once the guards were out of sight.

Jassan looked around. "The floor is sloping," he said. "I think the doorway will be on your side this time."

They felt along the walls on both sides, but nothing gave way.

"What do we do now?" he said.

"Try the normal doors," Emma suggested.

The pair tried the four doors they could see in the hall, but only two opened. One accessed the laundry and the other opened into what appeared to be an office.

"Dead ends," Jassan sighed. "What now?"

"The headpiece," she said. "Use Shvika's obruck. She probably uses it to open lots of doors in the palace."

"I don't know how to use these gems," Jassan said. "It would take me forever to figure out which gem opened which door."

Emma shook her head. "Just think about opening a door."

Jassan sighed, still unsure. But he closed his eyes and thought about one of the doors opening. He peeked to see nothing happening. He clamped his eyes shut again and thought about an invisible opening somewhere in the wall.

He felt Emma tap him on the shoulder and opened his eyes to see an archway that had opened on Emma's side of the hall.

The last visible door was guarded by two goblins with yellow hair.

"Hey, Shvika!" one of them jumped up and sprinted over to Jassan. "Here I thought you sent us down here as a punishment. But I haven't seen so much action in all my service as I have today! Who you have here now?"

"Morkni," the other guard said, "don't get us in more trouble. Don't mind him," she said to Jassan with a smile, "he's just happy to be helping." The yellow-haired goblin's smile melted slightly. "Is that Emmaleena? The Noble Princess?"

Emma tipped her head down, avoiding the goblins' eyes.

"Never mind who it is," Jassan remembered Shvika's raspy voice this time. "She's going to spend some time in the dungeon thinking about what she's done."

"What's she done?" Morkni asked.

Jassan glared at him as he thought Shvika might do when she didn't want to answer a question or to let him know it wasn't his business.

"Ok, ok," Morkni backed down almost immediately. "Mlika, let them in."

Both goblins bobbed their yellow-haired heads as the doorway between them melted away.

The hallway on the other side of the door was much rougher and Jassan could tell they were close to the dungeons. They entered a small room with a set of wooden stairs going up and a door at the top.

"I know I didn't go down any stairs," Jassan said.

"Another hidden door, then," Emma said.

They stepped to opposite walls again and ran their hands over them, hoping to find a way through. He didn't feel anything immediately and turned to see if Emma had, but when he looked, she was gone. He ran to the area she had been searching. Running his hand over the wall, his hand gave way through it.

"Who are you?!" the goblin on the other side of the hidden doorway was yelling at Emma. "What are you— General!" he said, ceasing his rant. "I didn't see you."

Jassan grabbed hold of Emma's arm. "I told you not to get too far ahead of me," he told her in his best raspy whisper.

"Why didn't we see you come through with her?" the goblin guard asked, only a little askance. The guard's long, unkempt hair was purple, with red on the ends as if it had been dipped in blood. But what really stopped Jassan was the goblin's size, much more substantial than either Emma in her human form or Jassan in Shvika's form. His thick, meaty shoulders nearly touched his ears and Jassan didn't know how the goblin man could even feed himself with such massive arms.

"What," Jassan trying to hide his stunned reaction to the guard's appearance behind mocking, "and leave her behind me instead? I don't trust humans *that* much."

"What are you doing with her?" Another goblin in the room stood up from the table where he'd been sitting. The second goblin's head was entirely shaved on one side with bright yellow hair on the other. "Isn't she a princess?"

Emma glanced down again. She was too recognizable, and she knew it.

"I'm locking her up in the dungeon, of course," Jassan said. "She and her friends who are already there will be questioned about their attempt to steal a gem from the royal jeweler."

"Her too?" the purple-haired guard said.

"What did she have to do with it?" the other asked curiously.

Jassan pursed his lips; they didn't have time for these questions. In hesitating, he spotted the hallway with the prisoner cells behind the two goblin guards.

"That's not your concern," he told the guards. "Your job is to put her in a cell, not ask questions."

"Of course, General."

"Right away, General."

Jassan realized his mistake when one guard reached for Emma and Emma glanced over at him in a panic.

"On second thought," he said, snatching Emma from the goblin's grip. "I think I'll handle this myself. Give me the key."

He held out his hand for the key, attempting the best haughty glare he could muster.

"Of course, General," the second goblin pushed past the other and slapped the dirty brown gem they had used on Eleka's cell into Jassan's hand.

Jassan pulled Emma toward the cells, but stopped to turn back to the goblins. "I will, of course, be questioning the prisoners while I'm down here," he said. "I expect you to leave us undisturbed until I'm done."

"As you wish, General," the first goblin said. "We'll be here if you need anything."

BOOM! BOOM! BOOM! Even down in the dungeons of Kirlik, the pounding on the mountain was louder than ever. Once the dirt and dust stopped falling, Jassan gave the goblins a curt nod and pulled Emma toward the cells.

"Emma!" Tyla shouted when they appeared in the hallway. "What are you doing with her?"

"Shvika," Eleka said, narrowing her eyes, "you know you'll never get away with imprisoning royalty. What are you thinking?"

Emma held out her hands to the twins. "Shhh," she whispered, "it's ok. This is Jassan!"

"Oh, good," Tyla said.

"We were playing it up just in case," Eleka added.

"Jassan?" Trivnor whispered from his cell.

Jassan smiled at him behind Shvika's face.

"Eww, I never thought about how creepy Shvika's smile would be," Tyla muttered.

"Did you get a key to the cells?" Trivnor asked.

Jassan held up the brown gem.

"Great," Eleka said. "What about the chain?"

"What about it?" Emma asked while Jassan moved from cell to cell with the guards' key, releasing the invisible barriers.

"The chains also have no keyhole," Eleka said. She pulled her chain taut to show the shackle.

Jassan checked to make sure the guards weren't visible, then darted first to Eleka then Tyla to release them with the brown gem.

Tyla watched him carefully. Once her leg was free, she rubbed her ankle. "Thanks," she murmured.

"Ok," Trivnor whispered, once Jassan had freed him, but they all continued to hide in their cells. "Jassan, why don't we have Shvika escort me? Perhaps she needs to take me in front of the king again."

"What about us?" Tyla said. "Can't you transport us out now too?"

"Let me get rid of the guards first," Trivnor said, pointing to the area where the goblin guards waited. "Then I'll come back for you."

Jassan made sure his disguise as Shvika was in place and marched down the hall with Trivnor at his flank.

When they reached the small room with the goblin guards, Jassan felt a hand on his shoulder. He turned to see the oversized guard with the purple hair smile at him. "Just where do you think you're going, Fraud?"

25

A CRACK

Jassan froze.

BOOM! BOOM!

The stone around them shook. The guards didn't move but everyone else looked up at the ceiling to see if it would fall in. The guard's enormous hand tightened, pinching into Jassan's shoulder.

BOOM! BOOM! BOOM! BOOM!

Everything around them rumbled long enough for Jassan to gather his wits. "What are you doing?" he snapped at the guard. He forgot the raspy voice, but the shaking walls were loud enough cover to make it passable. He roughed up his voice before he whisper-shouted, "Can't you see we have an emergency going on? Why are you impeding me? How dare you hinder official business?"

"'Official business' Kruh's beard," he cursed at Jassan. "You're an imposter. I just got word."

"Word from where?" Jassan shot back. "How can you be sure you weren't given misinformation to distract you from the real culprit?"

BOOM!

The guard's eyes widened a moment. Jassan was sure he'd struck a decent point with the man. But his eyes narrowed again and he pulled Jassan closer.

"Fine," he breathed in Jassan's face. "It's no crime to question an officer in Kirlik. I'll take you to the king and he'll decide."

"Fine," Jassan snapped back. "That's where I'm taking the prisoner anyway."

The weirdly oversized guard barked an order for the other guard to check on the other prisoners. As he dragged Jassan and Trivnor through to the next room, Jassan searched Trivnor's face. The older faerie's eyes drifted to Jassan's hand on his arm, then drifted to the guard's hand on Jassan's shoulder. Jassan received the message. Trivnor couldn't transport three beings.

"Take your hand off me," Jassan said, jerking away from the big guard. "I can walk my own prisoner."

"Not a chance," the guard growled, tightening his grip further and pinching Jassan's skin in the process. "I've been warned about you."

As the guard pulled them up the stairs toward the king's throne room, Jassan's heart pounded double-time in his chest. He tried to keep his breathing from showing his fear. Taking a deep breath, he realized that Trivnor could still get out and help the others.

He let go of Trivnor's arm and the faerie dissolved in a swirl of grey and white clouds.

"Get off me!" Jassan yelled. "Find him, you troll brain!"

The guard spun and searched the area. He didn't let go of his grip on Jassan but loosened it just enough for Jassan to kick at the guard's leg that was still on a stair and shove the top of him with all his might. The goblin fell on his face, then rolled down the stairs.

"I knew it!" the guard croaked once he righted himself. "Come back here!"

As the goblin guards charged up the stairs toward Jassan, he threw himself at the door. That's when his world fell apart.

Finding himself inside a wide hallway on the other side of the door disoriented Jassan. He fled, holding his hand to the wall on one side. He couldn't reach both sides of it so he prayed to Tartaku that the side he had chosen would have a hidden door to somewhere else. The goblin guard barreled through the door behind him. About halfway down the hall, the wall gave way and Jassan fell through the opening.

He caught himself in another hallway in time to see two more guards running toward him. He turned and ran the other way, feeling for another hidden door.

BOOM! BOOM!

He found a wooden door and prayed again that it would be unlocked. And real.

Tartaku heard him. Jassan pushed the wooden door open easily and slammed it shut behind him. The door didn't have a lock. Jassan raced through the large, furnished room only noticing out of the corners of his eyes that it contained some bookshelves, tables and soft chairs.

He saw a door on the opposite side of the room. Jassan dodged around chairs and a table, debating whether to duck under it, but three goblin guards made up his mind when they bolted through the door and came at him. He ran to the door and wrenched it open.

A vast hallway loomed in front of him. It was the main palace entrance. He stood on a mezzanine level. A beautiful stained-glass window towered over him on his right and over the massive doors one floor down on his left. He wondered if he could just transform into his dragon and take the quickest way out through the window to get away. But the palace shook with a deafening BOOM! and the window crashed in instead.

A colossal dragon wraith, twice the size of Jassan's own wraith form, exploded through the stained glass. Jassan stared, entranced by the dripping shadow billowing from the beast. The wraith eyed Jassan and dove toward him. Suddenly Jassan felt familiar hands on his shoulders. The hands pulled him to the ground just as the monster slammed against the wall behind him.

Two goblin guards pulled Jassan back to his feet. He recognized the two yellow-haired guards, Mlika and Morkni. The oversized purple-haired dungeon guard stuck out behind them but all eyes were on the giant wraith blocking their path down the stairs to the entrance doors.

Mlika pulled Jassan to his feet. Morkni stepped up to the dragon wraith who was trying to reorient itself to find its prey. A gem glowed in Morkni's headpiece as he put a hand on the wraith's belly.

Bright blue lightning shook the monster from head to tail. It wailed and thrashed, but kept its agency and didn't abandon its spot in their way.

"Whoever she is," Mlika shouted to the other guards, "get her out of here!"

Morkni pulled Jassan by Shvika's shirt up the marble stairs behind them. The dungeon guard and Mlika stood in front of the dragon wraith. One gem glowed on Mlika's headpiece as the blue lightning rattled the dragon wraith again, but the wraith stayed on its feet and even began to reach for the little goblin. Then the oversized dungeon guard stepped up to them. He yanked the obruck from Jassan's head and put it on his own head.

"Just proves you're not her," he growled at Jassan but kept his own eyes on the wraith. A different gem glowed in the headpiece and the monster put its claw down. Gradually, the beast spread his legs and his body sprawled out on the ground in front of the goblins.

Morkni sprinted up the stairs with Jassan in tow just as another wraith crashed through the palace entrance. The goblin shoved Jassan into one of the smaller hallways to the side as a third wraith flew into the palace through the entrance below them.

Once they were in the side hallway together, Morkni pointed for Jassan to follow him through a doorway. On the other side, they stopped to catch their breath.

"What are they?" the goblin gasped.

"Wraiths," Jassan panted, his head against the wall behind him.

"Wraiths?" Morkni said with a question on his face. But when Jassan didn't explain further, he said, "Well, they're too big to reach us in here."

Jassan shook his head. "Those are only the dragon wraiths," he said. "There are others in the form of humans, faeries and—"

BAM! The door shook and Morkni leaned his weight against it.

"Goblins!" Jassan finished.

The door Morkni leaned against shuddered with a massive force behind it. Jassan came to his side to help.

"What do they want?" Morkni yelled over the noise of pounding against the door.

After a moment, Jassan mumbled, "Me."

26

INVADERS

Morkni's face was a mask of confusion. "Who are you? You definitely don't sound like Shvika."

"Best you don't know," Jassan replied, hoping to keep his identity from the goblins, although he realized he hadn't been masking his voice for some time now.

Morkni nodded. A gem in Morkni's headpiece glowed and he stepped away from the door. The door continued to shake, but the goblin's face scrunched up in concentration. "This way," he said, turning momentarily to walk backward and keep his focus on the door before turning back to run.

Jassan followed the goblin through a long room with couches and several soft chairs. Finding another door before they reached the other side of the room, Jassan jumped through it without stopping. He left it open and soon the goblin followed him and slammed the door behind them. Morkni pointed, "Go!"

Jassan and Morkni ran down the long flight of stairs ahead of them. "I need to get out of the palace!" he said. At the glare he received from the goblin guard he added, "They'll tear this place apart to get to me!"

They turned a corner at the bottom of the steps and heard a crash and splintering of wood at the top immediately after they disappeared from view.

"I have to get out of here," Jassan repeated in a low voice.

Morkni shoved Jassan down the hall and they continued running. At the end, a door opened and they were back in the vast entrance hall again. The tiered space was filled with black, shadowy wraiths in all forms.

Morkni pulled Jassan back into the hallway. He panted, "I'm not supposed to let you leave."

"If I don't get out of here," Jassan said, "your palace and probably your whole city will be overrun and destroyed."

Morkni's brow creased as if in pain. The wraith from the top of the stairs was running down the hall toward them.

"I'll take your place in prison," the goblin guard said.

Jassan opened the door and watched the goblins in the entrance use their powers and ropes to restrain the creatures. But as soon as they subdued one, another would enter or another would free itself. The goblin wraith behind Jassan and the guard kept coming.

"Not if you lose me in the chaos!" Jassan shouted. "Don't let them hurt you!"

Without waiting for an answer, he opened the door and ran into the melee.

Dodging tails, claws and goblins, Jassan reached the main entrance doors. The walls behind him shook as he threw himself from the opening, high off the ground. Once in mid-air, Jassan transformed into his dragon. His favorite form was the easiest to use. He remembered Shvika's sash that Emma had placed on him and pulled it from over his head. The burly guard had taken her obruck from him so he no longer needed to return it. The sash appeared in his claw, but he dropped it to the ground behind him as he pumped his wings, heading toward Dasha's home.

Obviously, Shvika had been freed after he and Emma had knocked her out and tied her up in Dasha's kitchen, and she'd sent word out to the other goblins saying he was an imposter and demanding his capture. So, what happened to the rest of their friends? Were they still being held at Dasha's? Or were they being taken to the palace? Or somewhere else, considering the state of things he'd just left there? He knew he couldn't go back to the dungeon to find Trivnor, if he was even there, and get out of the goblin city. His only means of escape seemed to be to go somewhere that was familiar to Trivnor and wait for him there.

As his dragon eyes searched the sprawling city for signs of his friends, he noticed a new fire burning in the distance. He flew closer to it. Faerie and dragon wraiths took to the air behind him. He tried to ignore them and continued toward the fire, hoping it wasn't where he thought it might be. Wraiths in the streets looked up to follow his progress.

Jassan dove for the ground. He ran on four claws toward the fire. A centaur wraith jumped out from behind a building, clawing and kicking at him. He used his massive dragon tail to slam the wraith into the building and kept running.

Two faerie wraiths flew over another building at him. He raked his front claws across them, sending them spinning into the air to the far side of several buildings. Skidding to a halt, he forgot the wraiths. He stared at Dasha's home in flames.

Jassan ran the last few dragon lengths toward the burning structure. He hoped he might be able to resist the fire because he was in a dragon form. But as he reached out when he got close, the heat scalded his claw.

Nope, still a faerie, he thought.

Stepping back to watch the flames and wonder how to find his friends before more wraiths showed up, Jassan noticed a small piece of the fire lick away from the blaze. It continued across the street in his direction. The flame went out and Bubbles's purple scales slithered toward him.

"Bubbles!" he allowed himself a moment to breathe. "Where is everyone?"

As if in response, Bubbles slithered away from him up the street. Jassan followed at a sprint. The little snake could move swiftly over the cobbled road. She quickly turned a corner with Jassan's dragon legs pounding along close behind her.

"Jassan!"

Jassan spun hearing his name and he immediately wondered if he shouldn't have reacted so quickly in case the goblin guards had learned about him and were lying in wait for him to show up. Then he recognized the voice that said it.

He followed Bubbles and the familiar sound of his name. A barrel lid flipped off and clattered to the street. Jassan jumped but Bubbles slid ahead to the barrel. Burk's eager-looking human face popped over the rim.

"Jassan!" he said again. "Where have you been?"

"I could ask you the same thing!" Jassan answered.

Two faerie wraiths came screaming down the street toward them.

"Oops—gotta go!" Burk said, bursting from the barrel and bolting down the street away from the monsters. Bubbles slid up Jassan's dragon leg and wrapped around one of the spikes along his spine.

Jassan raced after Burk. Just around the corner, he turned into an alley and Jassan followed. In the blink of an eye, Burk changed to his dragon form, jumped over a brick wall, then changed back into his human form and kept running down the alley. Impressed by the move, Jassan stayed in his dragon form and raced after the swift-footed little human boy.

"Where's Trivnor?" Jassan panted as they ran.

"He's transporting everyone," Burk answered. He ran down another alley and abruptly stopped short of the end to flatten himself against one wall. Jassan could barely stop his dragon body from running past him. "We have to stay in this area so he can find us and get us out too. He said you should cut off your connection with the key so you can move around without being tracked."

"I can't," Jassan said. "We need my dragon form with everything that's going on. Plus, I can't change with Bubbles on me. And I'm not leaving her behind."

"Agreed!" Burk acknowledged.

With a bellowing roar, a dragon wraith dropped from the roof directly over Burk's head. Jassan didn't think. He dove at the creature before it could land on Burk, tackling it. He rolled over the monster once, but when it tried to land on top of him, he pushed his strong back legs into its belly and launched it into the air, far over the roofs of the buildings surrounding them.

"Yeah, you can definitely wait to change back," Burk said, sounding like they had proved that Jassan the faerie wouldn't be able to save him.

The pair watched as the dragon wraith rose again from the other side of the buildings. "This way!" Burk said, pulling on Jassan's dragon arm to urge him to follow.

They ran down the alley and jumped out into the street leading to Dasha's home. They could see four wraiths waiting outside the charred doorway. Three wraiths were tearing at other buildings and houses nearby. Jassan could hear the screams of the goblins hiding inside. Two more wraiths flew over the houses toward them.

"Where should we go?" Jassan yelled to Burk.

"I don't know," Burk said.

The four wraiths in front of Dasha's house turned their heads slowly to the young human and the dragon. "Come on," Jassan said, taking his turn to pull Burk's arm to get him away.

"But we have to stay here," Burk said, only allowing himself to be turned, "or Trivnor will never find us!"

Two human wraiths ran up the street from behind them. Jassan had not yet faced human wraiths, but they were coming from exactly the direction Jassan thought he and Burk should go.

"Oh, spit," Burk muttered.

Jassan pulled on Burk again. He turned to enter the alley they had come through before, but several dragon wraiths landed in front of them and blocked their way. Jassan grabbed Burk and shoved the younger boy behind him with his claw. "I don't think Trivnor will have anything to find."

27

LURE

In a tornado of clouds, Trivnor appeared next to Jassan. "Let go of him," Trivnor said, placing a grey claw on Jassan's dragon shoulder.

"No, not me!" Jassan cried. Before Trivnor could reply, Jassan pulled Burk forward and shoved him against Trivnor, pushing off his grip at the same time. Trivnor instinctively grabbed Burk. "Take him first!"

"No!" Burk yelled.

The dragon wraiths advanced on Jassan. Rather than waiting for them to overtake him, he chose the path of least resistance. He threw himself into the alley with the dragon wraiths. As one rose up on its hind legs, Jassan tackled it and didn't see Trivnor disappear with Burk.

Before he knew what was happening, Jassan ended up with the first wraith on top of him. He clawed at the monster's belly, but didn't do enough damage to slow it.

He grabbed the beast's front legs to keep them from raking across his neck and face. Pushing the wraith to the side, Jassan got his feet back under the creature. He pushed with his feet but forgot he still had hold of the wraith's front claws. He managed to flip the monster over his head on top of the other wraith.

In the tight alley, Jassan had to wriggle to get to his feet. He clawed at the walls on either side, hooking one claw on a doorway and ripping it free. Two more dragon wraiths turned the corner into the alley in front of him. Jassan heard screams from inside the building, but he took the door off its hinges with his claw and threw it in front of the newcomers. It effectively both distracted them and blocked their way. Jassan only hoped that the goblins in the building could find something else to keep the wraiths out.

The two wraiths behind him clawed at Jassan's tail, back and back legs, attempting to pull him toward them. He felt his skin tearing in several places as if he had run through the razor-sharp tellik bushes at home with bare legs. He screamed in pain.

Through a fog of pain, Jassan peeked to see a dragon bolt over his head. He thought for a moment the dragon was another wraith coming to kill him, but he realized the dragon was grey, not black.

The grey dragon landed on top of the second wraith, pulling at its head to divert it away from Jassan. "You have to get free!" Trivnor cried. Trivnor blew fire into the wraith's face so it couldn't see and it pulled away. As soon as the wraith untangled itself from the other wraith, Trivnor transported it away.

Left with one wraith clawing at his back and wings, and more moving down the alley toward him, Jassan turned to the one swiping at him. He turned over and bent forward to face the wraith. Not knowing how effective they would be, he still scratched his front claws across the snout of the monster hoping he could at least distract it.

They did the trick and the dragon wraith let go of Jassan's legs long enough for him to pull them away. He couldn't move away far enough or fast enough so he struck out with one leg to push the wraith away and gain at least some separation.

It worked, but Jassan stopped as soon as he noticed that he had pushed himself closer to the wraiths coming down the alley. He paused just long enough to take a breath, and Trivnor appeared in front of him.

"Thank Tartaku!" Jassan wept.

Trivnor placed his dragon claw on Jassan's dragon shoulder and the pair disappeared. The twisting whirlwind dissipated and Jassan collapsed against Trivnor. "Don't die on me yet," Trivnor said, scooping Jassan into his dragon arms. "And don't change just yet, either."

Jassan looked into Trivnor's black eyes. "I can't change now, anyway. Not with Bubbles on me."

Trivnor shook his head. "I'll take Bubbles. She's smart enough to have learned that by now," he said, "but we have to save the goblins first."

Jassan looked around and could see they were still in the city. Trivnor had only transported him to the next street over from where the wraiths had been attacking him.

"Can you stand?" Trivnor said, gently placing Jassan on his four legs.

Jassan pressed them into the ground. His knees shook and pain lanced up his legs and tail. Bright red blood dripped down his legs onto the cobblestones. He ground his teeth together as the pain burned through him. Once it eased a little, he nodded. "What are we doing?"

The wraiths from the alley and the rooftops had gathered close by and now turned toward the pair. This time, none hesitated and they all galloped toward them.

"We have to lure them away. If we disappear completely," Trivnor hurriedly whispered, "Kelraz will leave these wraiths to terrorize the goblins."

The clouds twisted around them again and they disappeared before they quickly reappeared farther down the street. When he landed himself this time, more pain shot through Jassan's legs. He moaned internally but held his tongue.

"They're drawn to living souls, remember?" Trivnor continued his explanation as they whirled away again in a cloud. "We're trying to lead them out. As many as we can get, anyway."

"Won't Kelraz follow us too?" Jassan asked, finding his footing again.

"Would you rather leave the wraiths to the goblins?" Trivnor asked earnestly and searched Jassan's face.

Would he? Could he? The wraiths would certainly keep the goblins away from him and his friends for a while.

A faerie wraith jumped from a building behind them. Three goblin wraiths followed it, two of them smaller wraiths who Jassan thought might have been children only moments ago.

No, he definitely couldn't leave the wraiths with the goblins.

Jassan's heart clenched harder than his teeth. A ripple of heat washed over him. He felt like he was being overcome by a raging dragon fire. He pushed past it as he gained momentum running through the streets with Trivnor. Blood splattered behind him, but he knew what he had to do.

He dodged the faerie wraith and the small goblin wraiths as they stumbled from the building. "Hey!" he whooped at them. "Over here!"

Trivnor ran beside him, keeping to his dragon form, and just as the wraiths turned toward them, Jassan burst past them to lead the pack farther down the road.

At another crossroads, more wraiths joined the ones continuing to gather. Jassan jeered at them and they followed along as well. Somehow, he was able to ignore the pain in his shoulder to wave them down and the agonizing pain in his legs to run.

"Just make sure they don't touch you," Trivnor said as Jassan dodged another wraith falling out of a window at him.

Suddenly the larger goblin wraith ran toward them and Trivnor blew his fire at it. Jassan assumed he was trying to slow it so the other wraiths could catch up. One of the little goblin wraiths ran straight through the flames and burst from the other side alight, with his entire body burning, still holding his clawed hands outstretched toward them.

"Bad idea!" Jassan hollered, dodging the burning hands.

Trivnor transported them away again when five or six immense dragon wraiths flew over their heads to land in their path. Reappearing well behind them, fresh pain stabbed Jassan when he landed hard. He slipped on the blood gushing onto the cobbles when his eyes glimpsed something up in the majikal sky. A gaping black hole yawned where there hadn't been one before. Several new wraiths descended into the city through the opening while a few others clung to the sky next to it, looking like they were floating upside-down.

Jassan pointed to the hole in the sky. "I guess we won't be going out that way," he said to Trivnor.

Trivnor followed Jassan's finger with his eyes, then jerked him out of the path of another dragon wraith before transporting them away again. "No," he said. "We're going to have to use more conventional means."

He raised his arm to point afar and Jassan could just make out the yellow banners hanging against the wall of the city.

"Come on!" Jassan screamed at the wraiths, momentarily forgetting the surges of blood pulsing from his legs.

But his legs didn't forget. As soon as he tried to run, they weakened. He tried to force them to move, but they wouldn't obey.

"Cut the connection," Trivnor said, running to his side. "We're getting close enough."

As Trivnor had predicted, Bubbles slithered down from his back and sprang from one of Jassan's spikes onto Trivnor's back. With an ache in his heart, Jassan imagined his own blue freckled skin and pointed ears and released the connection to the key. He knew he would be weaker and more vulnerable than ever. He looked down at his arm with the Moon Key attached to it and saw his own faerie face in the mirror before the pain created dark edges in his vision.

He tried to stand and run from the wraiths, but his skinny, shredded legs only twitched in agony. While he had been bigger and stronger in a dragon form, the gouges had been bearable. But once in his fragile faerie form, the same wounds were five times larger stretching over almost his entire legs and part of his back. "Don't try to move," Trivnor said. He used his grey claw to scoop Jassan from the ground. "I'll do the rest."

Trivnor limped through the streets with Jassan in his claw. Bubbles fell from Trivnor's back to wrap around Jassan's wrist. The pain forced Jassan to squeeze his eyes shut but he brought his arm into his chest. He felt every jolt with a shock of pain up his legs and back, but Bubbles warmed his chest. Trivnor didn't bother to transport them, but he couldn't move fast either. The trio finally stumbled in front of the largest of the portals. Trivnor hesitated.

"What are you doing?" Jassan asked.

"Making sure they see us," he said.

As he turned, Trivnor's shoulder moved out of Jassan's view. Behind them a solid mass of blackness with claws and fangs swarmed toward them. Jassan blinked and the whole world turned dark around him as Trivnor dove into the portal.

The cavern they entered was chaos. It was mountainous and the noise inside ricocheted off the walls. A few humans and goblins ran through the massive openings leading to other parts of Avonoa. Goblin guards ran in and out of the openings, either escorting fleeing goblins or blocking the path of the wraiths trying to get in.

Jassan spotted Emma and Burk. She was arguing with a goblin guard and pointing to one of the portals. When Trivnor appeared with Jassan in his arms, Burk grabbed the vial of healing tonic from her and ran toward them.

"No!" Trivnor said, changing back into his faerie form. He laid Jassan on the ground. "They're coming! We can't stop, we have to go now!"

Emma and Burk made it to Jassan's side. He had forgotten he was still wearing all three of the stolen and tattered obrucks Emma had taken from Shvika and given to him to hide and barely noticed when Trivnor pulled them from his head.

"We don't have time for that yet," Trivnor told Burk before he could open the vial. He turned to Emma and handed her one of the three obrucks. He said something in her ear and she ran to Gizi and Dasha with it in her fist.

Lokna appeared beside Jassan and Burk. "I'll take him," he said, then carefully picked Jassan up off the floor. Jassan winced and stifled a groan.

That's when the wraiths arrived. Black shadows poured through the portal opening behind them. The army of wraiths spread through the cavern like blood dripping into water.

Everyone screamed. Even, Jassan noticed, the fiercest of the goblin guards. As the wraiths swarmed and filled the space, Emma turned to run back to him and Burk at his side.

Three dragon wraiths sped toward her before she could move. She tried changing into her dragon form, but as she spread her wings to fly, Gizi wrapped her claws around them and clamped down. She pulled Emma to the ground just as the wraiths moved in place to tackle her and grabbed air instead.

"Burk!" she shrieked at the top of her lungs. Her cries echoed through the chamber.

"Gizi," Trivnor bellowed over Emma's screams, "get her out of here!" Jassan knew they were too far away to hear him and the only thing Gizi could see was Trivnor pointing a finger at them and waving it toward the portal, but the orange dragon nodded in understanding. Dasha clawed and kicked at the dragon wraiths attacking them.

Trivnor tossed an obruck at Burk then bolted toward the centaur twins. He threw himself over two attacking dragon wraiths, spun in the air, and threw the last obruck to them at the same time. Tyla caught it and pulled her sister into a portal and disappeared.

As Trivnor pulled himself out of the acrobatic spin another dragon wraith tackled him from behind. A goblin behind them saw their trajectory towards her and slapped her hand to the wall. A portal opened moments before Trivnor and the wraith slammed through it. The goblin kept her hand on the wall and Trivnor and the wraith disappeared behind the sealed portal.

"Trivnor!" Jassan screamed, reaching out with his good hand but unable to move otherwise.

Lokna pulled Jassan and Bubbles into his chest and ran for a portal. "Hold on!" he screamed. Jassan looked back at Emma being dragged away by Gizi and pushed by Dasha. He glanced down and saw Burk running alongside in his deep teal dragon scales, keeping pace with Lokna. Leaving his sister behind.

Lokna looked down at Burk and then slowed for only a moment to follow Jassan's gaze to Emma.

Jassan couldn't be sure who Emma was looking at, but he clearly heard her echoing plea. "Keep him safe! I'm trusting you!" Emma screamed before she disappeared into the black portal.

28

SHREDDED

"Emma was right," Lokna said in a low voice, watching the dripping sky. "There were too many of us. We had to split up and we all knew it."

Their little group lay in a deep depression. A drop of at least three dragon lengths had deposited them in a hollowed-out hole to hide from view of the top of it. Only pure happenstance or luck led Burk to fall into the hole as they fled from view of the portal and the wraiths.

"While you were busy flying back and forth and rescuing everyone," Lokna said, "the rest of us decided we had to split up. We knew all nine of us couldn't get to each of the lost keys without being recognized or discovered. Although we had planned on splitting into different groups than how we ended up."

Lokna pursed his dragon lips, which made Jassan think the dragon wasn't with the friends he wanted to be with.

After glancing at Burk, Jassan asked, "Who was supposed to be in the different groups?"

"We hadn't worked out all the details yet, but Gizi and I were going to go back to the Rock Clouds, not to it, you know, but near it," he said. "Emma, Burk and you were going to look for another key, hopefully closer to the Noble Kingdom to see if you could get any assistance there. Trivnor was going to go with Dasha and the twins. But with the wraiths all over us we had to scramble."

"Can we go find Emma?" Burk asked. He sat on the stone floor next to Jassan, dabbing potion on his legs while Bubbles swiveled over the wounds to help them heal.

Lokna shook his head. "Now isn't the time. If we go back to Kirlik or the portals, we'll be caught for sure, either by Kelraz, his wraiths or the goblins. Don't worry," he added when he saw the concern on the young boy's face. "She's with Gizi and Dasha. You know they won't let her get hurt."

Burk nodded but clenched his jaw. Jassan knew the young boy was attempting to be braver than he felt.

"What about us just taking Burk home?" Jassan said. "If he can't be with Emma, shouldn't we take him back to his parents?"

"No," Burk answered instead of Lokna. "None of us can go home. Kelraz would hunt us down. And I don't want to get tortured for information on where you are with that Moon Key. Or watch my uncle's kingdom get attacked and burned to the ground like the goblins'."

"The goblins know us, too," Lokna said. "If we went back to the Noble Kingdom or the Rock Clouds or even the Centaur Plains, the goblins and Kelraz would be waiting. Besides, we still have to find the other keys before Kelraz gets them. If he stays busy hunting us down, he won't be able to find the keys. Maybe we can either stop him or beat him to them."

Jassan hissed from the pain still burning in his legs until Bubbles twisted around them and cooled them down. Burk finally put away the vial. "I tried, Jassan. I don't know what else to do."

Jassan nodded. "I know," he said. "You did great."

"Did we even get the gem we needed?" Burk asked quietly.

"Yes," Jassan said, leaning back against the cool stone, feeling the hilt with the invisible sword still on his back and his spine conforming around it. "Trivnor has it."

"But Trivnor is the only one of us that doesn't have an obruck," Burk said, glancing at Lokna.

"Who has them?" Jassan asked. "We have one, right?"

"Yes, but…" Lokna slowly lifted the little golden circlet from the ground. The blue gem in it dangled precariously and the rest of the mangled gold didn't even resemble a circle any longer.

"Emma, Gizi and Dasha have one," Burk offered. "And Trivnor got one to the twins before they all…well…"

Burk couldn't finish and no one spoke for him. The groups had been split up but now Jassan, Lokna and Burk had no way of communicating with the others, while

Trivnor had no means of communicating with any of them either.

"So," Lokna sighed. "We rest. Maybe find some food. Get you healed up. Then head out to find the other keys. The others will be doing the same, but according to Trivnor, the key you have will help us figure out which way to go to find the rest."

Jassan looked at the little Moon Key. It was quiet and still. The cavern around them dripped rain and echoed the rustle of the forest. He didn't feel its attachment to him, let alone sense any indication of other keys from it. "I don't know," he said. "I don't think I know how to fully use it."

"Didn't Trivnor say it would pull you toward the other keys?" Burk said, trying to be helpful. Jassan just shrugged, which sent another wave of pain through his mangled shoulder.

Lokna lay down on the cold, wet stone. "It might take some time for you to figure it out. You can rest and heal until then."

"Until when?" Burk said. "This isn't a great place to stay. We're literally bait sitting in a barrel. What if some wraith stumbles in here?"

"Where are we supposed to go?" Lokna said. "Jassan can't walk and he can barely fly. He needs to rest and heal."

When the pain cooled enough for him to think, Jassan turned to Lokna. "We still need to find the keys, but you're wrong about not having anywhere to go," he said. "One of our homes is safe enough for us to go to…because Kelraz doesn't know where I live."

THE END

The adventure will continue in

THE CHAMPION OF JUSTICE

DRAGONS OF AVONOA

BOOK TWO

Note to Readers!

I hope you are enjoying the adventure in Avonoa as much as I enjoyed creating it! Although I love to write and create these stories, being an independent author is hard. I don't have teams of people ghost-writing, editing, formatting and marketing for me. I do it all on my own, so my only support comes from readers like you! Thank you for supporting me and my craft.

Another way you can support a lowly indie author like myself is to leave me a review. Feel free to use the link and/or QR code below to let others know how much you enjoyed the story! You can also pick up one of my other publications, the Avonoa series, or People of the Storm!

You can also sign up for my newsletter to be the first to hear about sales, signing events and new books! Sign up at avonoa.com, hrbcollotzi.com, or peopleofthestorm.com.

Or follow me on social media…
Facebook @hrbcollotzi
Instagram @hrbcolloti